*The*
PROMISE

*The*

# PROMISE *by*

## ESTHER KELLNER

THE WESTMINSTER PRESS

*Philadelphia*

To
*My Husband*
*and*
*My Daughter*

"WHO SHALL ASCEND INTO THE HILL OF THE LORD?"
— *Psalm 24.*

"WHO SHALL STAND AND JUDGMENT IN THE LORD'S
HOLY PLACE?"

# I

THE HEAT OF THE DAY WAS PAST. THE SHADOWS OF THE TREES HAD
lengthened and thinned, heat waves had ceased their devil dance
across the dry, alluvial plains. From the waters of the Persian
Gulf a hundred miles to the south came the first wind of evening,
a coolness upon the brow, a fragrance from many gardens, a soft
splattering sound, like falling rain, in the palm fronds.

Waking slowly, Sarai felt the sweet presence of early evening
within her brick-walled room. She lay drowsily for a time, hearing as from a distance the twitter of birds gathering in the tree
that shaded the court below. Then, coming fully awake, she was
suddenly aware of the day and the hour and sat up, knowing a
swift flash of joy. A shaft of red sunlight burst through a crack
in the wall beside her and she laughed and reached out and
caught it greedily, like a child.

At last I hold it within my hand, she thought, exultantly. The
sunset of his return!

For unless the gods willed otherwise, Abram's caravan would
enter the city gates no later than the first hour of darkness.
Throughout the day, slaves had toiled in the kitchen and workrooms preparing a feast worthy of the young master of the House
of Terah, and already there rose on the smoke from the supper
fires the smell of game birds turning brown, the fragrance of
freshly made bread. Sarai thought with satisfaction of the great
flat loaves, sweet and richly crusted, of the cakes and honey, the
baked meats and fruits. Surely such a supper would find favor
with any man, especially a man spent from the length of a journey, wearied by such cares as beset all merchants, and — it was the
hope of her heart — homesick.

She turned and lay, young and brown and naked to the shad-

9

owy coolness, across the low wooden bed with its yielding mattress, its decorated headboard. After the manner of a girl who is still a child, she cupped her pretty chin in her hands and kicked her small feet languidly. Her black hair lay like a veil across her back; her great dark eyes were full of dreaming. She was unaware of her beauty as a child is unaware, but both proud and conscious of the fact that lately she had come to the age of womanhood and thus, after the custom of the land, to the age for marriage.

"May Terah your uncle find you a husband of wealth and honor," Maacah, her slave woman, had said on that day. Then, being not only slave but also nurse, companion, guardian, comforter, teacher, and friend, Maacah added with understanding, "A kinsman will be his choice, it is said."

Sarai's heart quickened within her young bosom as she whispered the name. "Abram — may it please the gods — though never has he spoken to me in words of love. Yet until this very moon, I was not to be called a woman — not of an age to wed, to keep a husband's house, to bear his sons."

In this the house of her uncle she had dwelt since childhood, knowing but the dimmest memory of any other life. Within this memory there was, shadowy and vague, only the voice of her mother speaking with sorrow to some clustered women: "And where would I go, being now a widow, save to the House of Terah? Seeing that my husband has no kinsman to receive me into his care. Is not Terah the eldest of my brothers? And since the death of his wife — may the gods of the dust have mercy upon her! — sore is his need of a woman to direct the ways of his household and of his sons."

Thus, in this spacious house staffed by many slaves, Sarai had grown to womanhood, knowing as a family her mother, Terah her uncle, and his sons, Abram, Nahor, and Haran. "Daughter of the House of Terah," she was called and, for this reason, shown a more than ordinary deference. For in the city of Ur, and in others likewise, the name of Terah, being one of honor and wealth, commanded respect from every man, whether slave, scribe, merchant, physician, scholar, or priest of the temple.

Of the three sons of Terah, it was Abram whom she cherished

within her heart. Indeed, she regarded him with such devotion as both wearied and annoyed him. Yet he did not lack affection for the pretty child who was beside him only a little less often than his own shadow, and found it pleasant to confide in her when the mood was upon him. With the years, her devotion had become a tender love, which she sought to conceal from the eyes of the household, even from Maacah, lest he fail to return it and thus make her an object for pity or laughter.

Terah, being both aged and ill, could no longer bear upon his frail shoulders the cares of trade, and so it was to his sons that these matters fell, Nahor looking to the family interests in Ur, Abram setting forth with the family caravans. Indeed, Abram seemed always returning from one journey and departing upon another, and to Sarai his absences were weary lengths of anxiety and loneliness.

From the parapet edging the housetop she had watched his going, straining her eyes that she might follow his caravan into the haze of distance, whispering prayers for his safety to Nannar, the God of the Moon, the Exalted. She had caused to be made for him an amulet pierced with a tiny hole, that it might be suspended about his neck beneath the fabric of his tunic, above his heart. Such an amulet served to defend him from any evil eye or evil word, even from the perils of the *lil,* demon tormentors of men.

Such spirits of evil were everywhere. Sarai herself had heard their mocking voices in the storms, felt their ruthlessness in sickness and in pain, known the sound of their scurrying feet by night. No power could halt their entering, for they were like fog itself. They came with the wind and fell with the rain, entered with the dawn and with the dark, passing through doors however strong and walls however thick. Bearers of misfortune and sorrow and death, they snatched the child from its mother's arms, turned the love of a man from his wife, caused sons to desert their parents. Yet worse, they inflicted the curse of childlessness, which turned sick the heart of a woman and dishonored her husband's name.

For protection against such as these, many prayers were uttered, many offerings made to many gods, countless exorcisms invoked.

11

In truth, one could not learn all the incantations designed to avert evil, but there were some, powerful beyond all others, that were taught to children in their earliest years and repeated each day thereafter. These she said often, that Abram might go forth and return again, untouched by the forces of darkness.

Throughout the length of his journeys, dreams and fears and anxieties concerning him crowded her days. More than once, in the unrelenting heat of noontide, she had suffered a fearful vision in which she beheld him lost upon a desert wilderness, his waterskins empty, the men and animals of his caravan dead. Yet, with the coming of evening, when the palm fronds rustled in the cooling winds from the Persian Gulf, her mood changed, and likewise her reflections. And now her fancies conjured a far moon-drenched oasis where Abram lay, made wakeful by the memory of her face, while his men and animals, lately restored, slept in peace about him.

At other times, being neither driven nor solaced by things of the imagination, Sarai sank back into the reality and monotony of her days, watching one follow the other, slow and stupid donkeys, all alike. At night, sitting in the coolness of the roof top, she gazed upon the quiet stars and thought before she slept, To-morrow there may come a messenger announcing the day of his return.

Few girls had known a greater portion of loneliness. Since the death of her mother there was left to her only the companionship of Maacah, the slave woman. Terah, suffering many ills, seldom left the consolation of his bed. Nahor she saw but rarely, for he had taken in marriage Milcah, a kinswoman, and dwelt with her in another house. Haran, the third son, had died some years before, leaving a boy called Lot to inherit his portion. The name of Lot was not to be spoken with pride, for he was of such shifty-eyed weaknesses that the lowliest slaves looked upon him with contempt. Yet Abram dealt with him patiently and took him upon the journeys of trade, that he might have knowledge in the ways of business and thus learn the management of his inheritance.

Sarai had never been farther than a few miles beyond the gates of Ur, yet now, lying dreamily upon her bed, she sought to pic-

12

ture the return of the caravan. Closing her eyes, she ceased to look upon the painted stools and neat cross-legged tables, the cushions and rugs and mats, the lamps fanciful in design, where wicks were afloat upon the oil. All these she replaced in her fancy with fleeting visions of the countryside.

There were, Abram had told her, many cities like Ur, of simple flat-roofed houses, white beneath the sun, and narrow, twisted streets wherein one heard the calling of the water vender, the shouting of drovers, the jangling of donkey bells. There were palm groves and gardens and pasture lands and fields rich in grain and the bright, gleaming waters of many canals. She thought of the rich red glow of sunset across the plain, the swift-falling darkness, the men moving weapons within easy reach, alert to the immemorial danger of robber bands. And, in truth, there were many who would slay without mercy for such riches as Abram was bringing back. Fearing for him, Sarai knew a sick panic and, opening her eyes, spoke quickly an incantation addressed to Nannar:

" The evil word, the evil eye — God of the Moon, forbid them! Disease and sorrow and fever and death — God of the Moon, forbid them."

Yet who could say whether this god saw fit to hear her? Truly it was a prudent thing to pray also, even if briefly, to the household images within the room, and to Pa-sag, goddess of caravans. Then, hastened by the lateness of the hour, she climbed from her bed and occupied herself with the matters of dressing. The brick-paved floor was both cool and pleasant beneath her bare soles as she pattered to the great wooden chest against one wall for the finery which had awaited this hour.

" Now shall Abram behold me as a child no longer! " she said aloud, and her voice was rich in satisfaction.

With care, she made ready to color her smooth young face, spilling upon her bed her tweezers, the ear pick, the paint stick with its rounded tip, and a box hinged at one side, formed as a scallop shell from the sea. Within this box, in waxy little pools, lay the paints of a lady of taste, red and green and blue and black, precious and costly. For such paints as these, and for exotic scents from the lands far to the south, the life of many a caravan leader

13

had been spent and lost at last.

With the darker colors she shadowed her eyelids and added length to her great dark eyes, to the clean, high curve of her brows. Then, having tinted her cheeks, reddened her lips, and anointed her body with fragrance, she made rosy her nails and the palms of her hands. Gazing into her shining bronze mirror, she decided, at length, upon the pinning of her dark hair atop her head. Such a choice, she had discovered, gave her the look of a woman grown, likewise the chance of displaying her beautiful gold hairpins, only two days out of the bazaar.

She fitted her small feet into red goatskin sandals, put on earrings, bracelets, a necklace, an anklet, and then an undergarment thin and cool, passed beneath her right arm and gathered with a silver pin upon her left shoulder. Over this fell her gown, a tunic straight and slim, caught in at the waist by a wide girdle covered with designs of gold and lapis lazuli.

Footsteps brushed the brick passage beyond the room and then, quietly, Maacah appeared in the doorway. Sarai turned to her quickly and with eagerness.

"Behold, Maacah! Do I not, in the first jewels and eye paints of my life, appear as a woman grown?"

Maacah halted, astonished by the sight, for it was as if Sarai had cast aside childhood in the space of an afternoon. A pang, swift and aching, smote the slave woman's motherly breast. How swift and greedy the years! she thought, remembering that she had been a young girl when Sarai was given to her charge, and now she was graying of hair, stooped of back, grown thick at waist and chin.

"Maacah, answer me!" commanded Sarai, impatiently. "Am I a spirit, that you stand and stare at me and cannot speak?"

Smiling, the slave woman laid her broad and gentle hands upon the girl's slight shoulders.

"Truly my little mistress has come to womanhood," she said with an edge of sadness to her voice. "And since the death of your mother — may the gods of the dust give her peace! — you have been a worthy keeper of the house. Indeed, she would look upon you with pride, seeing how readily the slaves obey you, how cleanly the rooms, how well ordered the table."

14

"It is but fitting that I understand these matters," answered Sarai, " seeing that I will one day keep the house of a husband." She took up the mirror and, busying herself with the paint stick, made her voice both absent and casual.

Yet Maacah understood, and thought in swift gratitude, May the gods be praised, if indeed there is marriage between these two!

"It is to bear you word of Abram's return that I come," she said, gently.

Sarai turned swiftly, her face lighting.

" He has entered the city? " she cried.

" Even more," said Maacah, " for he is within the house, having been below for the space of an hour."

The mirror fell, clattering upon the floor.

" An hour? " Sarai's voice was filled with dismay. " And none came to awaken me, that I might welcome him? "

" So deep was the sleep of my mistress," answered the slave woman, apologetically. She added, " Nor was it a time for welcomes, seeing that he had not yet finished with the work of the day, and brought with him a scribe for some letters of importance."

Sarai bent and took up the mirror, and stood holding it in her hands. The radiance had departed from her face, and there was an edge of bitterness to her voice.

" Always letters of importance," she said. " Talk of trade and of caravans . . ."

" In the hands of his best scribe such writings are quickly done," said Maacah, with kindness. " Even now it may be that the letters lie finished and Abram awaits your coming. Thus, if you will but look within the Common Room below . . ." Of a sudden she turned her head, crying out, " Now surely has Azubah burned the honey cakes! " and hastened forth, her feet brushing with rapid sounds the bricks of the floor.

Alone, Sarai knew both hurt and disappointment.

" Day upon day have I waited," she whispered. " Day upon day have I waited — praying for him! " Which made the whole matter seem yet more unjust. " And, now he is returned, he sends for me not at all, but sits babbling letters of business."

15

Slowly and with dejection, she turned toward the passage. An ugly clay household god leered at her from his place by the door, where she had given him charge that no *Lil* might torment her, not even a demon of lesser disappointments.

"Muddy-headed blunderer!" she cried, in sudden rage. "Is it for this I have sacrificed before you?"

She snatched him up and flung him upon her bed, having no fear of incurring the displeasure of a god so impotent.

"Yet the fault is my own," she said to herself, "for his price was as nothing, and truly it is not surprising that a thing so cheap should be without worth."

Tomorrow she would go, not to the bazaar, but to the temple itself, and there purchase a guardian god to be respected. In truth, this poor thing of common clay had not the power of a gnat! Yet, as she glanced backward, a shadow crossed his ugly face, causing him to wink at her with brazen impudence, so that she fled in startled haste from the darkening room.

# II

THE CITY OF UR, ALREADY ANCIENT, STOOD BETWEEN TWO WATERS, having on one side the Euphrates River and on the other a shining canal of such width and depth that merchant ships were borne upon it. Half a million people were crowded into the square, flat-roofed houses which staggered up and down the narrow, crooked streets. These houses gleamed in the sunlight, being first plastered and then coated with a wash of white, for to wash a house in color was to invite such ill fortune as no man would bring upon himself.

The city of Ur was one of trade. Its streets, dust-clouded in summer, soggy with mud in winter, were full of bustle, noise, confusion, and color. In and out of the gates of Ur went merchants with their shouting slaves, their immemorial caravans. Ships brought fabulous cargoes to the water's edge, precious and beautiful timbers, delicate cloth, gold and ivory, silver and alabaster, unloaded and carried up the ramps by the toil and sweat of the slaves.

In the bazaars were small shops open to the street, where craftsmen worked at their trades. Cabinetmakers fashioned beautiful chests of cedarwood patterned with tracings of pearl and lapis lazuli. Jewelers made golden cups and lyres, golden beakers from which oil was poured into shallow clay lamps, anklets and necklaces, bracelets and rings. Smiths, lifting powerful arms knotted with muscles, toiled at their anvils. From the metalworkers came pots and razors, caldrons and mirrors. With the wares of the carpenters were bedsteads and tables, chests and utensils and tools. In the shops of the potters men kneaded wet clay underfoot and by hand, turning the shapes on wheels spun round by a foot lever, decorating and firing them at last.

Not the least among the craftsmen were the makers of cylinder seals, for these were of immense importance to the men of Ur, being their means of putting signatures to letters and documents inscribed upon clay. The seals were small and hollow rolls cut with intricate designs by sharp bronze tools, fashioned of quartz, jasper, carnelian, agate, obsidian, lapis lazuli, or, for poorer buyers, of materials as humble as limestone. Rolled across a damp clay tablet, the seal left a clean and narrow strip of pattern by which to identify the writer, the family or house from which he came.

Beyond the city grew harvests rich and bountiful, for the waters of the river had been turned into a network of shining canals spread forth in the land. Here, from year to year, toiled the brawny slaves of the state, filling the channels with water from goatskin bags, keeping the banks sound and strong. Here, fed and nourished by the water thus carried to their roots, were gardens, vineyards, palm groves, pasture lands, and fields of grain. Yet Ur was far more than a city of the farm lands, a market for the fruits of field and vine. Caravan routes of every land had threaded their way to its gates. Here passed all manner of foreign slaves and traders so that the streets, echoing many tongues, became a procession of colorful strangers and unfamiliar trappings.

High above the roof tops rose a building consecrated and holy, the ziggurat, terraced temple of Nannar, God of the Moon and

Patron of Ur. Four stories had the temple, each smaller than the first, each sheathed in enameled brick of a color different from the others. White, black, and red, it rose above all else, dominating the city, the countryside, even the far reaches of the plain, the trees upon its terraces giving it the look of a forest mountain. At the top was the shrine of Nannar, blue-enameled bricks edged in blossoms and greenery. "House of Light," it was named by those who looked to it with veneration — "Hill of Heaven" and "Threshold of Life." To its gates came the people of Ur, worshiping, prostrating themselves in the brick-paved courts below, gazing upward to the high priest serving at the high altar. Smoke from the sacrifice rose about him, the sound of flutes and the rhythm of drums accompanied him, and his voice came down to the worshipers in the ancient, chanted litany:

> "Lord, . . .
> Who created the land, foundeth the temples,
> Nameth their names . . .
> In heaven, who is exalted?"

And the people responded as one full, rising, and reverent voice:

"Thou alone art exalted!"

The people responded, and Sarai one of the first among them, for even as a child she had been deeply religious, praying anxiously and with humility that there would fall upon her head neither the wrath nor the vengeance of any god. In trembling earnestness, she echoed the final words of the priest:

"Look upon thy city! Look upon Ur!"

For the priest to climb to the top of the temple and worship in a high place seemed both natural and fitting to the people of Ur, for somehow there had come to them, from their shadowy beginnings, the memory of altars on a mountaintop and now, having no longer a mountain of earth, they had built a mountain of brick, that the tradition of their worship should be neither lost nor forsaken.

The ziggurat of the Moon God, though sacred beyond any other, was not the only temple in Ur, for there were hundreds of gods and goddesses to be feared and appeased. Some, like Ningal,

18

Nannar's wife, were images richly fashioned and adorned. Others were mean shapes of mud and gilt, standing in their own shoddy little street chapels, awaiting gifts and homage. Likewise of mud and gilt were the household gods which guarded the House of Terah and stood above the altar of the family chapel where Sarai prayed daily that Abram might be spared the enmity of all gods large and small.

The House of Terah, like the houses of all families of wealth, was of sun-dried brick, plastered and washed with white, built around a central court, brick-paved and open to the sky. Within this court grew flowers and a spreading tree, and upon it opened, by one means or another, almost all the rooms of the spacious house. There were two stories, the second with wooden galleries overlooking the court below. On the first floor was the entrance hall, a water jar for the washing of hands and feet, some drying linens. Likewise on the first floor, yet toward the back of the house, were the kitchens, storerooms, and workrooms, with huge brick stoves, open fireplaces, beehive-shaped ovens, and great flat millstones for the grinding of wheat into flour. Nearby were the bedrooms where the slaves slept on brick beds covered with straw. Along yet another side of the court was the Common Room of the men and, beyond, the family chapel where the dead of the House of Terah lay entombed beneath the floor.

Through an arch in one wall of the court were steps leading up to the second floor and, beneath them, a lavatory with a terra-cotta drain. The upper rooms, save that which was the Common Room of the women of the household, were family bedrooms, furnished in a manner of both comfort and charm, with carved and painted bedsteads and tables and clothes chests, with mats and rugs and shallow clay lamps.

The roof top, reached by steps still higher, was flat and walled and open, shaded at times by thinly woven mats. Upon such roof tops the women of Ur rested, gossiped, observed what came to pass in the streets below, sought the cool breezes which sprang up at sunset, and awaited the coming of their men.

Sarai's room, like the rest of the family rooms, opened into a brick-paved hall which led to the gallery across the second story and thence down the steps to the inner court. The gallery itself, being open to the sky, was still washed with the redness of sun set. Here, with her hand on the rail, the girl waited a little space, listening. From the kitchen quarters came the quiet voices of the slaves, the clatter of copper plates and ladles, the sound of soft, companionable laughter. Some birds nesting in the tree above chirped sleepily from the topmost branches. The court was empty and silent. Standing there, she felt her spirits ebb with the day. At this moment, as in all hushed evening hours, she was filled with a sense of sadness, born of the deep loneliness of her life.

Yet, with the sound of Abram's voice, her head lifted quickly and joy flashed like a light upon her face. Holding the skirt of her tunic with one small brown hand, she ran down the steps and across the court, pausing near the Common Room. This room, set aside for Terah, his sons, his guests, and his brethren, had been the scene of many talks of business, countless hours of laughter and feasting and fellowship now a portion of the past. Terah, after the manner of the aged, recalled such things no longer, but dozed upon his pillows or called fretfully for the broth and softened bread of his meals. The vast room was one from which festivity had departed. The luxurious cushions once brought forth to seat the guests had long gathered dust in the closet of the far wall. Only the rich and colorful rug remained. Abram paced its length as he spoke, absorbed in the dictation of yet another letter. The scribe sat cross-legged on the floor, his hand rapid in its deft twisting of a stylus as he inscribed wedge-shaped letters upon the damp clay. On one side of him was his bucket of washed, cleaned, and kneaded lumps, smooth and freshly made. On the other side lay a number of small, pillow-shaped tablets, each a letter completed and signed, each enclosed in its envelope of flattened clay.

Sarai's eyes passed the scribe quickly and with impatience, wanting only the sight of her kinsman.

"How weary his face!" she said to herself. "The heat of the sun . . . and the long journey. . . . And truly, he is thinner." Her heart was filled with solicitude, tender and maternal.

Abram was both young and pleasing to look upon, being broad of shoulder, narrow of waist, long and lean of flank. His features, handsome and highbred, reflected a sharp intelligence, in which gentleness and dignity had mingled. After the way of the land, he was clad in a short tunic, open at the neck, fastened down the front with plain stone buttons, cinched at the waist with a belt of carved shell. His hair, as black as charred wood within a brazier, was tumbled carelessly upon his head, and he wore, as became a man of his rank, a single large earring. At his waist was fastened a conical toilet kit, likewise a dagger of shapely design, richly adorned with lapis lazuli. A cylinder seal was suspended from a cord about his neck, swinging lightly as he paced. Nearby upon the floor, where he had cast them down, lay his headcloth and mantle, and Sarai, having a love of neatness, tightened her lips at the sight.

". . . one thousand donkeys," he was dictating, " purchased from a desert tribesman. These await shipment to you up the river. Five letters have I sent you concerning this matter, without a reply. How am I to do business? " He added, " The signature, ' Abram, son of Terah,' — and thus, for this day, are the letters of business completed."

The scribe nodded, finishing the last word. Abram moved forward and, taking the seal in his hand, rolled it across the base of the clay tablet, leaving a clean and sharp design.

" Let these be sent by the first courier, seeing that they are all of importance."

The scribe nodded, witnessed the signature, quickly smoothed the covering upon the tablet, and wrote that which would appear on the outer side. Then, heaping all the tablets into the bucket, he rose to his feet and uttered the courtesies of parting.

" May you live a thousand years, O Master."

" May you live a thousand years," returned Abram, absently.

Sarai drew back against the wall, silent and unnoticed, as the scribe shuffled across the court, made his way through the entry and out into the street. Scarcely had the porter closed the door upon him before Abram, hastening forth from the Common Room, passed her on his way to the brick stairs. She called to him eagerly, her heart beating fast with excitement.

" Abram . . ."

He turned and stared at her in the dimming light, beholding a graceful stranger whose presence both astonished and bewildered him. She went closer, and now her voice was rich in laughter, half-suppressed, as she reproached him.

"Is it that you have forgotten me in the months at Haran? No, now — surely my name still lives within your memory! Sarai, a kinswoman of your house . . ."

"*Sarai!*" Amazement was upon his face, and then affection, fond and indulgent. He laid his hands upon her shoulders, smiling down at her, and spoke with sudden tenderness. "Truly, I am happy to look upon your face — and the others of this household, likewise."

She answered him coolly.

"Yet you made no haste to greet us, but lingered within the Common Room, busying yourself with letters."

He laughed and embraced her lightly.

"Not by my own choice did I linger . . .," he began, in good humor. Then he shrugged and added, "But how is a woman to know the demands of business?"

Woman! It was a word bearing both surprise and pleasure. She did not answer at once but stood waiting, in the hope that there was more he would say. But when he had taken a step toward the stairs, as though to seek the others, she spoke in haste, that she might stay his going.

"The journey to Haran, was it pleasing?"

"As any journey of trade."

"So many moons have passed. Truly I thought you had forgotten those of your household, coming to look upon us as strangers."

"You are not unlike a stranger." He gazed at her curiously. "How long has my sister worn the garments of a woman?"

She shrugged lightly.

"So long — scarce do I remember."

"Let my eyes behold you."

He stood back, smiling, while she turned before him slowly and with pride, that he might behold the graceful line of her tunic, the gold and blue designs which graced her girdle, the flashing of anklets and earrings, the glitter of jeweled hairpins.

"In the street, I am veiled," she said, "seeing that I have reached the years of womanhood, and there are those who beseech my uncle for a contract of marriage to me."

" Marriage? " His voice was filled with astonishment.

Sarai shrugged.

" Is not marriage the way of the world? "

" Surely you are not yet of an age . . ."

" In truth, I am grown into womanhood," said Sarai firmly, " even as you are grown into manhood. And," she added, striving to steady her voice, " can it be said that Abram has no thought of marriage? "

For a little space he was silent, gazing upon her in the manner of the slave woman, with something of nostalgia and regret.

" So swift are the feet of time. As yesterday, it seems, that Sarai was still a child . . ."

" And not today? " she demanded, with eagerness.

" Nay." He paused, his face growing serious. " In truth, little sister, from whom have come these offers of marriage? "

With the steadiness of his dark, believing gaze upon her, the girl was unable to utter as much as a word. Indeed, the question filled her with fright. " Nannar, Exalted Lord," she prayed hastily, " close his eyes to my striving, let him know not the truth."

Aloud she spoke as one wearied unto death by the ways of suitors. " Let us have no concern with them, reciting their petitions, naming their names. Longer would it take than the evening itself."

Amusement, quickly stifled, shone forth in his eyes.

" May the choice be a man of riches," he said solemnly, " that marriage gifts in plenty be given to us all."

" Now does Abram speak of gifts," she answered, with merry impudence. " Is it that he has brought me some gift from the bazaars of Haran? "

For not in all the years of their growing up had he returned with hands empty of a gift for her. Indeed, there was a certain small chest in Sarai's room wherein lay a handful of colored shells from his first journey with his father's caravans, in the days of his boyhood. Yet now . . .

" The journey to Haran was no small measure of anxiety," he said, " troubled with a thousand matters to harass and delay me.

Caravans looted, an agent who was likewise a rascal, new demands of tribute from every petty official — in truth, there was no time for the thought of gifts."

Standing before her, he brushed from her uplifted face a blown stand of dark hair, but gave no sign that he perceived the hurt disappointment in her eyes.

"And how am I to choose a gift for Sarai, seeing that she has become a woman grown? The buying of gifts for a lady of fashion — indeed, this is a matter unknown to me. Still " — he reached toward the kit at his waist and a sudden smile flashed upon his countenance — " within the shop of a certain skilled craftsman, I beheld this trinket."

She cried out in wonder, seeing how it glittered, even in the dimming light, its intricate gold designs encrusted with stones.

"Abram! By every girl in Ur shall I be envied the wearing of such a necklace! "

He dropped it into her open hands.

"May it bring you joy."

"In truth," she said, half whispering, "it possesses a loveliness to be both cherished and remembered."

"As Sarai herself," he said quietly.

She looked at him swiftly, astonished and moved, and her heart quickened beneath the cool touch of the jewels, but he, turning from her, spoke casually and of another matter.

"In the bazaars of Haran may be seen craftsmanship beyond believing. Thus I bought also a chest — at a price above pearls — a wedding chest fashioned of cedar of Lebanon, inlaid with ivory and richly patterned with stones. Worthy, I think, of the princess herself."

"A wedding chest . . ." She echoed the words on a thin thread of sound, staring at him. He made no answer, and she perceived that his eyes were filled with distance, as though his spirit dwelt elsewhere, likewise his heart. Silence fell between them, empty and bewildering. She saw, with a measure of astonishment, that the light of the day was utterly spent. Darkness and shadow possessed the court, the leaves of the tree were black against the sky. Now surely the lamps were lighted in the upper Common Room and the supper meats stood ready in the kitchen. Yet . . .

"Is it," she faltered desperately, "that Abram has arranged a marriage?"

He returned to her, and spoke with sudden lightness.

"Has not Sarai herself said I was of an age for marriage?"

"I did not mean . . . I had not thought . . . In truth, it should have come to me, for within the gates of Haran dwell many girls of family, and of beauty." She drew a slow, shaken breath and asked humbly, "Is she beautiful then — the wife of Abram's choosing?"

"Beautiful indeed," he answered readily, "and one who shines forth in honor and goodness, as befits the mother of sons. For seeing that sons are the wish of every man's heart . . ."

Pain thickened her throat so that she choked, and her eyelids were scalded with the shame of tears. Yet, with pride as strong as defiance, she lifted her head and steadied her voice.

"Darkness is upon us. Let me summon Maacah, for surely you await the feast of your return."

She moved quietly and with dignity toward the arch which led, by means of a long brick passage, to the kitchen quarters beyond. But Abram, his hand suddenly upon her arm, stayed her departure.

"Nay. It was for you I bought the wedding chest," he said. And added, "Now see how it is with Abram . . ."

She stared at him with astonishment. "Is it that men too become suppliants in the presence of the beloved?" she asked herself, in wonder. For the eyes of Abram were filled with entreaty, and he stood before her in such humility that she was moved to pity, wanting to shield him from his own defenselessness. Thus, she turned to him swiftly, and was at once within the tender, dizzying realm of his embrace, knowing the smell of sun and herbs and dust upon the fabric of his tunic, the quickened breathing which moved his chest, the warm and shadowy refuge of his arms, the edge of his lips brought, seeking, to her own. In confusion of mind, she said within herself, "Perhaps I dream for, despite the prayers I have laid before the gods, surely it is not Abram who holds me thus!"

Then, with the touch of her flowing like wine within his veins, he began to kiss her as though he would say: "This is how I

25

have meant to caress you, my darling, out of the depths of my yearning when, on the long and weary roads, I beheld lovers turning to each other's arms beneath a moon . . . the joy upon the face of him whose hut, however humble, sheltered a beloved wife . . . the emptiness of journeys wherein I, of all the caravan, had none whose arms awaited my return . . . nights when rain whispered upon the casement of some foreign inn like the voice of loneliness. Out of the years of my love and need and desire for you, let me kiss you until I know your mouth in tenderness and in abandon, the softness of your cheek beneath my lips, the sweetness of your hair."

" Where the gods would take you, there would I be also," she whispered, " for in the love of Abram I am blessed."

For a moment, being filled with such emotions as find no release in words, he was silent, laying his hand upon her hair slowly and with tenderness, as though he caressed a child. Then, smiling suddenly into the dusk, he tilted her chin that he might look upon her face and asked, as though grave with concern, " But what of those who have offered, before me, rich gifts for the contract of marriage with Sarai? "

Her eyes grew bright with laughter.

" Not in truth did I tell of them," she confessed, "but only that you might behold me as a woman grown. In truth, no other man has looked upon me as at an age for marriage, since only this day, against your return, did I put on the garments and jewels of a woman. Only this day in the hope of marriage to Abram . . ."

She halted suddenly, stricken by the indiscretion of her own words and, shrinking from his touch, cried out: " Now, how is it that I have spoken of marriage? Only from my uncle should such words come! May his kindly heart forgive me, for truly his head would bow in sorrow to know my shame."

Abram stifled the smile which rose to his lips and drew her back into his arms.

" Have no fear, my darling," he said, solemnly. " No word of Sarai's shame shall pass my lips."

# III

THE ROOF TOP OF THE HOUSE IN HARAN LOOKED OUT OVER THE HOT and dusty streets into the shimmering hills beyond. Here Sarai rested often in the late afternoon, lying upon wide cushions shaded by an awning of matting. It was now five years since she had looked back upon the gates of Ur, aware that she might never behold them again. Yet in this knowledge there was little of sorrow, for all that was dear to her had come with her upon the journey.

Soon after the signing of her marriage contract the trade routes to the north had been closed by order of the king of Babylon. This was a blow which fell heavily upon Abram, seeing that much of the family trade dealt with the north. In the end, it was arranged that the House of Terah itself should be moved to the north, to the city of Haran, with Nahor, the brother of Abram, remaining behind to manage that portion of its trade left in Ur.

Within the quiet walls of their room Sarai and Abram had talked of the journey. It was late at night, and all others of the household slept. The lampwick glimmered low in the saucer, its oil nearly spent. Earlier, the shadows had leaped like black flames upon the ceiling, but now they massed and hovered, as quiet as a cloud. Sarai lay with her black hair spread forth upon the pillow, her face grave and thoughtful.

" The slave Maacah I would take, seeing that she is dear to me." She added, without shyness, " And she will impart to me her wisdom in the bringing up of sons."

Abram, leaning forward, kissed the edge of her hair.

" The slave Maacah," he agreed, with gentleness. Then, suddenly smiling, he added, " And the slave Azubah, seeing that the foods of her kitchen are such as would please the king. Indeed,

27

all our household shall go with us, and all among our kinsmen save Nahor, and the family of Nahor."

" Lot also? "

" And," he said, with significance, " the wife of Lot."

They were silent for a little time, thinking of her whose coming to the House of Terah had made it a place of strife and unrest. That Lot, being both weak and vain, should seek his friends among flatterers and inferiors was no matter of surprise, but they had not thought that such a one would be his choice of a wife.

The girl was the daughter of a lesser merchant who dealt chiefly in greed and dishonor, and who had bargained with her suitors so long, and with such gluttony, that the signing of her marriage contract was akin to the selling of a slave. She was sloe-eyed and languorous, with a skin as rich as the skin of a pomegranate, a body both shapely and graceful, a face beautiful in spite of its shadows of greed and striving. For possession of this girl, Lot paid a marriage price so great that he was regarded by all Ur as upon the edge of madness. Fearful of her displeasure, he cringed and was submissive before her, so that she despised him in her heart, and brought shame upon him by her undisguised contempt. In truth, his weakness was more than the men of the city could countenance, and many were the voices lifted against it. " Let my brother believe me, should the wife of my heart turn a single insolent glance upon me, she would be gone from my house before the rising of another sun! "

In the years of her girlhood, Sarai had yearned for the comfort of a sister, and thus looked with eagerness to the marriages of Haran and Nahor. Yet, in the matter of companionship for the daughter of the house, these were both unrewarding. The mother of Lot, scarcely remembered, had lain long within the dust of her grave. The wife of Nahor, fretful and sickly, was seen only, and then but briefly, at family feasts and funerals. Yet there was Lot, young and unwed . . .

" And surely," Sarai would say to Maacah, " when he has taken a wife, then I shall be done with loneliness. Abiding beneath one roof, we shall rejoice in our kinship, share the duties of the household, the bringing up of our children."

But this was not to be, for within the heart of Lot's wife there was no portion of sisterhood. Indeed, she conducted herself as a guest of whom the House of Terah was barely worthy. It was a matter of custom that every girl should be taught to perform the duties of the household, should know pride in preparing, with her own hands, special feasts for her husband, and for the most honored of his guests. Yet Lot's wife could not so much as boil a pot of broth. All household duties were distasteful in her eyes, nor would she look to the needs of her own family. Instead, she spent the larger portion of her days within the coolness of her rooms, while certain maidservants ministered to her body with scented baths, were busied with the moving of fans above her sleep, the gathering and bringing of fruits to stay her thirst.

For Sarai, life in Haran was not unlike the life she had known in Ur. The same loneliness afflicted her as in the days of Abram's journeys with the caravans of other years. As eagerly as then she awaited his return, knew joy at the sound of his voice, fulfillment within his arms. Their marriage had a quality of morning, of radiance renewed, rediscovered, and was of deep content, save that no sons had come to it, nor even daughters.

In the beginning she and Abram had spoken lingeringly of their firstborn, devising the manner of his care, his schooling, his name. Then Sarai would say, laughing as if such a thing were beyond reason, " If the child should be a daughter, rather than a son?" And Abram, with habitual gallantry, would answer: " Was not Sarai herself a girl-child? Why then should my head bow in sorrow at the birth of such a one? Nay . . ."

Since that time they had known the sorrows of five fruitless years and now neither Sarai nor Abram made mention of an heir save in their thoughts. The swaddling clothes fashioned by the hands of a bride lay unsought within the wedding chest which Maacah had closed upon them with sadness and finality, as one might close a burial cave. Yet Sarai, knowing what the chest concealed, felt stricken by the very sight of it. Her barrenness followed her everywhere and accused her with her shame. " Not even daughters . . ." She felt the eyes of other women upon her in both pity and contempt, and knew her name was uttered with cruel delight by such of the poor as find pleasure in the heartbreak of the rich. " Even in slavery, I am happier than she, with my child in my arms." " No, now, let us rejoice in our poverty rather than envy her whose goods cannot buy motherhood." " Indeed, she is beautiful, but what is that to her husband, seeing that she is barren? "

Yet she had never ceased to pray, in patience and trust, to the gods, the goddesses, and the ancestors become bones within their tombs, that a son might yet be born of her flesh and Abram's. Daily she sacrificed before the household images in the family chapel, leaving food and drink for their pleasure, kindling incense upon the altar below them. " Now, look upon thy servant."

Perhaps, said Maacah thoughtfully, some evil spell had been laid upon her. Perhaps Abram had an enemy skilled in sorcery who wished him to suffer the curse of going to his house of dust with none to raise up his name. For was it not true that when a man climbed above other men, an enemy awaited him on every step?

The other slave women agreed. Let the lady Sarai remember, said Azubah, a certain woman of Ur who, being under such a spell, was without children for the first seven years of her marriage. Then her faithful maidservant revealed that a sister-in-law had made a small clay image of her, flat and barren, over which to say daily incantations of hate. Whereupon the husband found and shattered the image, had his sister's curse rendered powerless by a skilled exorciser, and, since that day, his wife had borne eleven fine sons, and was ready to bear again on the day Azubah departed from Ur. See now how such things come about! The slave women could have told such stories from the setting of the sun to the first cockcrow, with scarcely the space of a breath between. Truly our master has an enemy, but if he summons the priests of the temple, surely they, being schooled in the exorcism of evil . . .

Still others declared his misfortune to be the deed, not of a sorcerer, but of some demon *Lil*. Such a one might have entered Ur with Abram's caravan after his last desert journey, since the desert was known to be the dwelling place of the worst of these. Here, they spread false water before the traveler, likewise the green palms of a false oasis, that they might lead him from the trodden paths and bring him to destruction. Their evil faces peered upon strangers from behind the rocks, the hills, out of the caves. They rode upon the sandstorms, dried the wells, maddened the camels, and loosed the winds. Every trader had seen such a *Lil* at least once, whirling with the desert dust toward those who watched in shaking terror and hid their faces at last.

There were also some who dwelt upon the mountaintops, afflicting with bitter cold and a sickness of the chest the stranger who sought the high reaches of their dwelling. There were some who waited in the depths of the great sea, that they might destroy men and ships. And there were some, yet more evil, who dwelt within the marshes and cursed all who came near them with a great shuddering and a wasting death.

To stay their powers and to earn fertility for herself, Sarai had placed throughout the rooms bands of cloth covered with mystical writings and exorcisms, yet the House of Abram was still without an heir.

In less than two years after the signing of her marriage contract, Lot's wife had borne, bitterly and with neither pride nor joy, two children, both daughters. These found comfort and tenderness within the arms of Sarai, even while they reproached her for her unfruitfulness.

On a late afternoon, shortly before the going down of the sun, Maacah came to the roof top where Sarai lay at rest within the shadow cast by an awning of matting. In her hands was a platter of wet, ripe grapes which she held forth with tender solicitude.

" May it please my mistress . . . if my lady will eat of the fruit, truly a cool peace will come upon her, even in the heat of this day."

Sarai looked up with gratitude.

" Maacah is kind, for indeed, the heat is pitiless upon me. And upon Terah more so," she added, unhappily.

They were silent, sharing a common anxiety. For more than the space of a moon, Terah had suffered an illness which came upon him suddenly and with great pain. And though he had wrestled with it throughout many burning days and sweating nights, he could not cast it from him.

" The look of death has not yet touched his face," said Maacah, with hope. Then, after a little time, she added, " Yet who can say, seeing that these things are with the gods?"

Sarai made no answer. Earlier, when she had gone to his room in the hope of ministering to him, she found him sleeping and in peace, but it was a false peace, Maacah said, drunk in an herbal potion which she, herself, had mixed for him. Lying upon his bed in the dim light, toothless and wrinkled, his mouth half opened, his body the shape of bones beneath the linens, Terah had seemed a mummy out of Egypt, as ancient and as desiccated. Yet who would say that death was upon him? More than once such an illness had seized him, and more than once loosed its hold upon him after many days.

"Surely Maacah, being skilled in the art of nursing, knows whether this sickness is a passing thing."

The slave woman shook her head.

"Such weakness and pain are not to be endured by the old. Should his days be ended before the false dawn, there would be no surprise in the heart of your servant, for a powerful demon possesses him."

Sighing, she turned away, crossed the roof top, and went down the brick steps to the second story, and thence down into the inner court. Sarai lay back upon the cushions, restless and troubled. It was a day of stifling heat. The sun burned like a torch set to the city. Down the twisted streets of Haran and out across the countryside, heat waves shimmered and danced in the blinding light and faded into cool lakes of false water far beyond. The world became a hush wherein all creatures gasped that they might breathe and sought the shelter of a roof, the shadow of a vine, a rock, a cloud, awaiting the night. Surely, on such a day, even a demon would choose to return to his own dwelling, remembering the coolness of a desert dawn, a shadowed well, a cave in the rocks. Yet with this one it was not so, for day upon day he remained within Terah's room, and the piteous old man knew peace only when Maacah induced in him, by means of potions, slumber so deep that even the *lil* were powerless against it.

Maacah, being a skilled nurse, knew many means and incantations by which to exorcise the evil spirits tormenting her patients. Indeed, countless demons had been vanquished by the potions she mixed, the rites she performed, the commands of her voice, but the demon holding fast to the bosom of Terah could not be dislodged. In vain she tied mystical knots above her patient, poured enchanted waters upon his head. "Let his illness be washed away!" she intoned. "Begone, thou evil one, and bear his misery with you!" But the demon remained to make Terah yet more ill, and certain of the slaves declared they had heard it laughing in the night, as though to deride the efforts of the household against it.

After a time, as Sarai restlessly pondered upon these things, she heard faint brushing sounds upon the steps and roused quickly, thinking Maacah had returned to bring word of Terah's death. But it was the wife of Lot who came, making her way to the roof top slowly and with ill humor. She wore a single thin garment upon her body, her hair was pinned high upon her head for coolness, her arms and ankles and delicate neck were without jewels. Behold, the heat within the house had driven her forth, even from the room where her maidservants waited to fan her as she slept. Throwing herself beneath the shade of the matting, she spoke with the petulance which was the larger portion of her nature.

"The ovens themselves are no less stifling than the House of Terah this day!"

Sarai smiled with understanding and moved upon the cushions, that she might make room for the girl to rest in comfort.

"Truly," she said, "it is an hour for seeking the coolness of the roof."

The mouth of Lot's wife grew sullen.

"If there is coolness in all of Haran, it is unknown to me."

"Later, with the sunset, will come a wind . . ."

"And still later, with the sunrise, new heat to scorch and wither us!" said Lot's wife, mockingly. She added: "Thus it has been throughout our years in Haran. Surely we have demons for husbands, that they would have us dwell beneath such skies!"

Sarai spoke quietly, striving for patience.

"Is it that they suffer less, our husbands, in the burning heat of the market place, on such a day?"

Lot's wife made no answer. Reaching forward one slim brown arm, she took from the platter a cluster of grapes. Slowly, while she spoke, she pulled them from their stems and crushed them, one after another, between the sharp whiteness of her teeth. Her eyes stared moodily into the blistered streets, empty save for a single caravan which stumbled in the direction of the bazaar, men and animals sickened by the dizzying heat.

" Now do my thoughts return to the cool shadows of Ur," she said, " to the sound of music made for dancing, and the glances of men who found me fair . . ."

Sarai looked up with astonishment. In Ur the sun burned even more fiercely, and the winds across the plain at noontide were like the crackle of flames beneath a cooking pot. Yet she made no answer, having come to know that those whose eyes look into memory often cast aside both truth and reality, that they may behold a more pleasing thing.

" In Ur I was no wife to live between high walls like a caged beast! In Ur other men than Lot offered the marriage price for me. Would that my father yet bargained, and that I yet laughed and danced, knowing there were many who found me fair . . ."

For a little time Sarai regarded her in silence. The girl, motherless and ungoverned, her beauty exploited by the greed of her father, had known greater freedom than was usual among the virgins of Ur. Thus, restrictions brought upon her by marriage were as walls confining her to a prison, closing out both youth and joy.

" In truth," said Sarai then, " there is a time for girlhood, and for the ways of a girl's heart, but that time has passed us on another road. Look not back upon it wailing and lamenting, like a foolish child after a toy outgrown, a cake eaten."

Within the face of Lot's wife there was no answering gentleness. She wrenched her shoulder from beneath the touch of Sarai's hand, and the rich curve of her reddened mouth grew yet more bitter.

" Would I had never known the road a wife must follow! For I am not such a one as can find delight in the making of swaddling clothes, the keeping of a house, the cooking of meals a man never ceases to devour! Behold, five years have passed since we followed the House of Terah to Haran. Within them, twice have I suffered the pain and ugliness of bearing, and for what but gloom upon the face of my husband because the bearing was of daughters, not of sons? What have I to do with sons or daughters? Their wailing and vomiting when I would have peace! Their calling after water in the night! Their soiling of my tunics with hands never clean!" She thrust forth her sandals and gazed upon them. "Behold my feet! In all of Ur were none more graceful! Is it that they were made for dancing to the tune of children's choking and wailing? Would a thousand times that these daughters of my bearing were your own! But you also would have sons, seeing that such a thing would be pleasing to Abram . . ."

"Even daughters," said Sarai, quietly, "rather than to be without a child."

The girl shrugged.

"It is the way of husbands, this wanting of sons," she said, with resentment. "If Lot would hearken to my voice and take a concubine! But, in this matter, he has refused to hear me . . ."

Sarai stared at her in silence, having no words to answer so astounding a burst of resentment. For all its honor and antiquity, the custom was one from which most wives shrank in dread. It was said that a secondary wife was the beginning of sorrow, yet Lot's wife spoke in the sulky tone of a spoiled child denied a honey cake.

"How is it," asked Sarai, in unconcealed wonder, "that a woman can wish to see a secondary wife in the house of her husband?"

"Never could she be equal to me," answered the girl placidly, "since I am the first wife of his choosing. For her it would be to look to the ways of my servants and the needs of my household, to receive my husband when his attentions have grown tiresome to me, to suffer the pain of bearing, even as I have done . . . and may do again. For," she confessed bitterly, "strong is the fear upon me that I have conceived another child. Still," she added, hope warming her voice, "with the help of the gods, I may yet cast it from me."

Beholding Sarai's face, she laughed lightly, insolently, and with contempt.

"Five years have we dwelt with our husbands," she said, "and you, who pray for children, are still barren of them! Can the gods hear nothing? " She leaned against the cushions and closed her eyes, a curled black lock lying, together with a jeweled earring, upon the apricot tint of her cheek. " Did I walk in the sandals of Sarai," she said, drowsily, " then, indeed, would I ask that my husband take a secondary wife! For seeing that you are barren . . ."

Sarai lifted her head, and the shame that burned within her breast swept upward on tongues of flame along her throat, across her cheek, to the edge of her rich dark hair.

" A son who is flesh of my flesh shall be heir unto Abram! " she said proudly.

Lot's wife smiled.

" The hope of Sarai is as broad as the desert," she answered, " and as empty."

# IV

THE HOUSE OF TERAH SLEPT AND THERE WAS NOTHING TO BREAK the silence save the lonely sound of a cricket chirping in the garden below the lattice of the window. Earlier the moon had hung in the west, as thin and richly red as a slice of a pomegranate. Now it had sunk into the sands of the desert beyond, and the night belonged to the stars.

The hour was very late. Some time before, Sarai had heard the haunting and familiar ritual performed at midnight by the temple priests who stood watch through the hours of darkness. Their magnificent hymn to the moon-god rose with the incense of the high altar and, like the incense, faded slowly, lingeringly, into the far blue reaches of the sky. Below them the sleeping city lay hushed and white, its feathery palms black-etched and still. A thin mist, rising from the river, drifted across the countryside. And into it, as quietly as shadows, moved the caravan of Abram on its homeward journey from Ur.

Earlier that day, a courier had brought word of his return —

" Before the false dawn, if the gods are kind . . ." And for the first time Sarai received her husband's message without a sense of joy. She saw the courier upon his way and sat looking, lifelessly and without pleasure, upon the small clay tablet in her hands. It was more than the space of an hour before she summoned Eliezer, the steward, that the household might be made ready, or sought out festive garments to wear for Abram's eyes. These tasks, each of which had been a delight to her in other days, now seemed burdensome beyond the doing. Indeed, it was as if she had grown incapable of everything save dejection. Tortured by the words of Lot's wife, she had brooded upon them until her days were lengths of solitary wretchedness.

Yet the thought of a secondary wife was not a stranger to her. Of late it had appeared often before her, in the manner of an evil spirit come to frighten and pursue her. When she opened her eyes to the morning, its grisly shape crouched beside her bed. When she would have eaten, it sat at her table, staring, so that hunger departed from her and a maidservant carried out, untouched, the food from Azubah's skillful hands. It kept pace with her when, sleep forsaking her, she rose to walk on the roof top or in the courtyard. Even with Abram's arms about her, she felt its chill touch upon her shoulder and buried her face against him, shivering.

" What is it, my darling? Has some illness come upon you? "

" Nay, nay," she shook her head, casting her eyes downward, that he might not see the glisten of her tears.

He smiled indulgently, as upon a child.

" A moon passes swiftly, and Sarai need not fear that harm will come to us. The men of my caravan are worthy of trust, and even though it staggers beneath its own riches, none will set upon it. For let Sarai remember the armed guard which marches beside us, our armed escort, strong and of vigilance."

His voice went on, fading from her ears and from her thoughts. " He thinks it is of his journey I speak," she said to herself, and knew gratitude that the truth was concealed from him, and she need not stand before him in the naked shame of her fear and guilt, in the futility of her prayers.

Not even Abram surmised the number of her visits to the tem-

37

ple which, in Haran also, was a citadel of the moon-god, the familiar ziggurat rising high above the city, its terraces glorified with shrubs and flowers. Into Haran, as into Ur, came daily processions of pilgrims driving livestock before them, carrying baskets of cheese and grain, bundles of linen and wool, skins of milk and oil and wine, measures of copper and gold, the tithes and taxes and votive offerings for the god. At the temple gates clerks inspected and weighed the offerings, recorded them on damp clay tablets, passed the pilgrims receipts on smaller clay tablets, and hastened them upon their way.

The temple area itself was like a smaller city, bustling with duties and activities set apart. Beside lesser temples of beauty, even magnificence, there were living quarters for the priests, slaves, and innumerable workers, among them cooks, sweepers, overseers, scullery boys, messengers, and scribes. Of scribes there seemed to be no end, for all matters were recorded upon clay tablets for the temple archives, whether a priest had sacrificed an ox, whether a farmer had paid in tithes two measures of barley, whether it was the judgment of the priestly court that a certain man, for striking his father, should have his hand cut off. Also inscribed upon clay were letters of credit, bills of lading, checks, balance sheets, mortgages, and other contracts of business, none being omitted, seeing that, both within and without the temple area, they were required by law.

There were storerooms for the goods brought to the temple gates, and for the finished work of the temple craftsmen, such things being used in trade, to earn the support of those within the sacred walls.

As the center of learning, the temple was open, not only to those who would enter the priesthood, but to those turned to other high callings, such as medicine and surgery. Certain of the priests served as teachers, others spent their lives writing and copying scholarly documents for the temple library, where vast numbers of clay tablets were contained. Others, interested in antiquities, gave their days to the temple museum. Some were masters of liturgical music, among them those whose office was the chanting of strangely beautiful laments for the dead. There were priestly judges who ruled upon cases brought before them, and whose verdicts were announced daily to those awaiting them in an outer court. Aside from the priests charged with temple rituals and sacrifices, there were exorcisers skilled in releasing those under evil spells, in purifying those who had transgressed, in restraining or driving out whatever *lil* possessed the ill or mad. Likewise of much importance was the order of diviners, who foretold the future by interpreting unusual happenings or dreams, by consulting the livers of animals, or by observing the movements of the stars.

These Sarai had consulted many times, imploring them to give her some glimpse of the future wherein she might behold a child of her own flesh in the House of Terah. One, an astrologer, said such a child had been promised her when the almond trees had many times flowered and borne fruit. Another said she was to be the mother of sons more numerous than the stars themselves. But the soothsayer who looked for guidance upon the entrails of a freshly slain fowl, shook his head as if in sorrow and would reveal no word of that which he beheld.

For the gift of a child, Sarai had made countless offerings, worn all manner of charms and amulets advised by the priests, purchased, to be sacrificed in her behalf, doves, a sheep, a lamb, a yearling calf, even a bullock. Other visitors to the temple prayed, within her hearing, " God of the Moon, grant me length of days, years of much abundance." But Sarai asked only protection for Abram and a child to raise up his name.

Desperately she consulted the elderly midwives and hearkened to their garrulous counsel regarding the most propitious hours and days for the begetting of sons. To the ears of Maacah came talk of magic potions which, taken at the changing of the moon, would make fertile the body of any woman, even her who had ceased to bear. These Sarai drank gladly and with hope, though the nauseous stench of them both sickened and revolted her. Thus, from moon to moon, she awaited a child and at last, in tears upon Maacah's broad breast, gave herself up to despair. But Maacah, ever rich in comfort, named wives made known to her in the gossip of the slave women whose firstborn had come only with their middle years.

Yet by such a marriage Abram was shamed before men, and

thus there grew within Sarai's bosom the gnawing fear that he might seek sons through another. How many men, she said to herself, have put away the most beloved of wives for such a cause? Indeed, their number was not to be counted. Nor was such a thing to be looked upon as an injustice, even by the eyes of the courts. Rather, it was seen as a duty, an obligation, a sacrifice upon the altar of family honor. In anguish she pictured the moment, saw the tall figure of her husband enter the room, looking quietly and with decision upon her, heard him pronounce the words by which their marriage would be ended. " From this day forward, seeing that you have borne me no sons . . . you are not my wife."

Night after night the terror was upon her, so that she shuddered, crying out in her sleep, and was sickened by day, and turned from the table without tasting food. Yet there came from Abram's lips no word akin to that which she feared. Perhaps he waits for me to make the choice of such a one . . . after the law of the land. . . . Such laws were well known to her, and to other women likewise, for, despite the sheltered manner of their lives, they were not without authority. Thus it was granted to them to plead before the courts, to employ labor, to have slaves as well as wealth in their own names, to share in family estates. There were laws, born of custom and need, for all manner of women, even those fruitful and those barren, and these came to sound upon Sarai's ears with the dull, repeated rhythm of the temple drums.

" *If a man's wife has borne him no children, and he takes to himself a secondary wife, that children may be borne unto him, the secondary wife shall not be made equal to the first wife, but the children of both shall share equally in the estate of the father.*

" *If, instead, the wife give a maid to her husband, that children may be borne unto him, the children of the maid shall be the legal children of the wife, and subject to her.*

" *If she gives a maid to her husband, and the maid has borne children, and afterward the maid has made herself equal to her mistress because she has borne children, her mistress shall not sell her, but shall reduce her to bondage and do with her as she will.*"

After a little time Sarai ceased to ponder these things and rose from her bed and began to dress. No longer would she divide the watches of the night between the phantoms of her misery and the sad, monotonous chirping of the cricket below. She put on her kidskin slippers and girded her tunic with a jeweled belt. Still combing the gentle darkness of her hair, she made her way through the passage, out to the gallery, and down the brick steps to the open court.

Hearing the light brushing of her feet upon the steps, Anun, the watchdog, rose at the entrance, growling low within his throat. She spoke gently and he at once bounded to her side, eager for the touch of her hand. Having shared the long, silent hours of her loneliness, Anun had come to be companion as well as guardian. He had been born in the stable and carried to Abram soon afterward by an enchanted slave boy. Thus he had never known the streets and was wholly apart from the packs of vicious, half-wild dogs roaming the city, fighting each other unto death over scraps of carrion and refuse.

When he was but a small puppy, one of the temple priests had laid a holy admonition upon him: " May thy jaw be ruthless, may thou rend and slay, may thou lap the blood of any who would harm this house." It was to be feared that Anun, under so strong a conjure, would grow into a slavering beast ever thirsting for kill. He was, instead, of great gentleness and devotion, even showing a desire to enter into the house with the family. This, however, being of ill portent, was a forbidden thing.

The court was lighted only by the stars. A faint wind stirred the leaves and touched upon the fragrance of the flowers which, opening by night, filled the air with heady sweetness. From without the walls came the tread of the watchman, muffled in the dampened dust of the street, and now and then, the sharp, quick sound of a donkey's feet as some man of Haran went his way.

Sarai sat quietly beside the far wall, her hand upon the massive head of the watchdog, her shoulders drooping. Of late her face had been grave and still, her eyes without light. When hope departed from her, there had departed also her feminine rejoicing in adornment. The delicate and beautiful fabrics fashioned by certain slave women, she laid within a clothes chest with her jewels, her scents, her eye paints, wearing, instead, tunics old and without charm, as one might wear garments of sorrow or repentance. For such as this, Maacah scolded her angrily. "How is it that my lady, being wife to Abram and mistress of his proud house, yet garbs herself like an untidy slave?" And tears came to the eyes of both, seeing that they shared between them an understanding of all things. Thus, for Maacah as much as for Abram, had she put on festive garments this night. The folds of the tunic, lying across her knees, had the gossamer delicacy of mist, the golden beech leaves of her necklace and earrings gave her a look at once shining and joyous. Yet she would have known but little more bitterness in the wearing of sackcloth.

Let the gods forbid that Lot should become heir to Abram, beside whom he was a figure weak and ludicrous. Abram was known, even to strangers beholding him for the first time, as a leader of men, having about him the quality of command in the bearing of a just king, a wise tribal chief, a conqueror whose warriors derided death in the following of his banners. He towered taller than other men, his shoulders broader and more massive, his stride longer, his head more proudly set. Those who loitered in the streets stepped aside for him, those who brawled were silenced at the sight of him, yet those who suffered sought his counsel and deliverance. To be wife to such a man was to know pride in abundance, but to give him no child . . .

Her dreary thoughts broke and were scattered by a sudden confusion in the street, the familiar and unmistakable sound of arrival, the voices of Abram and Lot, and then of slaves leading the animals to the stables behind the house. The heavy wooden door swung open and was closed again and the watchdog, leaping up, bounded across the court to greet his master, uttering throaty cries of joy. Despite the surge of excitement within her, Sarai did not hasten forth, but remained in the shadows, awaiting the departure of Lot. She heard Abram speaking quietly, silencing and soothing the dog. Looking into the dimness of the entrance hall, she could see the two men pause for washing at the great terra-cotta jar, could hear the splashing of water, glimpse the careless flurry of drying linens. For a moment there was no other sound. Then Lot spoke, as was his custom, with an edge of resentment to his voice.

"Never was a journey of such a length! My bones cry aloud with weariness, my eyes swim in sleep! "

The deep tones of Abram, rich in pleasant humor, answered him.

"Such soreness and aching forget themselves in the ease of a man's bed."

"This ease I will seek. Live forever, my uncle."

"Live forever."

With a yawn widely and loudly made, Lot crossed the court, quickening his pace so that he mounted the stairs in great leaps, the glimmer of his white tunic suddenly snuffed out in upper blackness. He hastens to her by whom he is despised, thought Sarai with pity. She pictured him entering the room, kindling one of the lamps, holding it above the bed that he might gaze with love and yearning upon the rich beauty of his sleeping wife, fearful that when he touched her she would rise in anger. How had he summoned courage to refuse the taking of a concubine? Courage had no portion in Lot. Yet those who love vainly often act in desperation.

A pang, new and agonizing, smote Sarai's heart. How many moons shall wane, she thought, before Abram hastens to another, and not to me? How many nights, waking to the sound of his return, will I wake also to the sound of his footsteps ascending to the room of the secondary wife, beloved for her bearing of sons? And again the panic came upon her, so that when Abram laid aside the drying linens and stepped within the court, it was in a voice faint and shaken that she called to him.

"My husband . . ."

He turned, startled, uncertain, as she emerged from the shadow of the vine upon the wall and sought refuge within his arms. They embraced with the silent tenderness of those whose love is as a tree, deep-rooted and enduring, by which they are sheltered, and which will live as long as they both shall live, and after. In a moment, tilting her chin so that the starlight fell upon her face, he asked with gentleness, "How is it that Sarai walks within the court at an hour when even the dogs of Haran are silenced in sleep? "

"Sleep would not come to me," said Sarai, lamely.

43

" All is well with the household? "

" All is well . . . save with Terah, whose sickness is unchanged. Yet, with the setting of the sun, he slept in peace."

Abram sighed heavily.

" May the night give him strength."

He stood in silence, his head bowed, as though recalling with sorrow the days of his boyhood and the giant among men who had been Terah his father. After a time, Sarai touched him gently, seeking to divert him from the vain griefs of such remembrance.

" What of the journey to Ur? "

" A fruitful journey, indeed," he answered, and turned to her, smiling. " Yet more tiresome than all the others, being filled with outrageous demands from petty rulers, endless bargaining with traders and officials, two tablets of importance shattered by a clumsy slave. But let us say no more of these matters, seeing that they are past and I am again within the doors of my own house."

" Would my husband have me summon a maidservant, that food may be set before him? "

" Nay, I have no wish for food."

He put his arm around her and they ascended the stairs together, yet as they came to the gallery, he halted and turned his back upon the passage to Sarai's room. Out of the dimness and silence he looked at her so gravely that her heart was touched by fright and stumbled within her bosom.

" Let it be that we go upon the roof," he said, " quietly, lest the household be awakened, for there is a matter that weighs heavily upon me. Until this hour no word of it has passed my lips. Yet now I would speak of it, I think, without waiting for the day."

The spark of fright flared up within her, became a torch which leaped and seared. This, then, is the hour of my destruction. My husband has turned his face from me. He will come no more to my bed. Yet surely he will not send me forth, seeing that there is none to receive me. Am I then to remain beneath the roof of my lord while he takes another in my place? God of gods, open first the door to my house of dust!

She found herself upon the roof top, standing numbly and without words, with no memory of having climbed the upper

44

stair. She felt the softness of cushions beneath her body and, of a sudden, the flare sank and went out, leaving within her mouth the taste of ashes, dry and dead.

"Let my husband speak," she said, dully.

Abram leaned forward, speaking intently, as one who follows a pattern of words many times laid forth in his thoughts. His eyes did not seek her own, but were fixed upon his rigidly knotted hands.

"It is a thing no longer to be shunned, seeing that it gives me no rest, keeping pace with me even in the length of the homeward journey."

See how it is with Abram, she thought, from the depths of her misery. Even as with me, these many moons past. Yet, hearing the gentleness in his voice, she sensed that he was striving to treat the sorry business kindly, to preserve for her some measure of her pride.

There comes to every man, he said, some burden of conviction which he bears in silence, concealing it even from the beloved, lest it be in error. Thus he, Abram, had guarded his tongue, allowing it to yield up no word of that which tormented him. Yet now, being certain of his own heart and the nature of his own duty, strong in judgment firmly settled and not to be shaken . . .

"No longer would I bear with the manner of our worship," he said simply.

Sarai's eyes flared wide.

"The manner — did my husband say — of worship?"

He nodded, slowly and without words and, being filled with his own thoughts, saw nothing of the stunned look in her face.

"Nay!" gasped Sarai. "This — it is *this* of which my husband would speak without waiting for the day?"

She sank back into the shadows, filled with sudden strife between laughter and tears. Yet the chill departed from her flesh, likewise the quivering terror. How loud and accusing the voice of guilt! she thought ruefully, and was returned to that which lay about her, the sky, the roof top, the city adrift in mist below. For a time she heard nothing that passed Abram's lips, but lay at peace beneath the healing touch of wind, savoring the sweetness of the night-blooming flowers, gazing upward, as in her childhood, at the glittering form of the lion crouched upon a serpent in the stars of the northern skies. Then the voice of her husband was strengthened within her ears.

". . . thus did Lot enter the chapel of Pa-sag, asking her protection upon our way."

She roused to the familiar name.

"I too have sacrificed to the goddess of caravans in my husband's name."

He moved restlessly, interrupting her words.

"To Pa-sag, to Nannar, to Marduk, to the family teraphim, to images and idols without end. In truth, when we consider our counting of the gods . . ."

"Can the gods be counted? Surely it is not known to us how many thousands of them hold our fate within their hands."

"And," he said gently, "if one god declares a man shall live and another says he must die?"

She stared at him in astonishment.

"Then it is the greater god who triumphs over the lesser — a thing known to Abram for many years past, since first he lifted his voice before the altar of sacrifice."

"In the simple and unquestioning days of my boyhood," he answered, quietly.

She stared at him blankly for a little space, her ears unable to receive his words.

"What — what is it that my husband has said?" she stammered at last.

He laid his hand upon her own, as if to comfort her.

"Let Sarai have no fear of Nannar's displeasure. In the temple of the moon — there, truly, he is both terrifying and awesome. Yet, seeing that he is but an ill-carved lump of wood, and can neither speak nor act . . ."

"*Abram!*" The word was a wail of panic. Flinging herself upon him, that he might be shielded from the eyes of the outraged god, she began to plead with him in terrified whispers. "Now, let my husband seek pardon for that which he has said, *quickly,* lest he be stricken with leprosy or even d —" her lips could not bring forth the word. She began to pray below her breath, hastily, and in desperation. ". . . let not your wrath fall upon him for, in truth, it is not Abram who speaks, but a man maddened by the length of a journey, the heat of a day."

"Nay." His quiet, unshaken voice stayed her fear, drew her to the shelter of his arms as to a refuge. "Surely it is known to Sarai that I would bring no evil upon her, that I would protect her utterly."

"And yet," she whispered, "how is it that the strength of Abram may prevail against the strength of Nannar?"

He soothed her as one would soothe a child, speaking in low and reasoning tones.

"Is he indeed a god of strength, seeing that when the Elamites sacked Ur he was borne, impotent and silent, from the gates of his own temple into the land of the enemy?"

She drew apart from him, troubled and confused.

"It is a thing of which I have no understanding," she faltered. "Oh, my husband, trouble me not with doubts, destroy not the gods of my youth, for truly they are dear to me."

"The goddess Pa-sag," he said, "a shape of mud. How is it that such a one may make safe our journeys? Are images of mud and gilt to have wisdom? Behold, on a certain day I watched a man who, in the Street of Potters, bought an idol that he might worship before it — an image of clay shaped but a little hour before, yet warm with the fires of the oven. Is it before such as these that men are to bow in worship — idols graven in ugliness and mud?"

Bewilderment stood in her eyes.

"If these idols are indeed without power, how is it that men look upon them worshiping, believing?"

He put her from him, and rose and stood apart, and spoke as one who, having labored in the fields of silence, offers the first fruits of his gleaning.

"There is within the heart of man a Voice which lifts his eyes unto the stars, a knowledge of Strength and Wisdom beyond himself — and herein lies his faith. Yet faith is a thing intangible, and man, poor creature under the sun, ever seeks comfort within the tangible, needing a symbol of his faith to see, to touch, lest he be afraid. Needing a symbol that he may say unto himself:

47

' Here is my faith — here before my eyes, within my hand — and thus it is not lost to me, nor by it will I be abandoned.' So have men prayed to idols, but their seeking is of another God — a God higher than clay — whose hands made both the heaven and the earth and cast the girdle of Orion in stars across the sky."

Sarai's voice was uncertain, troubled.

" Such things are beyond my understanding . . ."

" Neither do I understand, yet there is within me that which believes — and seeks to know."

He moved to the edge of the parapet and stood gazing out across the blurred white silence of the sleeping city into the hills beyond. When he spoke again, it was in the hushed manner of worship, and his voice rose slowly, gently, like incense offered upon the high altar of his heart.

" Where is the man whose soul has never pondered upon the mystery of Being, who never sought to know what lies beyond the silence of the stars? Ever a thousand riddles voice themselves within his heart! From whence comes man, and where is it that he goes — wrapped about with the dignity of death? And death, itself, wherein all men are equal, and from which no man is spared — is it a desert waste in which we perish, or is it that some green oasis waits for us beyond?

" This earth, this universe, bounded by wind and sand and stars — whose hands have shaped it? The way of the wind in its passing, the way of beauty within the smallest flower, the holiness of dawn — who has ordered these things? Who watches upon them, weaving the thread of existence into a pattern that eternity itself is powerless to change? Can any man declare that these things have come about by chance? Nay, I, Abram, seek — and I would find — this God, this Strength, this Glory, immortal and everlasting, whose voice abides within the souls of men! "

He stood in silence, his face lifted to the radiance of the stars, and she turned to him and beheld him as the striving of all of mankind against the oldest riddle of life.

# V

WITH THE WAXING OF THE MOON, TERAH'S ILLNESS WAXED ALSO
and, in the end, they fulfilled their days together. Long before
another crescent leaned out of the west, the old man lay within
the cool brick tomb beneath the family chapel, his cylinder seal
around his neck, beside him the bowl and spoon which would
serve him in the land of shadows.

Terah died just as the moon began its waning, a white and
gibbous shape among the stars. Shortly before the false dawn,
Maacah came to summon Abram, and the whispered urgency of
her words roused him quickly, even from the depths of his slumber. Sarai, stirring and half-awakened, heard them hasten down
the passage together and opened her eyes only in time to behold
the last flickering rays of the torch fade into the darkness. Like
all others of the household, she had been aware for many moons
that Terah's days were numbered. Yet now, the end being come,
she knew sharp grief in parting from him at whose hand she had
been given so much of kindness.

Thus she hastened from her bed, drew on a loose tunic, and,
pushing her long, heavy hair back upon her shoulders, made her
way down the darkened passage, shivering a little in the chill, the
bricks damp and cold beneath her unclad feet. Yellow lamplight
shone from the doorway of Terah's bedchamber, but, even as she
reached the threshold and would have entered, she was halted
by the sound of her own name in the old man's gasping voice.

". . . and if Sarai shall bear you no sons . . . how, then, may
the House of Abram live on . . . when you have followed me
into the dust? Thus do I counsel you . . . at the very hour of
my death: Take other wives . . ."

She stood stunned, one hand stretched forth, frozen in the

49

midst of movement. She heard the thin sputter of the lamp, the heavy beating of her heart. The silent moment lengthened, became yet more incredible. Then a chill that was not of the night seized upon her and shook her into reality. She drew back into the passage and huddled against the darkly shadowed wall, that those who listened might behold neither her coming nor her shame.

In the dimly lighted room Maacah stood silent, impassive, holding the lamp so that its wick burned bright upon the oil. Within the circle of yellow radiance lay the figure of Terah, as pale and wasted as a wraith beneath a moon. Abram, standing beside the bed, gazed upon his father gravely and with pity. His lips were edged with the white line of strain, and stark misery stood in his eyes, yet his will was not to be shaken by the sorrow of this hour, and he spoke without faltering before it.

" No other wife would I take," he said, quietly, " even in my misfortune."

The voice of Terah was lifted in sharp and querulous impatience.

" This taking of a secondary wife," he said fretfully, " is not for love, but for the begetting of sons. Being the custom of our people, the manner of our law, and favored by the gods . . ."

Abram lifted his chin.

" In the House of Abram there shall be no wife but Sarai, and still may we hold sons within our arms."

The old man pulled himself upward from his pillows and pointed a bony finger at the two who watched beside him. His faded eyes blazed with authority and, for the space of a breath, it was as if they beheld the Terah of other years, the giant among men. A sudden timbre of command in his voice strengthened and steadied the words as he cried, " *Take a secondary wife* . . ."

Then his shoulders sagged and were suddenly spare, and it was as if the mantle of authority had been snatched from his keeping and laid upon his son, leaving him as naked in death as in birth. But, knowing that this was good, and in accordance with the best years of his striving, Terah lay back, released the stern grip of the patriarch upon the thread of life, and thus, at last, knew peace.

Seeing that all was ended, Abram went slowly to his knees and, taking his father's frail hands, pressed them upon his lips and to his brow. Sobs broke from his throat, hoarse and rending, and, hearing them, Sarai knew at what cost he had denied Terah the promise, with what singular loyalty he had violated the precedents of countless generations. Tears came to her eyes. She moved forward swiftly and with compassion, but Maacah, looking up, motioned her away. " This moment," said the eyes of Maacah, " belongs to the dead and the living, to the father and to the son . . . and none may intrude upon it."

Obediently, the girl turned and went back to her own room, and there was within her no sense of rejection, but rather a sense of sweet tranquillity that warmed her veins like wine. Despite the sorrows of this unhappy night, she had been loosed from her wretchedness, unshackled from her fears. Not even briefly had Abram nourished the thought of a secondary wife. Nay, this misery had been grown by her own hand, rooted in her own jealousy and humiliation. And thus her grisly torturer slunk into the shadows and departed with the night. She lay across the rumpled bed, watched the morning edge in at the doorway, heard the first light calls of the birds, and knew more of peace than since the days of her childhood.

In the time that came to pass thereafter, her heart lightened, her eyes grew warm, and her spirit found many causes for rejoicing. It was as if she had cast aside the years and was again the bride of Ur, blithe and vivid, taking delight in all things. About her was the radiance of one who knows herself loved and desired, and, in the manner of all women seeking a new beginning, she turned to thought of adornment. The delicate and beautiful garments fashioned by the slave women were brought forth from the clothes chests to be fondled and admired and worn. She went to the bazaars, seeking new trinkets from the jewelers, new fragrances for skin and hair, new tints from the exotic lands of the south.

Of a sudden, all things seemed to conspire in her favor. The fierce heat was lessened, the mornings were sweet and cool. Abram, being occupied with business matters in Haran, did not accompany the caravan of the new moon, but sent Lot in his stead. Peace filled the household. The slaves worked deftly and without idleness. For many days there had been neither sickness nor strife among them. Even Lot's wife had been less troublesome of late, railing at her children and serving-women but seldom, finding fault with few matters in her joy at knowing she was not, after all, with a third child.

To Sarai the first hour of darkness was no longer a time for loneliness and nostalgia, but rather for a womanly content in the pattern of her days and Abram's. She felt a deep and joyous pride in the pleasant rooms, the quiet-mannered slaves, the flowering courtyard, the savory supper smells. Earlier, with the help of a maidservant, she had bathed from her body the heat and dust of the day. Now, anointed with fragrance and garbed in a tunic still sweet with sun and wind, she sat with Lot's wife in the upper Common Room. For a time, the two children of Lot had played upon the floor, but when one struck the other and both burst into noisy tears, their mother had shouted for a servant to remove them from her hearing. Whereupon, being borne to their own portion of the house, they ceased their woe and fell asleep, cuddled together as fondly as newborn puppies.

Three lamps burned in the upper Common Room, yet the corners were heavy with shadow. For the small and quiet household of Abram, a room so spacious was near to absurd. The house, having more than twenty rooms, had been built at the beginning by a merchant whose family included two wives, five concubines, nineteen children, two daughters-in-law, and three grandsons. When his family were gathered for a festive evening, together with visitors and servants, indeed the upper Common Room had been crowded to its very walls. Now, occupied by only two slight women, it assumed the look of a vast council chamber in which one's voice would be wholly swallowed by receding echoes.

A narrow rug, rich and beautifully wrought, was laid down the center of the floor. About the room were smaller rugs of equal beauty to be used as seats, numerous heaped cushions against which to rest, low stools, small tables, and great decorated chests. Here Sarai lingered often in the early evenings, enchanting Lot's children with stories and play, talking of household matters with the young steward Eliezer, hearing the complaints of Lot's wife, or savoring in solitude the quiet loveliness of the hour.

From below came the sound of the evening rituals, so familiar that she beheld them as though they passed before her eyes. Fresh green leaves were being placed upon the great clay water jars, that their coolness might remain within. The lamps, newly filled and with wicks newly trimmed, sent forth a yellow warmth not unlike the soft yellow star of Ishtar burning in the west. House slaves, in sandals and short tunics, passed to and fro, in and out, bearing platters of fruit, skins of wine, brushwood to mend the fires, braziers to warm the night. Such braziers burned in the courtyard until their first fumes were spent, and then, the coals sweetened with incense, were carried to upper rooms already chilled and damp. The sight of the braziers burning through the first darkness of the courtyard was a thing to be remembered, lovely, nostalgic. Their flames cast rich, quivering shadows on the brick walls, edged the vines and blossoms with light, summoned great and beautiful moths which came winging from outer darkness to perish within the coals.

A hush of waiting had fallen upon the household as it looked to the master's return. Sarug, the porter, scarcely more than a child, dozed in the entrance hall, with Anun, the watchdog, asleep beneath his bench. From the kitchen could be heard the slow bubbling of the great copper pots upon the brick cooking range, likewise the thin breathing of live coals in the open fireplace where the meats were roasting. There was a faint sound of knives and ladles and platters as the slaves went about the last portions of their work, but no laughter or light-hearted talk passed between them, for Azubah, the cook, had shouted for silence and now sulked within it, glowering and grim.

Azubah and Maacah were the same age, born in the month of Tammuz, of the same year. Both had served the family from their tenderest days, both possessed wisdom, loyalty, and skill, yet they were as unlike as the desert and the sown. Maacah was warm and motherly and of great gentleness, her patience as deep and unchanging as the Euphrates itself. Azubah, spare and angular and dour, knew little of patience and less of gentleness. Hers was the voice of wind rattling a dead palm. Her eyes and speech and face were as sharp as broken stones. Grimly, she crouched before the fireplace, her skin burned red by the heat of the coals, her hair become wisps about forehead and ears, her grease-stained tunic bespeaking her long combat with the roast.

From time to time she spat angry words into the fire and upon the table, where Maacah once again wet the grapes to keep them cool and firm of flesh. Once Eliezer came to the kitchen on a brief errand and, seeing him, Azubah fell back upon her haunches and cried with indignation, " Is the master not yet come? "

Eliezer, quiet of manner, answered her without inflection. " Not yet. Again delayed is the hour of his return."

He passed from the room, his dignity and calm making matters yet worse for Azubah's temper. Snatching one of the copper ladles, she cast it across the room, where it struck and shattered a pottery bowl. The other slaves did not so much as look up, having learned that her furies, if fed with neither interest nor protest, soon died and were forgotten. But Azubah was not yet ready to be silenced.

" Ten thousand plagues upon the sorrows of this day! " she cried violently. " Is it not enough that I should watch before the fire until my flesh is more redly scorched than the flesh of the sheep itself? Nay, it is not enough! The serving boy Jarah — may he fall into a well and never rise! — is so slow in his fetching of the firewood that scarcely a coal remains to keep the heat within the roast! JARAH! " she bawled suddenly, adding with bitterness, " The ears of that boy are stopped with ignorance and wax! "

Mirth, quickly stifled, glimmered upon the faces of those who listened. It was known to them that Azubah had a great measure of affection for the young demon whose merriment stirred and enlivened her days. Yet this was a thing she sought to deny, even before herself.

Jarah, dark-eyed and laughing, was an orphan of the desert sent as a gift to Terah from a trader of the south. In another year he would be called a man, yet now he was both ungainly and spindle-shanked, with the unkempt hair and unwashed hands and impish mischief of a growing lad. The eating of sweetmeats and the plaguing of Azubah were only a little less dear to his heart than Eliezer, whom he admired above all men. Even now, entering through the outer door with an armload of brushwood, he came softly and without sound behind her, his mouth working in mock grief before the fury of her words.

"And the master of the house, still does he linger — the gods know where — while the milk sours in the goatskins, the cakes crumble with age, and the meat is blackened in the waiting! "

Maacah, being accustomed to the rages of her friend, answered quietly.

"The tongue of Azubah builds mountains from a grain of sand, the eyes of Azubah see destruction forever at her elbow. Let my sister put aside her laments and strive for patience. In truth, the flavor is still within the roast and, seeing that darkness is upon us, surely the steps of Abram are turned to his house."

"How is it," Azubah grumbled, "that with each day since the death of Terah — to whom the gods of the dust be merciful! — the master has come late to his evening bread? "

"Truly his heart overflows with grief, and it is said he walks in the darkness and silence beyond the city walls, pondering this and other things . . ." Even Maacah was vague as to the reason, and her voice, faltering, dwindled into silence.

"Even in grief meals await the eating! " said Azubah, tartly. She jerked herself about, ready to seek the ladle she had hurled, and came face to face with the dawdling Jarah. "Face of a donkey! " she shouted. "Brain of a worm that crawls! "

In haste he dropped the firewood and leaped aside. With speed and agility to amaze the beholder, he eluded her blows, snatched a cake from the platter, and disappeared in the direction of the stables.

In the Common Room, Sarai also grew restless with waiting. For more than an hour she had busied herself with embroidering a strip of linen cloth which, when bright with a pattern of golden apricots, would border the hem of a new tunic. She bent close to the lamp as she worked, her dark hair edged with light, her fingers moving with the swift ease of flying birds.

Across from her, leaning gracefully upon some heaped cushions, was the wife of Lot, as lifeless in her indolence, as unreal in her brittle loveliness, as a splendid image. Indeed, she might have been formed in the Street of Potters from some rare clay, glazed and adorned and sent forth to serve as a goddess, a new Ishtar. And should she suddenly lift her eyes to find strangers bowing before her, there would be no surprise within her heart, but only annoyance that their homage had been so long delayed.

Amused by the fancy, Sarai leaned closer to the needlework, seeking to hide her face, but it was a small matter indeed that could escape the sharp and suspicious eyes of the other woman.

"How is it that Sarai smiles in secret delight?" she demanded, caustically. "Is it that some demon lover whispers in her ear?"

"Nay," answered Sarai, speaking with good humor, "if there is such a one within this room, it is in adoration of you, not of me, that he has come, seeing that you are fairer."

Lot's wife shrugged.

"Even a demon," she said, shortly, "rather than Lot! What is there of pleasure in adorning myself for Lot, seeing that he, poor fool, would fall down gibbering and worshiping before me even though I were as ugly and angular as Azubah! Nay — "

From below came the familiar sounds of arrival, the opening and closing of the heavy door, the voice of Sarug, childishly high and piping, the excited cries of the dog, the deeply quiet tones of Eliezer. Putting aside her embroidery, Sarai rose and hastened from the Common Room. Yet, even as she came upon the gallery, she was aware that a swift and unaccountable silence had fallen upon those beneath. Indeed, the only sound was her own gasp as, with questioning eyes, she sought and found the reason.

In the center of the court Abram stood wordless, his eyes as stunned and unanswering as though they were yet fixed upon that which had stricken him. Sarug, bewildered, was drawn apart from him in the manner of a child who senses a fear that is not to be named. Eliezer, startled beyond speech, had put forth one hand as if he would ask in anxiety, "How is it with my master?" and yet could not. There was no sound, no motion save the flare of the torches, the waver of fire burning in the braziers by the wall. Then Abram, lifting his eyes and beholding her, moved forward and flung out his hands in a gesture that besought her to understand that which he would say.

" So wondrous a thing . . .," he began unsteadily. " How am I to believe it has come to pass? Yet . . ."

His voice broke and he stood in silence, rendered helpless by a poverty of words. Sarai ran down the steps to his side. He has seen a vision, she thought, and suddenly she was made timid before him, awed and humbled by the look upon his face.

" In truth," she stammered then, " it is as if the heavens themselves had opened before you . . ."

He answered in the hushed manner of one who approaches the altar of sacrifice.

" This night it has been given to me to hear and to know."

Ever alert to the tides of the household, the slaves sensed some strange and unaccustomed happening and, ceasing their work, grew taut with listening. Maacah, putting aside the fruits, came slowly through the arch with Azubah behind her. The other house slaves followed, crowding the passage, pushing into the edge of the court. Even the little porter, relieved of his fears, drew near and gazed at his master with wide, expectant eyes. Seeing them, Abram showed no displeasure, but rather an elation at the thought of what he was about to reveal to them.

" Come forth! " he cried, suddenly. His voice rang down the length of the court, and they saw that the moment of his wavering was past, and he again possessed himself utterly. " Come forth, all you who dwell in the House of Abram — servants of the kitchen, handmaidens of Sarai, and surely my brethren." For, sensing the excitement below, Lot's wife had emerged from the Common Room and was standing upon the last of the brick steps. " Come forth and hear of this thing! " he cried. " That you may know wherein lies your destiny, and mine. For this night has the Most High God spoken before me; this night the God of heaven and earth walked before his servant, Abram."

It was such a tale as would never cease in the telling. A thousand years hence it would be unfolded again, and yet again, by those who write the annals of the past and those who read of them. Around the supper fires of a thousand caravans it would be remembered, while reddened light shimmered in the faces of the men, and went forth to perish in the darkness beyond. Upon a thousand feast days it would be given to the keeping of grave

57

and black-eyed children as a sacred portion of their heritage. And in a thousand streets it would be made known — streets where, for a coin tossed into a filthy hand, a man might hear marvels from a beggarly storyteller squatted by the city wall. It was such a tale as would never see death, but would share immortality, that all men might hear how, in generations past, he who was called Abram stood under the glittering skies beyond the gates of Haran and knew that God is one God, the Creator and Father of all.

"God of the moon," his heart cried out in wonder, "and of the sun, and of the everlasting stars; God of rivers and of mountains, of the desert and the sown; God of cool green cornfields, of fair blue skies, of lonely dusty desert roads — of all that is known to the eyes of man; of all that abides within the flesh of man: love and bitterness, strength and frailty, dreams and despair, birth and rejoicing, fire and ecstasy, anguish and death."

The stars burned white in the unending reaches of the sky, a vast loneliness brooded upon the empty plain, and a night mist crept out from the edges of the waters, and into the hills. Here in the swiftly fallen darkness, Abram, son of Terah, stood with the living presence of God and heard his voice.

How was it that the Voice arose? Was it out of the passage of the wind, the whisper of the sand, the murmur of waters in the deep of an ancient river? No man could say. Yet it was imprinted forever upon the fabric of this night which, out of all ages, had been chosen to bear the timeless and eternal words:

"Get thee out of thy country, . . . and from thy father's house, unto a land that I will show thee: and I will make of thee a great nation, and I will bless thee, and make thy name great; and thou shalt be a blessing; . . . and in thee shall all families of the earth be blessed."

Thus had God spoken before his servant Abram, but now, quenched by the blank and wondering stares of the house slaves, the splendor of the moment became as dust. How had he thought, holding it forth gladly and unsparingly, that they could partake of it by so sudden a means? Nay, a miracle was not a thing to be seized and divided into portions and shared like a loaf of bread.

"'Get thee out of thy country' . . . ," he began anew, and

dealt with the command deliberately, bit by bit, that they might understand. Yet the words, on his lips, were suddenly flat and tasteless. Save for Eliezer, whose clear, unwavering eyes were filled with perception, the slaves had ceased to hear him and become intent upon their own straying thoughts. Maacah, composed and erect, waited with forbearance for him to make an end of the matter. Azubah, slumped against the arch, dozed with the coming and going of her breath. Lot's wife had seated herself upon the steps and was giving her attention to a broken bracelet. Both Sarug and the watchdog Anun had fallen into slumber beneath the bench by the door. And Sarai, even while she received his words in the submissive silence of a worthy wife, gazed at him with eyes questioning and troubled.

Only a moment before, in the bright mesh of his wonder and joy, he had caught and held them utterly. How had the radiance abandoned him, the moment slipped from his grasp?

"Now, let words of wisdom be given to my lips," he cried, "that those of my household may hear and know: God is one God, living and eternal, no idol fashioned by the hands of men!"

And when it was thus that he began to speak, they were compelled, by the very force of his earnestness, to return to him out of the uncertain wanderings of their thoughts, the vague regions of their understanding.

"Know, my brethren, that these things be of truth: The idols you worship have no power, not even over the skin of a date stone. If you worship them, they will not hear your calling, and even if they heard, they could not answer!"

Sarai stared at him, chilled by the sudden sweat of fear. "Gracious Nannar," she prayed in despair, "have mercy upon him! Hear his words without wrath and, in truth, I will sacrifice a ewe lamb before you, to take away his sin . . ." And there was more she would have promised, had she not been distracted from prayer by the risen voice of her husband.

"There is no God but God. It is he who has stretched forth the earth and placed therein the steadfast mountains, the rivers, and causes the night to cover the day. It is he who sends forth from heaven the rain whereof you may drink. He causes the corn and the olives and the palm trees and fruits of many kinds to spring forth unto you. If you attempt to reckon the favors of God, you shall not be able to count their number.

"He has commanded his servant Abram, with all that belongs to Abram, to go forth into a new land. This we shall do, and Lot and those of his household likewise, if he would tarry with us."

Heads were lifted, eyes restored to life. Here, at last, was a thing to be understood. The entire House of Abram was to go upon a journey to a far land yet unnamed. Surprise, excitement, joy, and dismay passed among those who listened, according to their hearts.

"God is one God and, oh, my brethren, men have need of God. Thus let us rejoice that he will abide with us, and walk before us, and lead us upon our way. Return to your places, my children, and think on these things."

The slaves stirred obediently and, turning away singly and in groups, made their way back to such matters as they had abandoned. If a god had held speech with Abram, son of Terah, and promised to abide with him, then truly the master belonged to the chosen. Their voices rose and fell on murmuring sound, wave after wave of awe and respect.

"In truth," said Maacah, with pride, "the god of our master is a powerful god!"

"In truth," snapped Azubah, "the roast is as cold as a stone!"

# VI

An air of devastation had come upon the house. Portable chests lay open in every room, and about them were heaped and scattered those things which would be disposed within, and those which would be left behind. In the kitchen, Azubah and Maacah discussed whether a certain lamp would be needed, whether they would abandon the largest of the platters, the oldest of the drinking bowls. Scullery girls haggled over certain knives and ladles and pots. In the stables, slave boys bickered among themselves concerning the oxen, the sheep, the donkeys, the goats, arguing whether one had more strength than another, ate a greater portion of food, gave a lesser portion of milk, seemed prepared to die upon the way. Throughout the household, voices were lifted in dissension; laments were borne in with the noonday bread. It seemed to Sarai that with the passing of every hour a new dispute was unveiled before her, a new complaint revealed.

" Say to me now, my lady, is it true that we go, as Eber declares, to a land of demons? Woe, let me first be slain! "

" Behold, I am bent beneath the weight of age. My legs will not support me for the space of an hour altogether! How, then, may I follow a caravan across the world? "

" My lady, have pity upon me, miserable slave to the wife of Lot! How am I to make ready for this journey, seeing that such matters are unknown to me and that my mistress will give me no counsel concerning them; that she turns upon me with curses and blows when I speak of them and says that she will have my nose cut from my face if I again disturb her with questions? "

Even Maacah lost patience and came to seek Sarai in the Common Room, dragging by the wrist a weeping and struggling kitchen maid known as Urfa.

" May it please my mistress, tell this daughter of lunatics that we cannot take the cooking range, as she would have us do, seeing that it is built of bricks, one upon the other! Not even upon the back of a camel — "

It was a word ill chosen for, hearing it, the girl uttered a howl of fright and cast herself upon the floor at Sarai's feet. Being accustomed to the donkey caravans of the north, she regarded the great beasts of the sands as bearers of certain destruction, and it was only when she had been promised the privilege of walking with the herds that she would cease her wails.

Shortly before the noonday bread, a number of new slaves, brown and muscular young men of the desert, were marched to the house and delivered up to Eliezer. In their youth and strength, they were exceedingly well-favored, and already two of the maidservants had quarreled over the comeliest of them. Other quarrels flared in the stables and workroom. Indeed, the household had a nightmare quality, as though it were suddenly possessed by demons of idleness and strife. But with the coming of another day the confusion ended and matters were set in order, swiftly and fully, by the curt intervention of Abram.

With Eliezer beside him, he strode through house and grounds, a scribe hastening after them, recording matters yet to be decided, tasks yet undone. Certainly, the organizing of a caravan was not unfamiliar to a man who had made more than a hundred journeys in the name of his father's house. Thus, within the space of a single morning, he had sorted the animals, the slaves, the shares of labor, the clothing, the food, the goods, fixed the day and hour for their departure, and the manner of their setting forth.

Before the decisive commands of the master and the authority of Eliezer, the slaves ceased their dawdling and quarreling and fell to work. Garments and linens were laid within the chests, likewise uncut cloth and leather and goods of trade. Numerous skin bottles were made ready, to be filled at the start of the journey with wine and milk and water and oil, also skin bags in which would be contained large measures of grain and dried fruits, and the round, flat loaves of bread. Nor had Abram failed to make provision for the favorite kettles and platters of Azubah, the medicines and herbs regarded as indispensable by Maacah.

The oldest of the slaves had no wish to set forth from Haran, indeed were too frail for the making of such a journey. Yet they were not without worth in the eyes of a master, being women skilled in the ways of sewing and weaving, men wise in the tending of gardens and vineyards. In the end, Abram exchanged them for younger servants from another household, but first sought their consent, this being the way of the law. And in truth, two elderly slaves for one young and adventurous one was no mean bargain in the eyes of a man whose fortunes would depend upon the strength and spirit of his followers.

For Sarai, the swift-moving currents of the household possessed no actuality. She opened her eyes to the shining mornings, and closed them upon the sweet and gentle nights knowing: *Soon we shall go forth from this place forever.* But the thought was without substance, and floated from her in the vaporous, dissolving manner of a dream. Even when the rooms were barren of all that had given them comfort and beauty, even when the new slaves had come, the old ones departed, and the selling of the house was sealed and inscribed, the sense of unreality remained upon her.

Since the death of Terah, she had sought to write her own destiny in the stars, and Abram's also, saying to herself: "Here in this city of the northern moon, we shall live out our lives and come to our deaths and lie, one beside the other, in the cool peace of the dust beneath the chapel floor. And sons of our bodies, being given us at last, shall live out their lives as we have done, and come to know that which we have learned of life and death and love and striving. And they shall pour out libations of oil and water and tears upon our graves, and their children likewise, according to the endless pattern of existence." Such dreams, even shattered, were of the heart, and not to be cast aside as lightly as a broken clay tablet.

To her, Haran had never been either alien or unknown. Lot's father, her cousin, had been named for it. Her mother had once spent an entire summer within its walls. The caravans of Terah had made many journeys to its gates and being, like Ur, a city consecrated to the moon, it was as a second home, even to Nannar. To go forth to Haran seemed neither strange nor fearful, but this could not be said of going forth to a land unnamed, a place unrevealed. Where would they come to dwell at last? It was a matter that Abram left unquestioned, entrusted by his faith to the Lord he followed. But with Sarai it was otherwise, for she found only loneliness and anxiety in the echo of the words by which her husband had been commanded.

"Get thee out of thy country" — the white-walled city, the slow-moving caravans, the shape of the temple, familiar and awesome, against the hot blue sky.

"And out of thy father's house" — away from the little chapel where she had sacrificed many times before the household gods while, through the open door, the dawn poured out upon the altar a libation of sunlight. Away from the tomb of Terah which, remaining behind, would be unhonored by those who came next to dwell above him. Henceforth, there would be none to stand before his door and weep for him, and surely his heart of dust would sorrow at the thought.

Now she knew how much she had come to cherish, from the

roof top, the silvery-gray leaves of a certain olive tree, the manner in which the moons rose out of the hills beyond, the corner of the parapet where some doves had nested, tame to her hand. And she remembered the ways of the morning: the sound of a donkey's small, quick feet in the dust, the light laughter of women on their way to the well, the dampened shadows of the trees, the sweetness of the flowers, the voice of a mother singing to her child. Such little rivulets had fed the broad stream of her contentment, the deep peace of her heart. She looked upon the house with eyes of farewell, taking leave of it without words, lest Abram behold and know her sadness.

"Into a land which I will show thee"—a journey of no return, stretching surely to the very edge of the world.

It was known to all men, save those utterly without learning, that the boundaries of the earth were four in number—dawn, noonday, sunset, and midnight—guarded forever by four avenging angels and four deadly, sacred monsters. The world was watered by four ancient rivers, and enclosed in vast, lashing seas. Not infrequently some garrulous trader declared that upon these seas were islands, where dwelt men with pale skins and eyes the color of the waters. And if these tales were true, then such creatures were indeed demons, and not to be met without charms spoken or worn.

Thus, not only were powerful amulets laid within the wedding chest, but also the teraphim, small carven images of good fortune, protecting the family and proclaiming the authority of Abram as its head, being given only to the son of inheritance.

Lot returned with the caravan some days after the selling of the house, and was summoned by Abram to the Common Room of the men. They lingered here until the morning ended and they had broken the noonday bread, and the slave who served them said that their talk was not of setting forth together, but of separating their households entirely. This was no matter of surprise, for none who knew the nature of Lot believed that he would desire to share so rigorous and uncertain a venture. Yet even those who scorned his name agreed that he would find the parting from his uncle an unhappy thing. And indeed, when he at last came forth from the Common Room beside the son of

64

Terah, he spoke through tears, as though he said farewell.

". . . thus may fortune walk beside my uncle and all his household, and may the gods give him to arrive well."

Whereupon he embraced Abram swiftly and, turning away, hastened to his own portion of the house. Sarai, hearing his words, said within herself, " Now, may the gods be praised, *she* will be counted among us no longer! " And her heart was lifted up in guilty joy before it wavered and sank with the thought, Her children — what of the little girls? It would be no easy thing to look back upon their small, forlorn faces, to answer without tears the lonely waving of their hands. Yet, as matters came to pass, there was no need for her distress.

Late in the afternoon, a maidservant passing the room of Lot's wife heard her voice lifted in contemptuous, accusing anger against him. And when the lamps had been lighted and Lot had come, subdued and chastened, to the evening meal, it was to say before his uncle that he would, after all, depart out of Haran. Thus it was arranged that the two households should set forth in a single caravan.

To Abram, it was as if the finger of the Lord beckoned him southward, and they made ready to journey across the river, down past cities of hill and plain, into a land of desert and wilderness, even toward Egypt, rich and fabulous, a land of mud where people gave their lives to the dead.

The night before their departure was hot and sultry. In the Common Room of the men Abram was holding council, seated with Eliezer and Lot. Before him were gathered the men of the vast caravan — craftsmen, shepherds, drovers, herdsmen, camel drivers, slaves and bondsmen and personal servants, tillers of the soil, scribes and guards. Each was charged with the welfare of his own family, did he possess wives or concubines or children. They would travel, after the manner of all tribal parties, in orderly divisions. The leaders, each looking to the care and discipline of his own group, would be accountable first to Eliezer, then to Lot, and thereafter to Abram.

In the light of several lamps gathered within her room, Sarai knelt beside the last and most precious of her chests. With womanly pleasure in the delicate and beautiful, she laid therein the fairest of her tunics and veils, the brightest of her embroidered jackets and girdles, her cosmetic boxes and jewels and scents. Now all she possessed was made ready for the journey and, pleased that it was so, she sat back upon the heels of her sandals, brushing the sweat of her labors from her brow. Then, aware of some presence beyond the pool of lamplight, she glanced up and found Lot's wife paused in the doorway, gazing sullenly upon her.

Quietly and with courtesy, she asked, " Is there a way in which I may serve the wife of Lot? "

" I seek only sleep," answered the other woman, peevishly. " In the noise and discomfort of this plundered house, who is to find rest? "

Sarai made no answer, but took up a square of linen with which to cover the contents of the chest, folding it slowly and with care. " May the gods once again give me patience," she said in her thoughts.

" For days upon days," said the wife of Lot, " your hands have toiled in making ready for this journey. Indeed, one would think the House of Abram was without slaves. If we must depart, then let us depart, leaving the burden of the doing to our hand-maidens! "

" For me, it is no burden to look to the ways of my husband's house," answered Sarai, coldly.

Lot's wife shrugged.

" If the keeping of a house is a joy to you, then may you delight in it a thousand years! My pity is upon the manner of your pleasure." She moved forward and stared, unabashed, into the filled chest. " How is it that Sarai would take her paint stick, her ointments? Does she think to remain lovely, living in a goat's-hair tent? Such a thing is not to be! The softness of your cheek will become as leather under the sun, the redness of your lips will flow upon your chin like wine. In the space of a single season you will be as wrinkled by sun and wind as a woman stricken in years. Yet even though you were beautiful, when would Abram pay homage to his wife, seeing that his time is filled with paying homage to his strange God? " She added, with biting contempt: " How is a man to believe that which his eyes have not seen, neither have his ears heard, nor his hands touched? Is this not madness?"

The words brought Sarai to her feet in swift anger.

"With the faith of my husband so unpleasing in your eyes, how is it that you do not remain behind in Haran? For surely it is known to all that Lot had no wish to depart, that he consented to the journey for your sake alone?"

"Say to me now," answered the other woman, coolly, "do you think me so great a fool as to be unaware that, apart from his uncle, Lot is nothing, in the eyes of this city or any other? Thus I have counseled him: Except you go with Abram, how shall you possess either goods or riches? Therefore, remain with him, and depart from him only when you have obtained abundance, either by his wisdom or by his death. To me, this journey is an abomination," she declared, "yet I would follow riches to a land cursed by demons rather than dwell under fairer skies with obscurity and want!"

Sarai turned back to the chest, laid the folded linen over that which it held, and closed the lid. Sadly, out of her own thoughts, she asked, "Can the wife of Lot worship none but the god of ease?"

Malice glinted swiftly in the eyes of the other woman.

"Can the wife of Abram deny the faith of her homeland?" she mocked. "Nay, even while she feigns obedience to her husband, she does not receive his God! To Abram, who sees only with the eyes of a prophet, this is not known. But to me, since I see with the eyes of a woman, it is not to be denied!"

With derision set like a smile upon her lips, she gathered up the hem of her tunic and went from the room, and the light, musical jangling of her bracelets and anklets faded into the darkness of the passage.

Sarai stood alone, suddenly stricken in spirit and weary beyond measure. Even though she has accused me out of the hardness of her heart, she has spoken the truth, she thought.

Of a sudden, the upper portion of the house seemed echoing with silence. The hour was not late, yet already the women and children were closed within their rooms, knowing that they must rise before the false dawn. And now the winds changed, and a coolness was borne in upon the city from the sea, lifting the leaves of the olive tree, stirring the fronds of the palms, whispering in the dust of the street.

Surely Abram was wearied and in want of rest. She went out upon the gallery and looked down upon the empty, darkened court. A single torch burned in the entrance, where the porter and the watchdog took their rest together. Light still streamed from the Common Room of the men, across the trodden bricks and the orderly clay pots of flowers. Voices, rising and falling, mingled one with the other.

*Soon we shall go forth from this place forever* — and Sarai was chilled with fear of the unknown way before them. Yet with Abram it was not so, for the voice of the Lord remained with him and gave him peace. Such communion was beyond the reaches of her understanding. She could not fathom the nature of a God without substance, without shape, whose voice was a part of the silences, whose face was unseen by the eyes of men, whose words rose only within the temple of the soul. There was no teaching in all the land akin to this, nor was it commanded that all men bow before a single god.

Let every man choose for himself, it was said, such a god as will show him favor. No man can please every god, nor lives there a god pleasing to every man, for is it not true that he who smiles upon Lamech may turn his face with loathing from Sarug? Such are the ways of gods and mortals, my son. Let every man hear and take heed. Yet when it comes to pass that you enter a strange city, a far province, or an alien land, hasten to sacrifice upon the altars of that place, even though they be an abomination to you, that you may know the favor of its gods. For in truth, there is no god, weak or powerful, who does not admire a prudent man.

Such were the teachings of the temples, of the elders and the priests. With the echo of their voices about her, Sarai lifted her face to a sky now darkened and made oppressive by slowly moving clouds. "Concerning the Lord of my husband," she said to herself, "it might be a cautious thing to offer a prayer in his name."

Yet when her lips were opened, not so much as a whisper of sound issued forth. To the gods of the temples one prayed without wavering, hurried into words by the majestic ugliness of the images, the fear of giving them offense. But to lift one's voice to a God unseen, groping in the darkness and silence of the languorous night . . .

Oh, Abram, my husband, she thought in despair, how is it that you, a man above other men, should possess so unworthy a wife? Surely the stars have conspired against us both! In truth, as I would bear your sons with joy, so would I walk in joy before your God, knowing the same high faith that dwells within you. Yet how am I to do this thing, seeing that faith may not be beckoned like an unruly slave?

Suddenly the darkened clouds, massed one upon the other, were shoved aside as if by a mighty hand, and the moon came forth and stared down at her, white and cold. Terror, centuries old, seized upon her at the sight, so that she trembled and could scarcely give utterance to the words upon her lips.

" Nannar, exalted lord — " she began, stammering.

Without ceasing to stare upon her, the moon moved swiftly toward the roiled darkness of a heavy cloud.

" Hide not thy face from me! " she cried aloud. But the glory of the deity departed from her.

She whispered, " He has looked upon my guilt," and fled to the concealing shelter of her room, and wept in shame and in despair.

# VII

OUT OF THE BITTERNESS OF MANY YEARS, AZUBAH STARED INTO THE southern night. Hours before, at the going down of the sun, the disordered yellow sand and rocks of this wild countryside had merged with swift, concealing darkness. Now they crept forth again beneath the risen moon, and its light dealt tenderly with them, softening the edges of the parched and barren hills, tracing gently the jagged rocks, the dusty stream beds empty of all save the crouched shadows of the night.

The caravan passed as silently as a cloud, on the slow rhythm of the camels, the soundless tread of the herds. The children slept deeply, careless of the unceasing motion of the journey, and of the grim desolation which lay about them. The women, wearied by the passing of the hours, had tightened their woolen cloaks against the chill and fallen into slumber. At times they roused briefly and spoke, saw the wilderness unchanged, offering no promise of the oasis they sought, and, with an apathy learned of resignation, slept again.

Yet Azubah could neither sleep nor be comforted. The sight of the empty white moon above the silent waste filled her with unspeakable loneliness, so that, for companionship, she turned to recollections long thrust from her heart. For many years she had shrunk from thoughts of the past as one would shrink from the sight of weapons edged and wounding. Yet now, examining them at last, she perceived that time had made them blunt, and they were able to cause her little pain. Indeed, she could look into the days of her youth as if she beheld a life not her own, a woman not herself, considering them dispassionately, and with wonder. Say to me now — is it that I, the dour Azubah, was once a girl who laughed and sang, and who bore the gay and lilting name of Lia?

Such a thing was not to be, yet it was as Lia that she had been born and, she thought bitterly, once had died. She had been four years old when she was made a slave, sold to Terah by her ill and destitute father for the sum of five shekels. And surely my father loved me — for it was inscribed upon the contract tablet that when she reached the age of womanhood, she was to have a pleasing husband, either slave or freeborn.

As a child, Lia had been more than ordinarily winsome, the old ones said, light and quick upon her feet, slim and brown and spirited. The slaves of Terah had smiled upon her and made much of her and, in the years of her growing up, known pride in her. For, in truth, she was a girl with the body of a shining brown goddess, with flashing black eyes and swirling black hair, and a smile which brought the shapes of joy and mischief and tenderness upon her richly beautiful mouth.

Rahim, son of a merchant of the south, had seen her in the House of Terah and desired her for himself. And this was no matter of sorrow to Lia, for Rahim was young and lean and so well-favored that the oldest and ugliest of the maidservants peered at him from behind the arches, sighing. And thus, at last, Rahim bought her from the hand of Terah, a bargain not to be disdained, since the law required of him no more than the purchase price paid to her father.

Lia followed him to his lodgings as one would walk behind a god, her young face glorified before the world. Behold, I am chosen of a man both young and comely; behold, I am chosen of a husband freeborn, and thus loosed from slavery.

From the first she had loved him with all the ardor of her untamed heart, rendering up the fullness of her devotion as though she sacrificed upon an altar stone. Nor did she perceive that his own heart could be otherwise. In the simplicity of her youth, it was not known to her that the true love of a man might be the desert herself, whose charms were renewed with every dawn, whose mystery was never quite unveiled before him, whose voice could summon him back again, and yet again, to her embrace. And the heart of Rahim was indeed the heart of the desert, barbaric and inviolate, knowing neither charity nor compassion, veiling its own gluttonies with dreamlike mirages of enchantment.

When five new moons had risen, the latter rains were ended and summer returned to the land. It was at the season of the desert's flowering when Lia awoke to the still and heart-shattering morning. Rahim was gone. His caravan had vanished with the night. Wild and unbelieving, her hair streaming about her face, her unclad feet careless of stones and bruises, she ran through the streets, questioning those who might have seen him pass — the beggar by the wall, the taxgatherer at the gates, a leper who lay in the sun and wept for mercy. The caravan had set forth in the light of dawn, they told her, toward the southern desert. And truly the young master seemed to hasten, not furtively, but openly and joyously, as though there was one who waited.

" Let my sister dry her tears," said the leper kindly, for kindness men would take from his hands without shrinking. " Let my sister be comforted. Woe, the sons of the desert are wild and inconstant of heart! "

But not Rahim, not Rahim who had held her in his arms beneath the stars and called her his pet, his little gazelle, and laughed with her and caressed the sweetness of her hair and swore he would not let her go from him even in death.

The incredible days stumbled past. Growing big with her child, Lia sat alone, numbed and staring, and would neither eat nor sleep, nor dry her tears. A thousand times she besought the southern plain for some glimpse of Rahim, but at last she understood that this was not to be, and her heart grew bitter within her because she was still counted with the lowly. Were she highborn and of family, he would not have gone from her without the dignity of a formal declaration, providing her with a dowry, stating after the manner of the law, " You are not my wife." But even these poor rags of decency had been denied her. The daughter of a high house would have kinsmen to avenge her shame, but there was none to lift either the sword or the voice for the honor of a deserted girl lately a slave. Nay, she must seek her own vengeance, dry her own tears, find her own shelter and the food to stay her hunger. For women such as she had become, abandoned in their sorrow, the law opened a door and held it wide. " If a man run away, his wife may enter another house." Already the fat taxgatherer whispered the words, and his insolent glance had fondled her, so that she shuddered and fled from him, weeping. And with the sunset of that day, she returned to the House of Terah, her garments rent in her misery, ashes strewn upon the blackness of her hair. The child, born too soon of her heartbreak and despair, died with its first feeble cry and, at the same time, the girl Lia went forth from her heart.

" Call me Lia no more," she said harshly, " but instead, let Azubah be my name, for indeed I am forsaken! "

From that time forward she spoke of Rahim no more, but the flame of her anguish had smoldered until it destroyed, not only her tears, but the stream of tenderness which once flowed with sweet and lovely warmth within her veins. Now, after many years, none could say whether he still lived, or how death had found him at last, but there was an ancient saying, " He who loves the desert shall perish by her hand," and thus it may have been with Rahim. Yet it was known to all that, even in death, he would possess the temple of Azubah's heart.

This very wilderness must have been familiar in his eyes, she thought, for the men of his tribe had come here both in pillage and in trade. Surely, a hundred times and more, he had ridden this same way, gazed upon the same lonely hills, lifted his eyes to the same stars.

"Indeed, it was in his arms that I knew my first thought of this journey. 'My face shall be turned to the south,' I said in my dreaming, 'and camels as silent as shadows shall bear me to the land of my love, and overhead will shine the stars which he has shown me, the cluster of the seven small goats, the ox which bears a red jewel in his eye, the girded giant' . . . And am I not here?" she asked herself, in bitter mockery. "Has it not indeed come to pass?

"Yet," she added, striving to comfort herself with reasoning words, "from both masters of the house, I have known kindness, and from my lady Sarai, Maacah, Eliezer, even Lot. Truly, I am not alone, save in the realm of my spirit. And the lad Jarah is dear to me, for his father was of the desert also, and thus would my son have been, lean and young and laughing and brown — my son who died before I looked upon him, in the arms of Maacah who calls herself my friend, though I am friend to no one. But with Maacah it is otherwise."

Maacah had not been formed of song and fire and stars, but was a quiet clay, fashioned humbly, an opulent household image to be refuge to the motherless, comforter of the afflicted, healer of pain. That any man should be lover to Maacah was beyond credulity. Indeed, she seemed as wholly separated from such affections as the virgin goddesses of Ur, as cleansed and released from the turbulent petitions of the body. Since childhood she had been dedicated to loving compassion for all creatures, knowing them, not as male and female, but as fellow wanderers in loneliness and fear.

It was not the way of Maacah to strive against the gods, to question their wisdom or yet lament their injustices. She received each day into her hands as one would receive a basket of fruit from a vendor, quietly putting aside the bad, joyously making much of the good.

She had been born in the House of Terah and, throughout her

life, had made thank offerings for so fortunate a beginning. For none could say a slave was ever brought to death by Terah's hand, made crippled or maimed. Even in anger just and reasonable, Terah struck a slave no more than a stunning blow, and had never punished such a one by refusing him food and drink, or by exposing him, in the open fields, to the brutal castigation of the sun.

The slaves of Terah had entered his house by many roads, had sold themselves into bondage, were seized for the debts of their fathers, were leased, given in exchange for others, sent as surety and as gifts. A few were prisoners of war, foreigners who yearned after their homelands but who, being common and obscure soldiers, were not ransomed with the officers and statesmen. The greater number were freeborn, reduced to slavery by the ways of misfortune. It was a fate that might befall any man, for not even an astrologer could say, from season to season, whether he would escape both famine and plague. Indeed, many of the strongest among them had been struck down by hunger.

The father of Eliezer was such a one, no ordinary slave, but a man of learning and of family, freeborn in Damascus. Famine had reduced him to servitude in the first years of his marriage and, needing asylum for his young wife and the child yet unborn, he had sold himself to Terah for a service of three years. Yet when the term was ended, so strong was the bond of affection between himself and his master, that he chose to remain a slave rather than go forth in freedom. Meanwhile, his wife having died in bearing the child, he gave the remainder of his days to stewardship in the House of Terah, and to the instruction of his motherless son.

"Let my lord permit the lad to walk in the footsteps of the lowliest slave," he said, " that he may have understanding for all manner of men, and regard none unjustly, or without compassion."

Thus, before Eliezer entered the household to be charged with the duties of stewardship, he had served in the stables, the kitchen, and the fields, had been a seeker of brushwood in the hills, a shepherd among the flocks, and a guard in the armed escort of the caravan. Now, after many years, he again rode forth into the desert, and, of all the household, only Abram possessed more authority or knew greater respect.

The land to which they had come was of immeasurable desolation. Beneath the eerie light of the moon, the distant hills became as dust, soft and ashen and unreal, while from out their pale loneliness came the wailing of jackals, like the cries of evil ones wandering by night. And now the sand slipped beneath the tread of the animals as they plodded the steep ridges, up into the torn hills, down again to the shattered rocks, over limestone blistered and ragged and crumbling.

To Sarai, waking in soreness and weariness, it was as if she had never known another life. Nay, surely she was entrapped in time, moving neither forward nor backward. She had been born, perhaps a thousand years before, upon this same ill-natured camel and a thousand years hence would be within this same broken waste which, like the journey, seemed to have neither beginning nor end. How long the household of Abram had been upon the way, none knew save Abram himself, and Eliezer. She had long since ceased to number the days, even the moons.

This now was the land of Canaan, surely a land of many conflicts upon the tongues of men. A generous land, declared those from the hills above the Jezreel plain, a land enriched and beautiful where, in the seasons of harvest, wheat and barley rippled like the waves of the sea before the wind; a land of vineyards and fig trees and olive groves, and forests not planted by the hands of men. And in the time of spring, when the hills had grown white with flocks and the morning mists were lifted on the wings of the sun and shepherds called, one to the other, in the clear sweet air, who would wish to dwell elsewhere, even though he dwelt as a king?

A cruel land, said others, barren and shattered and stripped of verdure, even of sand, so that its naked ribs were laid forth beneath the merciless sun, and its streams were dried and become as dust, and men were brought to death in the untrodden reaches of its wilderness, their bellies swollen with emptiness, their tongues made black by thirst.

A savage land, said still others, where a river shaped like a serpent moved slowly southward to a sea salt and bitter, crawling

75

through untamed jungle growth, where dwelt all manner of scorpions and howling beasts and vipers of certain death.

Nay, said a camel driver encountered in a certain plain, it was a populous and wealthy land if one but turned to the west, to the edge of the Great Sea. Here were the roads of conquerors and princes and merchants rich in trade. Here in high, walled cities dwelt a people cast up by the sea in ages past, who ate the crawling things of the shore and sacrificed before strange, fish-shaped gods, whose men were fierce and warlike, whose women were beautiful and wanton. From a hilltop one might behold, standing forth against the clouds, the palaces of their kings, and the temples of their gods.

Truly, said Abram, these things might be said and not counted false, for the land of Canaan was a land in which the Lord had set forth some of all his creations. Thus the tellers of tales, the leaders of caravans, the keepers of inns, the shepherds of flocks, who counseled him along the way had not dealt in lies but had spoken, each of them, according to a different portion of the land.

By those who followed the broad and easy way along the coast and the Great Sea, tribute must be paid to a multitude of kings, chieftains, and taxgatherers. Such toll was more than a wandering household could bear, and so it was decided in council to keep to the wilderness lands instead. These, though of slender worth to tillers of the soil, would sustain many herds and flocks for a man of the tents, asking no return. Thus the caravan of Abram passed through the central region, down the length of the land, between the Jordan River and the Great Sea. Within this lonely waste lay few settlements to look with either resentment or avarice upon the sojourn of a stranger.

And now it seemed that the sandy places of the desert had come to meet them, widening and spreading before them as they climbed among the hills and heights. The scant remaining herbage dwindled and grew scattered and was lost in the wilderness dust.

The caravan was arranged after the immemorial pattern of a moving tribe, and thus preceded by a small party of armed riders. Lot and Abram and Eliezer led the main body, men who rode forth on camels or donkeys. She-camels followed, those which gave milk, those heavy with young, those whose foals ran beside them or were borne in woven crates upon their backs. After these walked shepherds and drovers with the sheep and goats and cattle and, behind them, pack camels bearing chests and tents, goods of the household and of trade. Near the end of the long and laden line were the women and children and, last, the armed men of the rear guard.

With each setting forth, they had chattered and laughed and known joy in companionship but, with the slow and laborious passing of the hours, had withdrawn, one by one, into the silence and solitude of utter weariness. From the first light of that dawning they had moved steadily southward, seeking a well, made known to them some days before by a camel driver encountered near a village of the hill country.

Once they had come upon an aged man, one who suffered from the holy sickness surely, for his eyes were empty of reason and his tongue thick and slow, as if unaccustomed to the syllables of speech. Beholding his gaunt face and wasted frame, Maacah brought forth for him such loaves as remained from the last baking. These the old man fell upon with shrill animal cries, tearing at their edges with toothless gums and broken fingernails, gnawing and rending and yarring like a beast of prey.

He was the first stranger they had met after entering the wilderness, nor had they come upon others since that day. Indeed, before another sun had risen, they were aware that a vast and unnatural silence lay upon the land, an eerie absence of life and movement, of birds, of animals, even of insects. They encountered no caravans, no women and children seeking herbs or brushwood in the hills, no lads with flocks, no men riding forth on errands of trade, not so much as a wandering merchant, or a hermit before his cave. Once, late at night, they had stumbled upon a village in the darkness and found it as silent as if all who had dwelt there lay dead within its walls. No watchman called out, no donkey brayed, no dogs ran forth, snarling and savage, to set upon the strangers. Indeed, as they waited, in listening silence, they heard only the chirping of a cricket by the wall.

" May the gods forbid that we linger here," whispered Maacah, " for the smell of death is upon this place."

Abram, turning in his saddle, called out the ancient salutation of the traveler.

"Let the men of the village hear me! We are wanderers in the wilderness, and far from our people . . ."

His voice echoed from the walls and lost itself beyond, yet not even a wavering light or a feeble cry came forth to answer him, to stir and shatter the immense, brooding silence.

After a little time Abram and Eliezer dismounted and, going forth in the light of torches, called outside the village walls until, coming upon the gates, they beheld these open to the night, revealing the emptiness within. It was understood, then, that all who once dwelt here had fled, driven by what forces of terror no man could say.

Since then no other village had been seen and, as they moved farther into the scorched and empty hills, the silence had not lifted, but had grown deeper and more oppressive. At times one of the men led forth a small hunting party and, on such a day, Eliezer had shot a gazelle, but this was the last time they had seen animals, though they could hear jackals and hyenas at night, and once Jarah had chased a jerboa into its hole. Throughout this day they had encountered only silence and emptiness. No antelopes fled before them, no birds or even lizards. Indeed, there were not even tracks to proclaim that such creatures still dwelt within this barren loneliness.

And now, being both cramped and chilled, Sarai sought release in movement and, stirring cautiously, pushed aside the folds of her headcloth, that she might gaze about her. The lad Jarah, she perceived, was sleeping so heavily that his cloak had fallen from his shoulders entirely, leaving him exposed to the bitter cold of the night. For several days past, he had sickened and refused bread, though he thirsted after water continually.

"Then let my portion be given him," said Azubah quickly, "for what is this water to me, seeing that it swims with flies and smells like a camel!"

And truly, thought Sarai, that which we bear within our waterskins is no drink to be taken for pleasure.

Roused by their voices, Lot's wife stirred, pushed from her face the heavy hair which had tumbled down in the hours of her slumber, and shivered in the chill. After a little time she asked, with undisguised derision, " Say to me now, do we still seek the well of the camel driver? "

" Within an hour we shall come upon it," said Sarai quietly. " As far to the south, the stranger told us, as a man may travel on a single skin of water. Thus Abram has said . . ."

" Abram has said, Abram has said," mocked the wife of Lot. " How long before you learn that no man knows whereof he speaks? Within this region of torment there is nothing so precious as a cup of water. Is it to be believed, therefore, that these people will suffer us to drain their wells? The camel driver lied. We shall come upon no well this night, nor yet before we perish in the heat of tomorrow's sun! "

" Still your tongue! " said Sarai, shortly. " Such words rouse fear in the hearts of the slave women."

" And in the heart of Sarai also," Lot's wife answered. Yet even while she spoke in derision, her voice seethed with anger. " What but destruction awaits us in this miserable land? " she demanded. " What but . . ."

Her words were lost in sudden clamorous shouts from the men of the advance guard. Those of the caravan roused and stirred, straining forward, that they might behold what had come to pass. At the same time Eliezer rode back to Sarai's place among the women, drawing his beast to a halt beside her.

" Let my lady have no fear. It is for joy that they shout. The oasis of the camel driver rises against the southern stars."

Yet, as Azubah grumbled afterward, how was such to be called an oasis? A few palms broken by wind and storm, so that they were shorn of fronds entirely and stood stripped and naked beneath the moon, as desolate as the shattered land about them. A stone trough filled to the brim with dust, a stream bed dry and clogged, within it rocks which once had glistened with living water but now lay entombed beneath outlines of sand.

The well was a black and open pit in the whiteness of the sands. Indeed, it was both strong and very ancient. Who knew what hands, toiling in the dim recesses of the past, had shaped its rock coping, had fashioned the stones of its lining with hand-holds by which a man might descend when the waters had ebbed, fill his goatskin, and climb forth again. Surely it had quenched the despair of many, and they had drunk not only of its cooling waters, but also of strength, of promise, of the stream of life itself.

" Is it to be wondered," Sarai asked, " that men fall down worshiping before this place? For surely an angel of mercy abides within these waters."

" The angels of this place have long slept beneath the wilderness dust," said Eliezer, " their hands scarred with years and toil. And truly such men are a blessing to the very earth, seeing that they built not for themselves alone."

So great was the weariness of the household that there was but a murmur of talk among them; they thought only of sleep. The children, borne in the arms of mothers and maidservants, did not so much as stir from the depths of their slumber, nor knew at what moment they were laid within the tents. Abram directed the setting of the watch fires, the posting of the guards. Having looked to the animals, the shepherds and drovers rolled themselves in the warmth of their cloaks and slept.

Stumbling with weariness and aching for sleep, Sarai drew from her body the garments of the day and lay down upon her bed mat. Out of the silence which had fallen upon the encampment rose the familiar sounds of the night, the crackle of fires, the shrill chirping of a cricket in the spilled dampness by the well, the whisper of sand. When Abram had put out the lamp and stretched himself beside her, she moved beneath the woolen coverings, sought the warmth of his body, the sense of his nearness, and slept.

Surely it was but a little time . . . the space of a jackal's howl, a camel's groaning, at most no more than the time required for burning a single armful of brushwood, before she heard the voice of Eliezer lifted at the tent door, the murmuring sound of his apologetic words, and then Abram answering, in tones swiftly cleared of sleep, " Say that I will come . . ."

Yet surely hours had passed, for dawn was breaking a rosy light glimmering between the earth and the edge of the dark goat's-hair tent. In the dimness she saw her husband rise, taking up a tunic with which to cover his body, girding his waist with a swift, sharp motion, pushing back his tumbled hair as he went forth to meet the steward.

May the gods forbid that it be morning . . . for I am still weary beyond the telling . . . The thought rose, wavering, within her mind, dissolved and rose again. And then Abram had returned and his hand was upon her shoulder, lean and hard and insistent, compelling her from sleep.

"Summon Maacah, and come with her to the first watch fire beyond the well."

She lifted herself and stared at him, anxiety upon her lips.

"Jarah?"

"Nay, it is a Canaanite girl, found at daylight by one of the guards. She lies as dead, yet there is life within her, and within the child also."

Sarai rose from the warmth of the bed mat, shivering in the dawn chill, girded herself in a tunic, and hastened from the tent.

The redness of morning had colored the wilderness, edging the purple hills, the broken palms, the ancient stones of the well. Beside a watch fire burned to ashes, and still upon the shepherd's cloak wherein she had been borne to this place, lay a young girl native to this land. Her eyes were closed, quiet, with lashes fallen in shadow upon her thin and pallid cheeks. Yet, even in her unnatural sleep, she bore the weary look of one who has lived out such a length of wretchedness that death has long since ceased to be a thing of dread. Her garments were rent until it was as if she were wrapped in rags. Her feet, small and bare, were marked with clotted blood. In her arms, as though lifeless, lay a small and shrunken child.

"It is a boy child," said Sarai to herself, "and it is dead."

Yet when she reached forth and touched him, she felt that his body had warmth and that his heart yet moved, though feebly, and she perceived that his lips had the strength to shape themselves for a cry.

Maacah dealt gently and skillfully with the girl.

"Hers are the wounds of thirst and hunger," the slave woman said, "and of despair."

Sarai lifted the child to her own bosom and wrapped him within a fold of her cloak and went to sit apart upon a stone,

81

caressing him with the tenderness of her hands, uttering small sounds to comfort him. She commanded Urfa to bring warm milk and, from one finger, delivered it drop by drop into the small, seeking mouth. And it seemed that, even as she watched, the child was strengthened and made whole. His eyes, as black as cinders, fell open, and a faint cry came from his lips.

Presently Abram stood at her side and gazed down upon her and asked, " How is it with the little one? "

" Behold, he smiles for you! " cried Sarai, and they looked at each other and laughed together.

If the girl should die . . . thought Sarai. And suddenly the desire, ruthless and unrelenting, possessed her utterly. This child would then be as our own and, day after day, would lie within my arms. And those who passed the tents of Abram would cry, " Behold the fruitful wife! "

Yet even at this moment, in the first risen light of the sun, a shadow fell beside her, and the voice of Maacah shattered the brittle fancy.

" The mother of the babe is afraid, and weeps for it. Let me then bear it to her arms . . ."

She will not die, thought Sarai, and the old despair returned to her. She will not die, neither shall this child be mine. Nor any other . . .


# VIII

WHEN ABRAM SPOKE TO THE GIRL IN HER OWN TONGUE, SHE CEASED to be afraid, even for her child, and was submissive, being borne to the tent of the slave women. Maacah and two young maidservants dealt with her kindly, giving her food and drink, rubbing her thin body clean with sand, bringing her a fair tunic, and wrappings for the babe. And the maidservants, pleased with this grave, childlike creature, would have bound up her hair, but she would not have it so. Instead, she tended it with her own hands, and refused that it be other than loose about her face.

But for the coming of this girl, the household would have lingered a little time beside the oasis. Scarcely had she the strength to walk, however, before she besought Abram, in a passionate outpouring of words, to hasten their going forth.

" Let my lord believe me," she cried, " within this place there is only death! Let my lord behold the silence, the ruin, the merciless burning of the sun! Truly, such famine and drought are upon us as cannot be remembered by any who now tread the earth. Our fields are empty, our flocks are dead of thirst, our wells are stopped with dust, and from those among us, both aged and young have perished. If my lord would indeed save his life, and the lives within his tribe, then let him go down into Egypt, whence many from these hills have fled, for in Egypt there is corn in abundance, likewise grazing lands, and a Pharaoh who is merciful. And let me set forth with the caravan also, seeing that I am not such a one as can make this journey alone."

Now the stillness and desolation of the land was to be understood, likewise the hills emptied of game, the houses emptied of villagers. And the old man of the wilderness, thick of tongue and vacant of eyes — if indeed the holy touch of madness was upon him, it was the madness of one abandoned, in the extremity of his years, to hunger and desperation.

" I am within your tent," said the girl, quietly. " My life and the life of my child are yours, to serve you and those of your tribe until we have seen death."

" And what of your husband? " Abram asked. " The father of your child? "

It was as if she had veiled her eyes, so swiftly was the fabric of caution drawn between her glance and the gaze of Abram. Yet she spoke without faltering, and her voice held truth.

" All those lie dead who were dear to the heart of Elisheba."

Thus did she reveal her name, though not deliberately, Abram thought, seeing that she appeared to wish she might recall the word when she had uttered it. Yet she did not flinch before him, but continued to kneel, humbly and with dignity, awaiting his will.

" From this day forward, Elisheba and her child shall be counted among those of the House of Abram," he said, at last.

Whereupon she embraced his feet, and wet them with her tears.

With the dawning of the next day the tents were dismantled and the animals led to their places. A word from Eliezer, and loads were cast upon the pack camels. The riders mounted and sat silent and waiting, the drovers and shepherds stood in quiet readiness with their flocks, the men of the guard moved into orderly ranks and halted. Then, when Abram had made a sign to them by wrenching his spear from the earth, the caravan set out into a countryside empty of all save rocks and sand.

It was as if the sun had burst into the sky, an eruption volcanic and violent, pouring forth heat which, within the space of an hour, had rolled upon them in molten waves.

" Surely even the wild goats pant for breath on such a morning," said Maacah with pity.

" Has any goat survived this hour? " demanded the wife of Lot. " The head of Maacah is filled with sand if she does not know that we alone, of all creatures, have remained alive within this burning desert. And before the setting of another sun, we shall have perished likewise . . ."

Let her speak as she will, thought Sarai, for indeed I am too ill to contend with her this day . . . Since the first hour of the journey, pain had lashed her eyes as though with fire, and her ears had been filled with a shrill, persistent ringing. Now a sickness gnawed between her ribs, so that she became limp with weakness, drenched with sweat. And there were many others stricken in the same way.

And now the rolling hills sank into a waterless plain beneath an even greater burning of the sun. The heat of the rocks was cast into the scorched faces of the household, and wind as violent as a roaring fire rushed upon them. Their eyes were reddened in its blast, their brows crusted with sand, their lips cracked and swollen. Near the hour of noontide they beheld, along the rim of the sky, a great oasis where palm trees floated, cool and green, above the false waters of the sands. And many were near to weeping at the sight.

Then the grave and gentle Elisheba turned to them with pity for their wretchedness and spoke in words of consolation, saying, " The night will be cool, and full of stars, and there is a well which awaits us."

" How are we to believe the words of her mouth? " demanded the wife of Lot, with scorn. " Was she not lost upon the wilderness? "

" May it please my lady," said Maacah quietly, " the girl was not lost, but only weakened by thirst and hunger."

Urfa's pale eyes bulged.

" Who can say," she cried suddenly, " that she is not a daughter of the evil ones, and seeks our deaths? "

" May your tongue wither! " Azubah burst forth, but already the temper of the slave women had altered. Alarm rippled among them on a thin thread of sound which thickened and strengthened and rose, seething, to the very edge of terror before Abram lashed at them with a curt command. And when they had fallen quiet, he did not speak at once, but held the silence of disapprobation before them, his eyes dealing deliberately with every face before he lifted his voice.

" Those who scorn the native girl and her child will be left behind," he said, coldly.

The murmuring ceased and did not rise again, but disquiet remained with the caravan and with the day, bringing forth vague suspicions and fears not to be named.

Thus, when the wind arose, at the going down of the sun, and a pillar of fire came before them, Urfa was not alone in her shrieking. Indeed, many of the men uttered howls of fright, so that the animals were stricken with panic and broke from the caravan, among them the camels which cast their loads as they fled. And among the servants of Abram, some fell upon their faces, imploring deliverance of their gods and promising, in exchange, gifts far beyond their poor powers to bestow. Some wailed and covered their faces and were loud and voluble in regretting their sins; others flung themselves upon the earth and clawed at the sand and rent the fabric of their garments. Nor did they cease their laments when the pillar vanished, whirling beyond a great rock, and appeared no more. Only when Abram commanded them before him and they saw him calm and untroubled did they emerge, one by one, from the terror which possessed them and draw near to the place where he waited patiently and in silence. And when at last he turned to them, it was neither in anger nor in reproach that he spoke, but in the quiet,

85

reasoning tones of a father who comforts terrified children.

To those of the desert, he told them, such a pillar of fire was not frightening, being neither unexplained nor unfamiliar. Indeed, he himself had looked many times upon these sights, as had the men of his bodyguard, his camel drivers, his slaves. Lot also had seen such pillars of fire, likewise Eliezer, Namtar, Heber, Sarug. " Come forth and speak, all of you, and say how it was that you beheld this thing, and how it possessed no power to do you harm! For a pillar of fire is no evil being of the desert, but a spindle of dust whirled round by the wind and reddened by the setting sun. See now, the wind has departed, and the pillar likewise! "

In the end his words were believed, and thus a new murmuring rose among those of the household. " Truly our master is a man of courage! " . . . " Say to me now, could we follow one richer in wisdom and learning? " . . . " Nay, the pillar is not to be feared. I said this myself, from the start! "

It came to Sarai, listening, that these were not the first people, wailing and heedless of reason, with whom Abram had dealt, subduing their terror by the compelling essence of his voice, the singular nature of his understanding. And she was able to perceive the wisdom which had been laid up for him, day upon day, while he entered the gates of countless foreign cities, held speech with many tribes, witnessed the ways of mankind in all conditions under the sun.

To look upon him now was to behold a stranger, a man of the sands such as gazed with loathing upon any walled place, and stuffed his nostrils with wool before entering a town, that he might not be afflicted with the stench of civilization. Indeed, it was as if Abram stood astride the wilderness, knowing a kinship with the barren earth, the burning sky, the silent reaches of the hills, beholding therein his destiny and, with it, the destiny of his people.

When at length the camels and donkeys had been recovered and their loads restored, the caravan set forth again, moving yet farther into the brooding loneliness. About them lay a silence so immense that their spirits faltered before it, and the smallest sound from out of the past was to be remembered with longing, even the wailing cries of night, the furtive rustling in the dry and shattered brush.

With the last hour of the day they reached the well made known to them by Elisheba, a cistern in the sands. The water was stale and warm, and gave forth a sickening stench, yet it had not been fouled by animals, nor defiled by carrion. Thus it was water which did not contain death, and — let the spirit of the well be praised! — it was abundant.

Suddenly aware of it, the animals crowded ahead, quivering with thirst, tormented by sun and flies, panting and choked with dust. As a symbol of halting, Abram thrust his spear into the earth and, beholding this, those of the caravan rejoiced, for who among them would forget this bitter day? All suffered pain-encrusted eyes, skin burned to the dryness of sand, and lips burst by heat, so that blood welled from their open cracks.

The household, long past the days of its awkwardness, made camp swiftly and with ease. For the women was the unloading of the pack camels, the raising of the tents, the kindling of the supper fires, the making of the supper bread. Children and young girls bore water from the well and ranged forth in search of such brushwood as might remain, dry and thick with dust, in some empty stream bed. And when all the caravan had stilled their thirst, when they had eaten bread and known rest, the shape of the world was altered before them, and the journey was no longer to be looked upon with dread.

Then the murmuring of the encampment, a small flame of life and voices and movement among the women, flickered and faded and went out, and their tents were silent and in darkness. The moon had not yet risen, and the night, black and unshadowed, pressed close about them, but the full, clear voices of the men beside the fire spared them from utter loneliness.

It was the way of the men to remain together until whatever late and star-filled hour brought sleep upon them. But this night the company had been gathered for but a little time when a matter of astonishment came to pass, for out of the blackness of the night and into the redness of the fire strode a Canaanite man. Behind him were others, grouped and silent, their presence perceived only when the light leaped forth and traced the curve of an ear, a jutting chin, the gleam of a forehead, the muscle of an arm, the line of a thigh.

It was as if they were formed of shadows, so swiftly and soundlessly did they emerge, being upon the gathering before their coming was known to the guard, before voices could be brought to silence, or fires quenched under handfuls of sand. Halting at the edge of the darkness, the leader folded his arms upon his chest and called out the greeting of the sands:

" Behold, we are wanderers in the desert, and far from the tents of our people . . ."

Whereupon Abram advanced to meet them and spoke with a dignity befitting the noblest of tribal sheiks:

" From wherever you come, O strangers, be welcome here! "

Within her own tent, Sarai drank deeply of serenity, savoring it as though it were living water, cold and sweet.

" Truly," she said to Maacah, " these small matters — the quenching of my thirst, the breaking of evening bread, the shelter of a tent, the return to cleanliness — these small matters have given me peace. Yet in the burning light of this morning's sun I would have doubted the gods themselves could heal my afflictions! "

They smiled at each other with understanding. It was known to them both that the slave woman could not rest until she had looked within the tent, before she had asked, " Is it well with my mistress? "and performed certain small, unnecessary services for Sarai's sake. And even when there was nothing further to be done, she lingered.

" Should my lady desire another pillow — "

" Maacah is gracious, but I require none other."

Only by deeds could the slave woman express the fullness of her devotion.

" A broth of herbs to summon sleep — " she began.

" Nay," said Sarai, kindly. " Let Maacah serve herself, for she is very weary."

And at this moment there came a movement upon the threshold of the tent and the voice of Azubah called, in guarded tones, that she was the bearer of news.

" Is it not enough that I must see to the baking of bread for this multitude?" she grumbled, when Sarai had bidden her enter. "No, it is not enough!"

Whereupon she revealed that strangers had come out of the darkness, as silent as camels, and that they now sat before the watch fires of Abram, each appearing as a man who could devour a whole sheep. Yet the master had commanded only bread and curds for them, and this was a joyful thing to her, for she was already wearied with the cooking of evening meals and the tending of the ailing Jarah.

"Woe!" she sighed, seating herself upon the clothes chest. "I ache as though trampled by a thousand camels!"

"What manner of men are the strangers?" Maacah asked.

Azubah shrugged.

"Who can say, seeing that it is not the custom of the desert to question wayfarers? Merchants returning from Egypt, one might believe, seeing that there are sounds of donkeys in the darkness whence they came. Yet, like all natives of these sands, hairy of face and filthy of body!"

"Let us look upon them," said Sarai suddenly. And, turning, she quenched the flame of the single lamp and filled the tent with darkness that they might gaze, unperceived, upon the scene beyond.

Their gaze fell upon the leader, a man of years equal to those of Abram, tall and spare, having a tribal look about him, his face darkly brown, his hair black and wildly unkempt, his eyes narrowed as though by years of shrinking from the glare of the desert sun. And of his face, which was both long and lean, Maacah whispered, "Behold, he has the look of a jackal!"

"And the smell of one also!" said Azubah, shortly.

Perhaps he had come from Egypt, seeing that his body was neither ill-clad nor wasted. Easy of manner and glib of speech, he spoke as a teller of tales, being quick and facile with the words of Abram's tongue. His men, a silent and grizzled gathering, ill-clad and ill-favored, sat behind him and spoke not at all, but ate and drank with the wolfish savor of those who have long known famine. And, indeed, it was of the famine that the leader spoke, weaving the tale of its beginning as swiftly and lightly as a skilled woman might weave a piece of cloth:

89

On the fifteenth day of the month the sun had gone out and had not reappeared for the space of an hour. The omen was of the veriest evil, said the temple priests, and afflictions would fall like locusts upon the land. And truly the rains descended from heaven in a flood of such violence that the seedlings were destroyed utterly, likewise many of the flocks. Let my brother believe me, even the cubs of the wild beasts were swept from their dens! And the sun which shone thereafter was of such burning that the countryside became as a brazier alive with coals, and the waters were dried away, and many of the wells, and the hot winds came from the southern sands and parched what remained of growth, and famine fell upon the land.

Where there should have been grain, there was only want; where dew should have glistened in the morning light, there was only dust. The peasants looked upon their fields and wept that the labor of their hands should have been in vain, and prayed the forgiveness of their gods for whatever sins among them had brought about this bitter castigation.

Without wheat and barley and the rest of the corn, how was a man to barter — indeed, how was a man to survive? Not a tuft of grass remained for the herds and flocks, and it was the greater part of wisdom to slay and eat them, seeing that they must surely die.

The famine being widespread, neighbor fared no better than neighbor. All knew hunger and thirst, and came to walk with desperation. Indeed, seven moons had risen since the people had looked upon bread, and now neither curds nor cheese remained to ease their cramping hunger. Olives and fruit were scant comfort to those nourished since birth on milk and meat and richly ripened cheese, but where was a man to find meat? Truly there were animals of the chase that had not perished, but a Baal had whispered in their ears that they must hide themselves within the rocky caves and come forth only in darkness, and thus they were not to be slain.

Like their fathers before them, the men of this land had turned their faces southward, to the land of Egypt, where grain had been heaped, measure upon measure, to the height of the loftiest sycomore, in the storehouses of the pharaohs. A few had made the journey there and bought grain for their stricken villages, but these, returning, had been plundered by bandits who sold the grain at so towering a price that only the rich could taste of it.

Now little water remained within the wells and no flocks upon the hills. No herbage, however sparse and thorny, was left to tuft the rocky highlands. All fields were dust beneath the sun and, seeing that hunger does not go forth alone, but shares its pillage with pestilence and violence, who was to escape? Women, out of anguish and despair, lifted their voices and wept. Children stared with dull and sunken eyes into empty bowls, their bellies big with hunger. Two lads, coming upon the carcass of a kid in a field, fell upon it and ate of it ravenously, for it smelled only faintly of death. But there was a demon within it and the lads were stricken with a great swelling and vomiting, and died in the way that the scavenger dogs sometimes died, foaming and writhing and arching their backs.

And now there came forth the priests of the land to rebuke the people, and to ask what transgressor among them had brought about this disaster. And there was none to answer, each man declaring himself innocent of the doing. Whereupon the priests entered the stone enclosures of their high worship places and prayed amid smoke and fire, with the sound of chants and drums and the gashing of their own flesh, to the Baalim, their gods. And sin offerings were made, men bringing their firstborn sons to be cast into the fire or slaughtered upon the altar stone, that the purity of innocent blood might wash out the stain of sin upon the land.

Woe, there was a certain slave girl of whom a tale was told! Let my brother believe me, she refused obedience to her master, the father of her child, and fled with the child and hid it in the wilderness, that it might not be made a sacrifice. And her deed brought even greater wrath upon the land, for the burning wind strengthened, the dust thickened, and lions grew so bold that they came forth from their caves in the hillsides and entered a village, seeking blood. Say to me now, if that girl is found, should not her throat be cut and her entrails burned upon an altar? Th teeth of the leader gleamed in savage pleasure at the thought.

"Would that I might do the deed!" he said. Yet, seeing that

the Baalim had been offered so gross an insult, who could say that even this would appease their wrath?

For the famine had worsened. And at last, abandoning their villages and carrying nothing save the little water or wine which remained to them, and the children whose bones were like welts upon their bodies, the people of the land set forth, traveling by villages and by families, bound for Egypt and the purple mountains across the Jordan. Had not this exodus come to pass some days before, then surely the caravan of Abram would have been set upon and plundered, for hunger could alter the most humble of men, making them bold and desperate.

Even upon the edge of the desert, a stranger might barter, in other years, for oil and grain and grazing lands, but in this season of bitterness there was none to hear his voice. Who was to barter with an abandoned village where vipers curled upon the doorsteps and a vulture sat in every man's tree? Nay, he who would save himself must go down to Egypt and remain there until the days of wrath were ended, the gods appeased. And should he encounter bandits upon the way, then let him yield his goods without protest, lest he lose his life, the leader said.

" For within these hills are outlaws without mercy! " And having spoken thus, he rose slowly, insolently, before the company. " Behold them before you! " he sneered, and his eyes were narrowed to glittering, his mouth a thing of evil.

The words brought Abram to his feet, Lot and Eliezer also. And now the strangers seemed, without so much as a movement, to close in behind their chief, and the moment was deadly. Beyond, in the fetid darkness, a hyena moaned.

" Truly the courage of my brother lies in the bloodless surrender of his goods, if he would live to enter the grasslands of Egypt." The words were mocking and contemptuous.

Then it was as if Abram had measured the leader by a single unswerving glance and found him without stature. Truly, this man had eaten of his bread, partaken of his civility, yet there remained the law passed from mouth to mouth down countless generations, given from father to son, inscribed upon clay by kings and priests and judges: " Thou owest nothing to a bandit."

And so he answered, with words level and unhurried: " In

truth, the paying of tribute is an ancient custom, and one which I have honored many times. Yet, since the scanty substance I now possess is needed to sustain my household, no portion of it shall be rendered up to him who stands before me. Nor is he the first outlaw whose demands I have denied. Thus, let it be understood that I stand defenseless before no man — and to none will I yield the bread of our mouths as tribute! "

And then, with utter contempt, he spat between the feet of the leader. At the same time, his hand fell upon the dagger at his waist and his men rose like shadows around him, so that the circle of firelight was crowded with them, humble wanderers become practiced warriors within the space of a sign. Beside the measure of their purpose, the silent and disciplined readiness of their bearing, it was as if the robber band dwindled and grew weak. But its leader sprang forward, snarling through clenched and broken teeth:

" By the beard of my father! I will have your herds and flocks, your grain and oil, and such of your wives as it may please me to possess . . ."

Whereupon Abram struck him across the face with such violence that blood spurted forth and stained the sands where he fell. And, dragging him upward, Abram tore the dagger from his hand and held it against his throat and spoke to his men.

" A single move and your leader shall die the death! And if your faces, or the face of this verminous wretch, ever come before my eyes again, then I swear you shall not live long enough to cry out for mercy! "

Whereupon he flung the leader at their feet as one would cast carrion before the dogs. The others, poor-spirited and quailing, shrank together, awaiting a word of command. And when it came, a guttural sound forced between bleeding lips, it bade them depart. Now they seemed to retreat and, without sound, dissolved into the darkness and were gone from sight.

In the sudden stillness Sarai and her slave women turned again into the tent, nor did they seek to conceal their trembling. And Azubah vowed fiercely to pass the keenest of her kitchen knives among the women of the encampment, that they might share in its defense when the bandits returned.

"Let my sister be comforted," said Maacah, with a slow and wise smile. " I have looked more than once upon the face of cowardice. They will not come again."

But afterward Abram ordered the fires made brighter, and strengthened the guard, and gave Eliezer charge over those who would stand watch through the night.

# IX

Not since the days of his boyhood had Eliezer stood guard beside the watch fires of a sleeping caravan. It was in the twelfth year of his life that he made his first journey beyond the gates of Ur, and stood his first watch with the sentries of the night. And no trust, before that hour nor since its passing, had been so grave a matter in his eyes. He had moved resolutely up and down the fires, taking unto himself a bold and manly stride, feeling that in his hands alone rested the defense of the caravan, the lives of its men, and the fortunes of Terah. And even when his eyelids burned with the yearning to sleep, he remained stanchly alert, sensing an intruder in every shadow, hearing a stealthy footstep in the thinnest whisper of sand.

He was a youth made awkward by the very urgency of his desire to serve his lord with honor, and his head was full of the dizzying, unobtainable dreams by which the solitary hours of boyhood are glorified. In his fancy he wrested a spear from a ruffian who would have plundered the caravan, slew a marauding lion which had set upon the flocks. And afterward, also in his fancy, he stood forth with seemly humility while Terah his lord cried out for all to hear, " Behold a lad who is even now a man among men! "

In truth, the howls and shrieks and wails of the wilderness smote him with terror, and he shook so fearfully that a dagger would have fallen from his hand. Yet the dreams remained before him, sweet and high.

Remembering, the man was stricken with a sharp nostalgia, a

sense of irrevocable loss that not one among them had come to pass. Now, surely, he said within himself, the richest years of my life are left behind me and, knowing this, I yield at last the truth which is the common sorrow of all: I am no princeling of the gods as I did dream, but only sullied clay, as other men.

And as his thoughts returned to the things of his boyhood, so now they returned to Ur. Ur was the city of his birth and of his growing up, and therefore dear to his heart and to his memory. Out of the uneasy night, he recalled the room that had been his own, the bed upon which he had slept, a lamp by which he had lingered late at night recording matters of the House of Terah upon the tablets. There was a certain hymn from the temple at dawn, a bird which sang in the olive tree, a peddler who had sold pomegranates rich and red and juicy beyond all believing, the staring clay god to which he had prayed, departing upon his first journey . . .

Time had borne from the face of the earth nearly all who rode forth in that caravan. Yet others had come in their stead, and so unchanging was the pattern of existence that the scene that now lay before him was scarcely to be distinguished from the scene that lay beneath the dust of years — the desert mist, the unalterable stars, the sleeping herds, the men sprawled within their cloaks upon the sand, the slow-moving shapes of the guards passing against the redness of the fires.

Yet, borne upon the loneliness of that alien night, out of the mist and out of the past, there floated toward him faces diaphanous and dissolving: Terah, the beloved master . . . his own father, a man mighty of heart . . . the gracious mother of Sarai . . . Haran, by whom Lot was begotten . . . Milca, sultry maidservant, and the first girl he had known in desire. There had been others, now shadowy and nameless, girls with seeking lips and wanton eyes, encountered at the festivals, within the villages, the bazaars, the inns. Many had stirred his blood, but never his heart, and among them there was none beloved.

"How is it," he asked himself — when he had moved to the edge of the fire and back again — "how is it that love comes at last to the heart of a man, love for one woman above all others? Times without number, I have perceived it. Even though a man has taken to himself a host of wives and concubines, there is one among them who possesses his heart. How does this come to pass, seeing that the beloved is often less beautiful, even less fruitful, than the rest? How is it that they are bound, one to the other — by what strange filament of understanding, what insoluble bond? "

The watch fires had begun to smolder and grow faint. Presently he would brighten them with such thorns as the women had been able to recover from the sands, with brush gathered along the way and heaped upon the backs of the camels. From out of the desolate reaches of the sands came the sudden wailing of hyenas. A jackal, venturing near the encampment, tainted the night with a smell of mold and filth. He thought, in wrenching despair: The stench of jackals in a land of wasting death — is it for this we have abandoned the green loveliness of our homeland?

Suddenly he was warned and made alert by the whisper of God which comes to those in peril. He beheld no movement, heard no sound, not so much as the pressure of an unclad foot upon the sand or the motion of a linen tunic. Yet he knew there was one who lingered behind him in the darkness, who gazed upon him from the shadows and perhaps sought his death.

Quietly, he moved forward, giving no sign, neither altering his stride nor turning his head. Yet from the edge of his glance, he discerned a shadow, darker than the rest, which moved with stealth and halted beside a clump of thorn. Should this stranger come upon me suddenly, leaping from the bush, hurling a spear, at least I shall be spared surprise, he thought.

His hand did not lift from the dagger at his waist but tightened upon it, his muscles grew taut and ached with waiting. Now he had turned and was again approaching the thorn and, seeing that danger lay in wait for him, surely it was wisdom to attack. With the lith violence of an animal, he sprang from the night upon the crouched figure, hurling it to the sands with such force that it gasped once, and moved no more. The struggle had been so swift, so soundless, that not even the guards perceived it. And now that it was ended and the figure stilled, a vast silence spread about him and, in the ringing loneliness, he heard the beating of his own blood. His arm, arrested in the midst of a dagger thrust, was still above his head, and the weapon hung loose in his hand as he stared upon the fallen stranger.

"Have the bandits then sent a child to spy upon us?" he asked, bewildered.

Seizing the small figure, he drew it toward him, and the starlight glimmered from a quiet face framed in thick, dark hair.

"The Canaanite girl!"

His lips could scarcely shape his astonishment. And while he knelt at her side, she opened her eyes and gazed up at him in terror.

"My lord, I beg of you," she whispered desperately, "neither hold nor betray me, but let me go forth, seeing that it is for the sake of your master I do this thing — and for the sake of the household, likewise . . ."

"Where is the child?" he asked her then.

"He is with Maacah, and I — I have said to her that if I should die, then let him be given to your care."

"Wherefore?"

"You have no son, yet you are such a one as would bring up a youth to stand as high as any man, and this is what I would wish for my child, seeing that he is dear to my heart."

She was utterly spent and choked with tears. And lest she be heard by the sentries, he lifted her and bore her beyond the firelight and stilled the piteous sobs of her lips against the fabric of his tunic. She was so small and light that the moment recalled his boyhood, when he had helped to lead the flocks of Terah and, more than once, had borne a frightened lamb to safety in his arms.

"Let my lady be comforted. Let her cease to weep. Let my lady believe me, no harm shall befall her."

He felt strangely elated and yet confused, so that he was unaware of his own words, and spoke in syllables murmuring and incoherent. And when he had placed her upon the sand, he did not leave her in her wretchedness, but crouched beside her and touched, with pity, the soft darkness of her hair.

The moon had begun to rise, large and pale and infinitely lonely, and in its light he beheld her clearly, the slight and childlike body, the small toil-marked hands, the ears delicately shaped and deeply cut with slave marks concealed until this hour. And he remembered that she would not suffer the maid-servants to touch her hair.

" How is it," he asked gently, " that you seek your own death? "

" The Canaanite," she gasped out. " My face is known to him, for he has seen me at the inn of my master, where I served food and drink to those of the road. Should he behold me within this camp, then truly the son of Terah would die. It is an in-exorable law, from which there is no escape. For Abram has given me asylum, though I — I am not freeborn."

Urgency quickened his voice.

" Yet when we have entered Egypt, and truly we are at its very gates . . ."

" How is it that I had hoped for deliverance? " she answered, dully. " My face is known to many, and there is a bounty of no small worth for him who will seize me in the name of my master. Even the priests desire my death. Thus, let it be."

" Nay! " he gathered her into his arms and held her against his breast as he had held the lambs. " You shall not go forth to perish, but return to the refuge of the tents, and I will take to myself the child of your heart, and he shall be as the flesh of my flesh, and you also, little sister."

How is it that love comes at last to the heart of a man, love for one woman above all others? He laid his face against her own and thought within himself: To the end of life, were it required of me, I could cherish her as now, gently and utterly, without desire. And he said aloud, " This night I have found my beloved," and kissed her mouth.

And while the sentries were concerned with replenishing the fires, he bore her back to the tent of the slave women and left her within its shelter.

Before the dawn light glimmered along the edge of the sands, a thousand images of her had risen in his fancy. He thought how it was that she had toiled at the inn of the ancient caravan road, even — it was not to be doubted — since the days of her child-hood. He saw her striving with the heavy water jars, kneeling in sweat and weariness before the cooking fires, hastening to set wine and smoking meat and new bread before those whose feet had turned to the gates of the inn — thieves and rascals, lords and elders, officers, merchants, emissaries — the multitude of the road. From them she had learned his own tongue, the tongue of the north which was the voice of trade.

And there were other images that came before him, so that his blood rose, hot and disordered, to pound against his impotent anger, his unavailing hate. He beheld travelers, coarsely jocular, calling to her in terms intimate and familiar, even obscene; her owner, at whose name terror and revulsion stood forth in her eyes, seizing her with neither tenderness nor pity, begetting upon her a child he would have slain. How had she fled with the little one and sought the wilderness, in what hour of darkness and silence, by what desperate a means?

And when morning had stirred the gathering from sleep, he hastened to bear the matter to Abram.

". . . thus it is known to us both that the woman of whom the Canaanite spoke is the woman received into our tents."

"The harboring of a runaway slave," said Abram slowly — "this is not the act of a prudent man. Yet I would not see her delivered up to the priests of the ungodly. Let her be given, instead, to some household of Egypt wherein she may find sanctuary as well as peace."

The breath of Eliezer quickened in his throat, and the proud contours of his face tightened.

"May it please the son of Terah," he said, "let her remain with the caravan!"

"Wherefore?" asked Abram, in surprise. He added mildly: "Would this be wisdom? Seeing that the priests seek her death, who can doubt that she will be discovered? If not upon one day, then surely upon another, and when that time has come to pass . . ."

"Let it be upon me!"

"Nay," Abram spoke kindly. "I would not have Eliezer risk death for the sake of a runaway girl."

"Let the wrath be upon my head!"

Thus was the truth torn from his breast upon a wild and desperate cry, the truth and the anguish, the ecstasy and the fear. The words, hurled forth in violence, fell like stones about them.

And afterward, in the swift and staring silence, each heard the whisper of his own breathing. Sudden detached sounds intruded upon the moment — the shouting of a herd boy, the groaning of a camel, the voices of some women returning from the well. And when Abram again lifted his eyes, there was upon his face an understanding and a regret. So does life deal with every man, even with you, Eliezer.

"May it please the son of Terah," said Eliezer, desperately, "I would cleave unto this girl, and to no other. Therefore, let her be given to me in marriage. This very day, without waiting further, since who knows at what hour disaster may overtake us?"

Abram stood without words, his shoulders bent beneath the weight of his reluctance.

"Thus shall it be," he said, at last, "though it is no happy thing in my eyes, and not according to my heart. Because of the love I bear him, I am distressed for my brother — for how is he to escape the judgment and the death? Yet, also because of my love, let it be as he asks."

A great joy lighted the face of Eliezer, and he fell down before the son of Terah and embraced his feet.

# X

UNDER THE MERCILESS STARE OF THE SUN, THE WATER SANK YET lower in such wells as remained to them, and gusts of fiery heat were driven endlessly upon their burned faces. On every side vultures rose, gorged and loathsome, from some grisly feast. Again and yet again, the shadows of their wings were imprinted upon the path of the caravan as they drifted and hovered above it in their quest for death. Once Abram scattered a host of them from the body of a struggling gazelle and, granting the animal mercy with a swift thrust of his spear, saw how its living eyes had been plucked from its head.

No single cloud, however small, obscured the blinding light of the sun. Near the wells, lions lay in the parched and shattered scrub, awaited the coming of desperate animals from the hills and caves, fed upon their starved haunches and drank from their veins. The sands were littered with the remnants of bloody feasts, horns and ribs picked clean. There were other bones also, not of animals, but of children, and skulls which remained of tragedies not to be named. And always the vultures, flapping boldly, glutted and reeking with carrion.

The earth quivered on such waves of heat that it was as if the Most High God had set the hills to trembling. Sweat ran down the faces of the travelers, drenched their bodies, soaked to streaming wetness the fabric of their garments. The eyes of the camels were crowded with flies, their coats appeared scorched and afflicted with mange. The herds and flocks were shrunken beyond believing, for many of the animals had died, and others had been slaughtered that the household might not suffer want of food. At night, the pungent smell of jackals was close about the camp, and their lean, gaunt shadows slunk away beneath the moon. Each day rose as a new shape of misery, bruised and bewildered, dreadful to be met.

Out of her wretchedness Sarai thought with dull and unrelieved longing: To lie beneath these sands in death, unwearied and unknowing, in the coolness and dark. Yet, worse than the burning sun, more terrifying than the scattered wake of famine and death, were the empty reaches of watching silence, the vast and whispering loneliness.

Then, at the dusk of a certain day, the household glimpsed a light near a cave in the rocks, and Lot thought it the watch fire of a hermit. On still another day, near the going down of the sun, they beheld a column of smoke rising, tall and blue, from the barren hills on the right.

" A merchant bound for Egypt," Abram surmised, " by one of the caravan routes near the sea."

These two, the hermit's light and the merchant's fire, Sarai held fast against her fears, taking comfort in the knowledge that the tribe of Abram was not utterly alone in this awesome waste, that there were others who had suffered its miseries and survived, who had traveled its length and breadth and did not perish. Indeed, just beyond that very rise, across the empty stream bed, around the boulder, one might come upon other tribes, other faces — shepherds, holy men, caravan leaders, even soldiers of the frontier. Yet, gaining the rise, passing the stream bed, coming upon the boulder, one beheld only ravaged emptiness scarred by the suns and winds and droughts of uncounted centuries.

Then, as they approached the caravan roads of the coast, some of the heat abated. A cooler wind reached out to them, smelling of waves and salt, and there appeared the cairns of stones which would lead the traveler to Egypt. And as one cairn was left behind, another was seen to rise ahead, so that the way was not to be mistaken.

Thereafter, the heat lessened, and the taint of death came only with certain winds. Each sunset offered a new well, and now there appeared other travelers bound for the land of the pharaohs. These had come southward along the straight, unbroken coast and had looked only lightly upon the famine, yet their mouths were filled with tales of its desolation and destruction. Thus, night followed night, and the watch fires glowed upon the faces of men gathered together in hunger for companions, and for word of the world beyond. Each caravan unfolded some new matter of astonishment before the others, and many tales were told of Egypt, for among the strangers were those who had both journeyed and dwelt therein.

Despite the famine that was upon them, those of Abram's household had turned their faces to the Nile country slowly and with reluctance, for who would wish to enter a kingdom of the dead? Thus was Egypt known abroad, and the very name conjured images dim and terrifying, not to be sought. In Egypt men lived only for the dying, and gave their days to the building of tombs which would wall out time and decay.

And of the many tales that were told, the strangest was of the great stone monster. . . . Beside the desert, upon the edge of its silences, crouched a lion in a headcloth, it was said, holding between his huge and carven paws the mystery of ages without number. He had been given the face of a king, imperious and cruel, with eyes staring and remote, gloating upon some barbarism unknown to the beholder. Here, from everlasting to everlasting, the monster lay, disdaining the generations of men who scurried at his feet in unvaried patterns of birth and growth and mating, who strove with puny arrogance against the tides of eternity, and departed with the seasons of time that others might creep forth to scurry in their stead.

At the going down of every sun, new thorns were kindled, encampments spread forth, and yet other caravans seen to approach, led by the sight of smoke rising in the quiet air, by the yellow light of cooking fires, the hastening of their camels and donkeys which, nearing the well, were beckoned by the spirit of the waters. And soon the night camps began to be crowded with animals, clamorous with strangers, heavy with the stench of sweating and unwashed bodies, with the smell of foreign foods and alien wares. Merchants and their slaves, camel boys, couriers, caravan leaders, peasants and craftsmen, physicians and vagabonds jostled one another and the animals likewise, that they might partake from the well. And when all had drunk, and broken the evening bread, and the women were within the tents, then new tales of wonder rose upon the smoke of the watch fires, and always the talk returned to Egypt.

Truly there were, within the Nile country, greater marvels than could be numbered in the space of a thousand years. " Let my brother believe me, there is a harem of the pharaoh magnificent beyond the telling! " How many wives and concubines had been led beyond its walls no man could say, but so many eunuchs were needed to guard it that, were they assembled before the eyes, the company would obscure the earth from Shechem to Zoan.

Here dwelt women gathered from every margin of the world in the king's unending and unscrupulous search for perfection. And many honorable men — even those of high houses — had been slain because he desired their wives. " Woe, if my brother possesses a wife of beauty, then let him take heed and declare her his sister, lest he never again behold the gates of his own city! "

It was a tale which spread among the travelers with the swiftness of a plague and which, by the setting of another sun, had been passed from every mouth. If my brother possesses a wife of beauty, then let him take heed . . . In the tents of the women it was received with a fluttering excitement, evoking both anxiety and delight. Yet the wife of Lot regarded it with bitter disdain.

" It is not I who shall be led forth to dwell in a palace! " she declared. " Nay, the gods deal spitefully with those who understand the nature of their own desires." Yet, even as she spoke, her hands were busied with scents and jewels and delicate garments which had not been lifted from a clothes chest since the departure from Haran.

Some of the most ill-tempered and ill-favored women of the household twittered with alarm, lest they be borne away to the royal harem. Indeed, the wife of Heber vowed to conceal herself within a grain hamper, and to thrust a dagger between her breasts rather than suffer an Egyptian guard to drag her forth.

" Though only a king weak-witted and drunken could desire such a toad! " Azubah remarked sourly.

Among the men there were those who commanded their wives to veil their faces henceforth. There were others who, out of the placidity of years and wisdom, smiled to hear of the matter and knew no alarm.

" Indeed," said one, " the wife of my heart has borne me nine sons, and is as beautiful as a gazelle in my eyes, yet I should be astonished if the king beheld her as other than an aging foreigner with a loose tongue."

Yet there were many of the men who, being consumed with jealousy of a certain wife and seeing her as desirable beyond all women, feared they would meet death for her sake. Thus, more and more heeded the words of the strangers so that, in the end, it seemed doubtful that any caravan had ever borne toward Egypt a greater number of brothers and sisters than did the caravan of Abram.

Both Maacah and Azubah had grown fearful lest Sarai be desired of the pharaoh, and Urfa lifted her frenzied voice with their own, declaring it was revealed to her in a dream that Abram would die by flogging, for the sake of his wife. Even the shy Elisheba came forth and, kneeling at the feet of her mistress, implored in the halting accents of her soft, foreign voice, " Seeing that this tale has come from the lips of many travelers, and that my lady is beautiful beyond other women, may it please her to have prudence . . ."

Sarai's eyes dealt tenderly with this girl who was wife to Eliezer and beloved of his heart. Indeed, the radiance of the love between them was made known before the world, lighting their faces, giving a tremulous, shining quality to their laughter and their words. See how it is with these two, she thought, even as with Abram and Sarai, in the days of Ur. And she knew a sudden heaviness of heart, a sense of unavailing regret.

"Let my mistress be comforted," Maacah told her. "Is a wife less dear to her husband for being numbered in his eyes with the fixed and abiding blessings of the gods, the beating of his heart, the coming and going of his breath, the rising stars . . . ?"

Yet despite the solacing words of the slave woman, Sarai was stricken with loneliness as she stood apart and beheld the stalwart form of Abram moving among those of his household, giving orders as to the sharing of a well, the slaughter of a fallen ox, the punishment of a thief. In the midst of men fearful lest their wives be seized in the name of the king, he alone gave voice to no concern. It was as if concern for the caravan possessed him utterly, and, in the last portion of the journey, his manner grew even more detached. For a space of days, they had scarcely spoken together.

Yet when the household had entered Egypt, he made it known that it would please him to break the evening bread within his own tent.

At the going down of the sun, the caravan halted near some marshes which fluttered with vivid wings, and trees stirred by quickened winds against the last reddened light of day. In the well before them was water, sweet and of fabulous depth, so that all drank and were filled. And so abundant were the grazing lands that the animals lay down upon them, the encampment was spread forth above them, and the floor of Abram's tent was carpeted in fragrant grass as rich and deeply yielding as a rug from the weavers of Damascus.

The tent was made festive as Sarai moved about it, lighting the fairest of the lamps, hanging aloft a spray of scented herbs, casting a length of richly patterned wool upon the cushions. And when she had bathed, it was in a fair tunic that she girded herself, the darkness of her hair spread forth upon her shoulders, a glimmering of gold upon her wrists and at her tender throat and in her ears.

Night was upon them before he came. Having entered, he paused, stricken by the sudden radiance of the lamps and, standing there, drew one hand slowly, heavily, across his brow.

"In truth, I am weary beyond the telling . . ."

She saw, with sudden compassion, how harshly the journey had dealt with him. His skin had been burned to darkness by the unrelenting sun. His face, thin and strained, was afflicted with a look of years, and there were certain unfamiliar patterns of weariness about his eyes. Thus she hastened to heap the cushions for his comfort, to bring forth the food she had made ready for this hour, the dates and curds, the heated wine.

And not until he had eaten and was at peace did she disclose that which burdened her heart.

"There is a tale from Egypt — surely it is known to my husband . . ."

He cast a swift and smiling glance at her.

"Truly it is known to me, seeing that disquiet is upon all the caravan because of it."

It is now that he will speak, she thought suddenly. It is now that he will speak and say how both fear and torment have possessed him for my sake . . .

Yet he uttered no word further, but was silent, absorbed in thought. Beyond the encampment, the lonely sound of frogs rose from the marshes. Crickets chirped in the grass, and a bright-winged moth flew in toward the lamps and began casting itself against the wall of the tent with soft, monotonous thuds. Sarai roused and spoke insistently.

"What is the will of my lord concerning this matter?"

For a little time, he was silent, considering her words. And when at last he spoke, it was in the grave and careful tone of one who lifts his voice before the council.

"Often such tales are but the idle tattle of the bazaar. Yet, seeing that you are fair to look upon, proclaim yourself my sister."

"Wherefore?" she asked, quietly.

He spoke as one astonished.

"Have I not a duty before the Lord to save myself for that which he requires of me?"

106

She was silent, stricken to the heart by the nature of his answer. And now it seemed that the evening beside him was falling into decay before her eyes. The wicks were burning low upon the oil, the herbs had lost their fragrance and smelled of dust, the hour was nearly spent. Yet he had uttered no word to fulfill the longing within her. Surely those of his followers who counseled their wives in this matter had spoken otherwise. " Proclaim yourself my sister," they had said, " that we two may be divided neither by the king, nor by anything save death, seeing that my heart lives only because of you."

But with my husband, it is not so, she thought, in painful heaviness. Seeing that his life is given to the Lord, even now we are divided by realms of the spirit unknown to me.

Twice had the Lord revealed himself to Abram upon the journey into Canaan. At Shechem, a vale centuries old, where terebinth and mulberry trees flowered in the shadow of the great mount of Gerizim, he had renewed the words of his promise: " Unto thy seed I will give this land." And Abram built an altar there, that this might not be unremembered. And afterward, among the shattered rocks and stony hillsides of Bethel, farther to the south, he had built yet another altar, and gone apart to it and taken counsel with the Lord and known his will.

But Sarai heard not the voice of the Lord, nor fathomed the devotion of her husband to his name.

Often her thoughts returned, with longing, to the gods of her childhood in their distant temples and chapels and sanctuaries, too far from Canaan either to hear her voice or receive her offerings. She had long since bidden them farewell. And of all the household images before which she had sacrificed, only the family teraphim remained, buried beneath the weight of garments and linens in the wedding chest.

" Let them be preserved," Abram had directed, " not because they possess divinity, but because they signify the right of inheritance."

Thus they lay in darkness and silence, unaware of what passed above them, perhaps even unaware that they had been borne out of Haran.

But with Nannar, shining deity of the night skies, it was otherwise. As all men knew, he departed from the terraced temple with every sunset, to sail above the margins of the earth in the splendor of his galley, the moon. Wherever the caravan journeyed, Nannar journeyed also, casting the path of his own glory before him, beholding all that came to pass among men.

Again and yet again, Sarai thought in her distress: He who worships before the Lord of Abram may worship before none other, but I dare not stir the wrath of Nannar against me. Yet, if I do not seek his God, it may be that my husband will turn from me utterly.

The night was still. The silence of peace was upon the encampment, for the winds were sweet and the afflictions of the desert lay behind . . . the waterless plains, the stench of death, the howling animals of the dark, the wraiths of famine and destruction which had journeyed beside them. "In this moment of deliverance, I should know only joy," she said to herself, but the words were cold and comfortless and without persuasion.

And then, in the diminishing lamplight of the tent, Abram stirred and spoke from the edge of sleep:

"When it comes that we encounter other guards of the frontier . . ."

"Then I shall declare myself the sister of Abram," she answered obediently. And bitterness rose unbidden to her voice as she added, "Lest my husband be slain because of me, and his destiny remain unfulfilled."

He opened his eyes in mild astonishment and then, suddenly smiling, reached out to her with tender understanding.

"Declare also," he said, "that I would not have us divided, neither by the king nor anything further, since my heart lives only because of you."

And the uneasiness within her wavered and was quenched utterly as he drew her to his breast and began to kiss her mouth.

# XI

NOW THE MISTS OF SUNRISE HAD LIFTED AND THE BIRDS WERE CALL-
ing to one another in the marshes and a golden light had come
upon the land, edging the fronds of the date palms, the reeds of
the waterways, the wet and shining leaves. The passing caravans
of the night had departed with the first dawn, but there was still
to be seen of them the soiled and trodden grass where they had
camped, the warm and smoking ashes of their fires.

Sarai had returned to her tent bearing a cool and brimming
water jar, but Urfa, the languid kitchen maid, still lingered at
the well with a pitcher to be filled for Azubah. The caravan had
made no haste to depart from this place, seeing that it was one
of abundance, and two moons had come to pass since, entering
the land of Egypt, Abram had declared before them all: " We
are a high house from a proud and ancient city, with a destiny
promised us by the Lord himself. Therefore, give care to your
animals and to your goods, and make yourselves and your children fair and clean, that we may appear before the Egyptians as
men of dignity and honor, not as mean and disorderly wanderers
of the sands."

The guards of the frontier had given him leave to sojourn in
the grasslands until the famine ended, for such was the will of
their king. But they had voiced no curiosity as to the women of
the caravan — indeed, had displayed not so much as an idle
interest in them, either for their own sake or for the sake of the
pharaoh. And thus the clamor concerning the royal harem de-
clined.

At the threshold of her tent Sarai halted, gazing in wonder at
a sudden, swift-rising stream of dust upon the plain. And when
she had shaded her eyes against the brightness of the morning,

she beheld a large number of archers approaching — Egyptians, lean and brown and fleet, their eyes fixed and remote, their feet bare and strong and rhythmic, each man so like the others that it was as if they were all kinsmen. Clad in white jerkins, they bore the shields and bows of archers, and it was apparent that they were guards preceding a traveler of rank.

At the same moment a wild and terrified cry rose from the lips of Urfa.

" A thousand warriors are upon us! " she shrieked, and cast her pitcher upon the stones.

After the archers came runners, swift, muscular, intent, and then carriers bearing two royal chairs in which reclined two princely Egyptian youths. With them were slaves, scribes, body servants, astrologers, physicians, and advisers. After these came other runners and then, at last, a rear guard of archers so like the first as to startle the beholder.

Sarai watched, her eyes taking pleasure in the colorful sight. The folds of her tunic, being driven against her body by the morning wind, gave her the graceful and shapely lines of an exquisite carving, and one of the youths, beholding her thus, turned swiftly to the other. Whereupon a command was shouted and the entire company halted with an instant obedience and precision terrifying to behold. Urfa, seeing what had come to pass, flung herself upon the earth before them and howled for mercy. After which one of the officers, being commanded by the older prince, detached himself from the ranks and, going forward, hauled the gaping maidservant to her feet.

" Who is she who stands before the tent? "

" S-Sarai, s-sister to Abram, s-son of T-Terah."

He cast her from him and she fled, shrieking, to fall at the feet of her mistress and, when the Egyptians had passed, to cry out her sorrowful tidings.

" Behold, the name of Sarai was required of me! Behold, they have looked with favor upon my lady! Woe, the life of our master has reached its latter days."

Her laments brought the women forth from the tents and cast panic upon the household. And before the sunset of that day there were many who implored Abram to depart from Egypt and turn back into the way by which they had come.

"How are we to do this thing?" he asked, in tones of quiet reasoning. "We have neither grain nor flocks to sustain us upon another journey. Should we turn back to the stricken lands with so little of substance, then, truly, all our caravan would die. Nay, this matter is in the hands of the Lord, and, seeing that we abide in his protection, neither Sarai nor any other among us shall suffer ill from the Egyptians."

"Let my lady have no fear," said Maacah, but the familiar words were without conviction, and her voice was shaken with uneasiness.

"Only in curiosity did the princes speak," declared Azubah, boldly. "Even now they have ceased to remember the matter!"

Yet before many days had come to pass, there arrived a certain official, splendid of bearing and of wig, escorted by archers, eunuchs, runners, and slaves who bore an empty carrying chair. The lady Sarai, sister of Abram, would set forth within the hour for the royal palace, by command of the courageous and invincible lion, the mighty and fertile bull, beloved and immortal scion of the gods, the pharaoh of Egypt.

For a space of five days, Sarai had dwelt within the Court of Women, awaiting the hour when she would be summoned before the pharaoh. Her journey to the palace had been swift, for those who bore her carrying chair were royal runners, well chosen, and their hard bare feet thudded upon the roadways at a pace so smooth and fleet as to fill her with wonder.

More than once they had come upon a village, clean and white and of good order, spread beneath date palms which stirred in the freshened wind and cast damp and wavering shadows upon the roof tops and before the doorsteps. She had looked upon brightly painted houses as colorful as blossoms, had beheld flowering trees of a splendor beyond the telling.

Past the village lay a rich and fertile countryside patterned with sun and shadow. Not since the days of Ur had she looked upon orchards and vineyards thus burdened with the weight of ripening fruit, cattle thus fattened with grazing, fields of such bountiful yield. Along the marshes, reeds moved in the quickening wind and ducks took flight against the sky. At the riverside women knelt and beat their linens upon the rocks to the rhythm of their singing. Small boats glided past, with colored sails mirrored upon the stillness of the water, as silent and beautiful as the phantoms wrought by the desert heat.

Indeed, this was no land heavy with death wherein people gave their lives to melancholy rites performed in shadows and whispers. It was, instead, a land flowing with joyous spirit poured forth upon all within its boundaries: the men, in tidy white aprons, bearing geese to market; the young wives with their babies in carrying-slings before them; the children leaping and running at games in the streets.

Darkness had fallen when the runners gained the palace of the pharaoh, and Sarai was conducted to the Court of Women. She stepped from the lowered chair into the light of torches flaring upon dark and unknown faces, upon a scene alien and unreal. And in truth, she was possessed by terror, yet she held her head proudly and went forward with the imperious step of one who would say, " Behold, I am no woman from a shameless tribe of the sands, but the daughter of a high house, wife of Abram, son of Terah, whose city of Ur is named among the greatest of the earth."

The light dealt cruelly with her eyes, after the soft and starlit darkness, yet she was aware of broad copper gates and stately steps, of torches flaring upon richly polished woods and high brick walls, of guards stiffly erect, immobile, in short white jerkins, their chins thrust forward at matching angles, their eyes fixed and unmoving.

She was led through a long colonnade fragrant with a thousand flowers and radiant with lights held in the hands of lamp bearers. Painted vines climbed the columns and, on a ceiling as blue as the fairest sky, painted birds rose into painted clouds, their look of beauty and reality bestowing an air of enchantment upon the place.

After a time she was brought to a small entry, where a certain eunuch, round and bald and ruddy of countenance, sat before the folds of a drapery heavy and ornate. These, being swept aside by one of the guards, revealed a room vast and rich beyond believing. Sarai entered slowly and the fabric of the drapery fell behind her, closing her in.

Suddenly, she knew a wild desire to flee, to fling aside the patterned folds and rush past the eunuch and down the pillared halls, and seek the garden. Surely, in the shadows, she could hide herself until the hour of dawn and thus find her way beyond the city, back to the grasslands of the encampment. Now, suddenly, she was no longer a daughter of Ur, but a woman of the desert, alert to danger, defiant of restraint, familiar with the ways of finding concealment, of moving by the bright, guiding patterns of the stars.

Yet when the eunuch had cried out in his shrill, hysterical voice, the guards would rush forth, and shouts would rise to the very roof top: " Behold, the woman of the north has fled! " And they would pursue her in the clamorous manner of wild spearmen upon the heels of a terrified gazelle. And though she gained the refuge of the darkness, the concealing shapes of the garden, how was she to pass beyond the guarded walls? Nor could she return to her husband with the shame of disobedience upon her. Nay, it was a thought incautious and foolish, impossible of the doing. And, knowing these things, she abandoned herself to despair and wept bitterly.

As with all women, when she had wept, she suffered less heaviness of heart. Thus she cleansed her face of tears and turned at last to gaze upon the room, her eyes rising from the tiles of the floor to the scenes which adorned the walls, and the patterned colors of the ceiling. About her were richly covered couches, mats and cushions deep and yielding, low inlaid tables strangely carven, one having a pedestal which simulated a captive in chains. The drapery which had been drawn aside for her was embroidered heavily and magnificently in brilliant blossoms and golden butterflies. Against her coming, a number of exquisitely wrought lamps had been lighted, the rooms perfumed and arrayed with newly gathered flowers.

Beyond the room was a bedchamber also lighted by lamps beautiful in design, and scented with flowers and incense. She went forward to gaze in wonder at the carven bed covered with delicate linens, the cross-legged chairs padded in fabric heavy with embroidery, the dressing chest, its countless mirrors and combs and jars and pots and cruses.

Lifting one of the mirrors, she gazed within it and beheld a woman unknown to her. Her eyes were reddened and made swollen by dust and heat and weeping. Her face bore marks of utter weariness, her tunic was both rumpled and soiled, her hair roughened by wind and sand, hanging in disorder. Should the pharaoh behold her in this moment, then surely he would cry out in scorn to know she had been called worthy of his court, would return her at once and with distaste to the tents of Abram.

So alert had she grown to the ways of danger that she heard the first faint motion of the drapery behind her and turned swiftly upon the sound, fear filling her eyes. Yet it was no king of Egypt who stood there, but a slave girl who, coming forward, made obeisance and, with a softly slurred accent, spoke in the tongue of the north.

"I am Hagar, your servant . . ."

She was a girl less of beauty than of grace and appeal, being small and exquisitely wrought, with skin the tawny color of sand beneath a reddening dawn. She had the alien face of an Egyptian, the proud head, the richly carven mouth, the dark eyes tilted beneath darker brows as cleanly curved as crescent moons.

" By command of the pharaoh, I wait upon the lady Sarai, for surely she is weary from the length of her journey, and would rest. But let her first be bathed and arrayed in fresh garments, and given food and drink . . ."

In the quiet kindliness of her words, Sarai heard the voice of Maacah and, this being true, gave herself into the hands of the slave girl utterly. Whereupon two dark maidservants were summoned and when they had bathed her in showers of scented water, she was arrayed in a thin linen garment and brought within the lighted bedchamber. Her hunger fled before the measure of her weariness, and though they would have served her bountifully with food and wines, she fell upon the cool ease of the great bed and slept before they had finished the uttering of the words.

Into the hands of Hagar, she learned, was delivered each maiden summoned by the king, to be garbed and anointed and adorned after the fashion of Egypt before he received her. And few came unwillingly, for the name of the pharaoh was great, the magnificence of his palace known abroad, his own charm and comeliness the gossip of every bazaar. Yet so exacting was his choice that many found no favor in his eyes and were returned to their families, though not without gifts of fabulous worth.

The harem of the king, guarded by eunuchs, was large and sheltered all manner of women: the wives and concubines, likewise their children; house servants, nursemaids, midwives, and personal slaves. It was a vast household, and increased with the passing of every season. The eunuchs, squat and fat and indolent, gave the monotony of the hours to eating and drinking, or lifted their voices in coarse jests and shameless gossip with certain slave wenches.

From the rising of the sun until the first shadow of darkness, women lingered in the vast harem garden. Indeed, there was no hour of the day when they were not to be seen, in varying numbers, walking in the shade of the high walls among the luxuriant trees and shrubs and flowers, sitting beside the sunken pools where lilies bloomed upon the waters, tarrying with games, embroidery, laughter, and murmuring talk. And, in truth, they seemed singularly companionable, with no greater dissension or jealousy among them than might exist between sisters, and much of the same tenderness.

There were, among the newer wives, those who had not yet learned the Egyptian tongue, but spoke in the alien syllables of their own lands. Many, as though to assuage homesickness or loneliness, had brought with them pets to be fondled and schooled and given extravagant care. A certain small monkey clung about the neck of his mistress, a beautiful girl from an island in the Great Sea, and moved the others to shrieks of delight with his mischief, so that they fed him nuts and sweetmeats and made much of him. A gentle brown girl of the sands, heavy with her first child, had a little fawn from the tents of her father, and it was said that she clung to it as though to a memory. Several owned brilliant birds, which spoke in the tongues of men and uttered, in raucous accents, the words of their homelands. A dark, aloof princess from the land of Kush kept a half-grown leopard beside her. And there was a great likeness between them, both moving with a haughty feline grace, regarding the world with a cool stare from narrow green eyes, possessing the tense and restless bodies of the untamed.

With the late hours of the morning and the early hours of the evening, Hagar summoned the two maidservants for bathing and anointing the sister of Abram. With swift and practiced fingers they stripped from her body the jeweled gifts sent by the pharaoh, the shimmering necklaces and anklets, the earrings and finger rings and bracelets — and these baubles, however precious, were so common to their touch that they tossed them aside without concern for them. In the shadowed coolness of the apartment Sarai was led to a small bathing room. Here, ewer after ewer of scented water was emptied upon her, so that her long hair made flat, black patterns against her throat, upon her shoulders, over the slim contours of her back, and the water streamed down her body and ran beyond sight into a sunken basin beneath her feet. The maidservants dried her with scented linens, anointed her with perfume, and dusted her flesh with a powder of fragrant roots.

To the women of Egypt were known a thousand means of prolonging youth and illusions of youth, and those who served the Court of Women possessed great skill in such matters. Beholding so vast an array of potions, oils, washes, salves, powders, scents, poultices, balms, and tints, Sarai was unable to voice the measure of her astonishment. One of the maidservants, swift and delicate of touch, tinted her face and the length of her eyes, reddened her lips and nails, the palms of her hands, the soles of her feet. The other dried and arranged her hair and, with scented linen, polished it to brightness. Flowers, exquisite of form and fragrance, were brought from the garden that they might be placed in her hair, against the pillow on which she slept, beside the plate from which she dined.

With the weariness of the desert still upon her, the memory of its burning heat and merciless sands unshaded by as much as a rock, Sarai rejoiced for a little time in these pleasures. Say to me now, would not the wife of Lot burst with fury, beholding me thus? Yet, with the fall of night, loneliness and disquiet returned to her. In the yellow flames of the lamps she saw the wavering

116

supper fires of the encampment and, beyond the door, the dusk of the walled garden became the dusk of the tents. As one bereaved, she cried out in anguish of heart, "How is it with my beloved?"

And, rising to her feet, she would have paced the length of the room, had not the voice of Hagar spoken across the silence:

"Let my lady hear and understand. I too have known the sorrow that comes to a woman who is far from the things of her heart and in the midst of strangers."

Sarai turned slowly, her face questioning.

"Surely Hagar was never a stranger in the land of Egypt . . ."

"Yet to the palace of the pharaoh I came as a stranger in fear and in sorrow when, the caravans of my father being lost, we were sold into slavery for his debt. But, with age and dishonor upon him, my father died on the very day of the selling, and now there is none alive who is kinsman to Hagar."

The hands of the slave girl fell quiet, her eyes were distant with loneliness. Then, returning slowly to that which lay about her, she took up a slender cruse and began the filling of a wine bowl.

"Still, at the hands of the pharaoh, I have suffered no unkindness," said Hagar, suddenly, "and with Sarai it will be the same. Already he has sent gracious gifts to the tents of Abram, and with the coming of another day, when he has looked upon my lady's face . . ."

Terror, warm and sickening, rose in Sarai's throat.

"At what hour am I commanded . . . before the king?"

"Indeed, he would have received the sister of Abram this very day, had not a sudden misfortune come upon him. But pain has stricken his eyes, so that he sits as one blinded, and the astrologers and physicians attend him. Yet this is but a passing thing, they say, brought about by the fierce glare of sun on the streets when he visited the temple. And with the coming of another day . . ."

But when five days had come and gone, there was still no command from the king. Each morning Hagar brought word of some new delay that had risen before him: a plague of locusts had fallen upon his fields and he had gone forth from the city to give orders concerning them; an ambassador had come from a far land and must be royally received; the astrologers had spoken against the day; his favorite sister had sickened of fever and sent for him.

Thus Sarai remained within the Court of Women, and each day crept like a beetle to its end. When darkness fell, the golden drapery was pushed aside and slaves entered to kindle the lamps, to bring fresh flowers opened by the afternoon sun, to perfume the apartment with herbs and incense. Later other slaves came, bearing a table laden with food. When it had been lowered to the floor, Sarai seated herself upon the embroidered mat beside it while Hagar, taking up a spread and lovely fan, came to stand behind her.

"I am weary," she said then, "with meals eaten alone. Surely the best seasoning for any food is companionship. Is it forbidden that Hagar share this meal with me?"

"Whatever my lady wishes shall be done — for thus the pharaoh has commanded."

"Then let Hagar sit before me."

The slave girl obeyed, silently and passively, yet her voice, when she spoke, held a quality of breathlessness, as though she sought to conceal the full measure of her delight.

"Not since I dwelt in the house of my father have I dined thus — as a lady dines."

Sarai had grown accustomed to the profusion of foods set forth for her pleasure — platters of fish, a roast of antelope, small birds basted with honey sauce, a whole roast goose, countless vegetables, seed-crusted rolls, crisp and flat loaves of bread, honey cakes, figs, dates, flagons of wine, baskets of grapes. She and Hagar broke the wings from the roast goose and, sitting cross-legged upon the mats, ate delicately from the fingers of the right hand.

"Seeing the abundance before me, one would believe I possess the appetite of a crocodile."

"If my lady will taste of the little birds — truly, they are delicious of flavor, having been fed upon honey and nuts."

Thus their voices were mingled in bright, unburdened chatter. They spoke of the ways of Egypt and of Ur, the harvests of the Nile, the famine within the land of Canaan. And Hagar told how it was that the pharaoh had compassion upon all who were stricken and ordered that they, with what remained of their flocks and herds, be received into the grasslands of Egypt. And so it was done, even against the laments of the priests and the sorcerers. These had long foretold that out of the tribes of the north would come One who would rule, not only Egypt, but the world itself. Yet the pharaoh refused to halt the Canaanites at the gates, saying, " It shall be written of me in the Book of Ages that no man went hungry under my rule."

Indeed, he was a king to be named with pride, a man of justice and mercy. Neither he nor his deeds would be forgotten, seeing that he built from everlasting to everlasting. And as for the magnificent palace wherein he dwelt . . .

" Behold," said Hagar with pride, " not even the tides of eternity shall wash away these walls."

The meal was ended at the late hour of moonrise. Slaves, being summoned by Hagar, removed the table, poured water over the hands of Sarai, brought drying linens scented with the fragrance of flowers. And when they had gone, an immense silence came upon the apartment. Some of the lamps had been quenched and the shadows had darkened; the passages beyond the door seemed untrodden and empty. Insects chirped mournfully in the moon-drenched garden, and the faint, sad notes of a harp came from a distant chamber where some concubine of the pharaoh sought to dispel her loneliness.

Here time was like the Nile itself, flowing, slow-moving and languorous, through color and fragrance marvelous to behold. There was about it the quality of a mirage, beautiful, illusionary, not to be believed. To the stranger, Egypt was like a legendary oasis found only on the lips of some teller of tales whose feet had never trodden the harsh places of the earth, but who walked upon clouds of fancy entranced by his dreams. Yet, with the passing of still other days, Sarai was concerned no more with wonders, but only with her discontent at being apart from her husband, and with the anxiety of her waiting.

Quietly, and with understanding, Hagar brought forth many things with which to seek her interest: an exquisite design to be wrought in gold thread; a lion cub, sprawling and playful, purring beneath the touch of her hand; a game in which carven pieces, scarlet and white, were moved about a patterned board.

And when they had wearied of games, she sang the songs of her native land, accompanying them with notes plucked from a small scrolled harp. Or she told the ways of the gods of Egypt — how a man who sinned could not live after death, but was hurled into the jaws of the devourer, an avenging monster of perpetual appetite. And there was much more that she told — stories of beginnings, of war and love and tenderness and sorrow, even the tales of adventure shaped by the lips of her nurse, in her childhood.

". . . and, lifting his head, the terrified sailor beheld a great serpent with golden scales, and eyebrows of lapis lazuli . . ."

She sat opposite Sarai on a richly woven mat, speaking lightly and with merriment. Her hair, long and black, was parted behind her ears, so that a broad and shining lock was brought forward, and lay upon each shoulder. She wore a simple tunic which followed chastely the high curve of her young bosom, the delicacy of her waist, the clean lines of her thigh. Her small brown hands were tenderly made, and she moved them easily as she spoke, giving grace and expression to her words. Truly, thought Sarai, she might be one of the dark goddesses painted upon their walls, a ruling princess, a temple dancer, the favorite wife of a great king. For the joyous spirit of the brown Egyptian girl had given her an illusion of beauty singular to behold. And the heart of my sister is a gracious heart . . .

Thus the days faded slowly, one into the other, until the old moon had sunk beneath the sands and a new moon hung in the west, sharp and bright, like a golden sickle awaiting the season of harvest.

"Now surely the pharaoh remembers me no longer," cried Sarai in despair. "Yet until he has received me and given me leave to depart, how may I return to the tents of Abram?"

It was an evening wretched with discontent, and more than once she had paced the length of the great room, speaking with Hagar, who sat near one of the lamps, intent upon the sewing of a fair girdle.

"Shall such a one be returned to the tents of her brother?"

smiled the slave girl. "Nay, my lady shall remain within the palace to the end of her days, and be to the pharaoh the wife above all others — the beloved." And she spread forth the girdle, to see how it fared.

Hearing these words, Sarai could no longer abide the shame and sorrow that rose within her.

"May the king forgive me," she said miserably. "I am no sister to Abram of Haran. I am his wife!"

The needlework fell, unheeded, to the floor beside Hagar's sandal, a stitch half formed, the thread still in her hand. She stumbled to her feet, unable to give voice to her dismay, and thus they stared at each other.

"Wife!" said Hagar. The word was flat, and without reality.

"There was a caravan —" faltered Sarai. "Truly, it is no easy thing to explain. A caravan whose leader spoke in warning . . ." And she told how it came about that they feared for the life of Abram. "Yet how am I to lay the truth before the king, seeing that he, a man of justice, has known deception from us both?"

Her words had scarcely ceased to echo within the room before the golden drapery was hurled aside and a figure, commanding above all others, stood in the doorway. Uttering a little gasp, the slave girl sank to the floor.

"Exalted ruler . . ." she stammered.

"Let Hagar depart."

He spoke in the tongue of Egypt, but his words were made known to Sarai by the gesture which accompanied them. Swiftly, and in silence, Hagar went forth. Surely my heart is bruised with the strength of its pounding, thought Sarai. Yet she waited as though unshaken by his presence, motionless, with proud and deliberate gaze. Not before all the kings whose hands have lifted the scepter of this land will I show myself fearful and trembling.

He who stood before her bore himself regally, yet not in arrogance. The length of his tall and muscular body gleamed in the lamplight as though it had been shaped by gifted hands from some richly dark and burnished wood. His face was at once austere and gentle. The linen of his short, girded tunic, delicate of weave, was imprinted cleanly upon the shadows, and upon the bronze sheen of his flesh. He wore the high crown, a pair of wide, jeweled bracelets, an ornate jeweled collar which lay upon his chest and covered the breadth of his shoulders.

"The lady Sarai," he said, and his voice held no mockery, but was gracious and mild. She had thought to return his gaze coldly, but now, humbled and chastened by his courtesy of manner, she bent her head.

"By the words of Sarai's mouth many things have been made clear before my eyes." He smiled a slow and bitter smile. "Surely it is no matter of surprise to you that a prudent king should wish to hear what passes within his walls. Indeed, the length of his days may depend upon the strength of his ears."

He came forward with a light and unhurried stride, casting the fabric of the drapery behind him.

"Lift your face, wife of Abram, that I may behold it fully."

She obeyed, raising her eyes to meet his own and, as they stood thus, there went out from her the delicate, quickening sense of kinship which rises between those who, even while they come together for the first time, perceive that they are not strangers.

"In truth," he said, gently, "word of your beauty is no idle tale told by a garrulous camel driver." Then, with gracious interest, he asked, "In what portion of the northland lies the homeland of Sarai?"

She spoke with pride.

"I am a daughter of Ur, city of the moon, and wife of Abram, son of the House of Terah."

"And how is it that the tribe of Abram has sought asylum in Egypt?"

"My husband had thought to dwell in the land of Canaan, but famine fell upon us and drove us forth, and cast us upon the mercy of the pharaoh."

Sudden displeasure surged upon his face.

"Should a man believe that one who would grant him an oasis in the wilderness would also slay him for the beauty of his wife?"

"Yet," she said quietly, "this tale was given to our ears many times."

He turned from her and sighed as one disheartened and wearied.

"How has such a thing arisen, seeing that I have striven, day upon day, to follow the paths of justice?"

In truth, thought Sarai, it is as Hagar has declared. He is a man of righteousness, and possesses a mighty heart. And had I never looked upon the face of my beloved, I would rejoice that I was chosen by such a one.

"Indeed, it was unknown to me that she whom I commanded to the palace was the wife, not the sister, of Abram. Yet now I perceive that the gods sought to warn me, sending plagues and omens upon me, filling my days with unrest. Let them be appeased. With the first light of morning, Sarai shall be restored to her husband. Camels and flocks shall go with you, as with every guest of the king who is returned to her people. And it is my will that you shall bear, in your departure, some gift of your own choosing."

"The pharaoh is gracious," she answered slowly, "but seeing that I have received his pardon, I desire nothing more. For surely this is more precious in my eyes than any other gift he might render."

He turned to her imperiously.

"Nay. It is my command that Sarai make the choice of such a gift as will bring joy to her heart."

A sudden thought came to her, audacious and stirring. Yet she answered humbly, almost fearfully.

"Then — if it pleases my lord — I would have the girl Hagar as my own. Often my heart cries out for the kinship of a woman gently born, a companion of the spirit. The girl Hagar is of family, and there is between us a sisterhood."

He regarded her gravely, and with understanding.

"Hunger of the heart is not unknown to me. Therefore, let Hagar be within your hand, to dwell henceforth within your tents." His gaze, gentle and unhurried, lingered upon her uplifted face. "The beauty of Sarai is the beauty of a womanly heart, of one who should be the mother of nations. Such a one I have sought through the length of these unrewarding years. But am I to seize you from the arms of Abram? I would not dishonor my name with such a deed. Yet," he said slowly, "seeing that the basest enemy of every man is himself, let Abram and all his household go up out of Egypt and return to it no more. And may the gods abide with you and give you peace."

He paused before her, as though he sought to remember that she had stood, tremulous and lovely, in the silent room where golden flames wavered among the golden flowers. The sense of his nearness again rose up between them, and she saw how it was that he turned and went apart from her, even while he would have received her into his arms.

# XII

HAGAR COULD NOT SLEEP FOR THE EXCITEMENT THAT POSSESSED HER. With the first dawn she rose from her bed mat in the tent of the slave women and, taking up a water jar, stole forth into the waxing radiance of the day.

About her lay the broad encampment of Abram, now made vast and affluent by the gifts of slaves and goods and animals from the hand of the pharaoh. The sentries of the night had ceased their watch and were gathered about a small fire, eating bread twisted upon a stick and baked hastily, incompletely, to stay their morning hunger. They lifted curious eyes to the Egyptian girl, perceiving her strange foreign beauty, her tender grace, the quality of bearing that gave her a look highborn and apart. And they would no sooner have called out to her in familiar greeting than to a daughter of the king.

Accustomed to the sheltering walls of the palace, Hagar shivered in the dawn chill. She was still clad in the slender tunic of Egypt, the delicate sandals, and her amulets sent forth glimmers of light and thin, silvery tones as she walked. Over her hair she had swept a length of wool given her by Sarai, so that her head was sheltered from the dew, her shoulders warmed against the cold.

The sun was rising, casting a thin and reddened veil of light upon the grasslands, the rushes, the streams by which the land was watered, glorifying the edges of the trees, the backs of the fattened kine in the field beyond, the wings of a great white water bird rising suddenly into the morning. The girl lifted her face to the heady sweetness of the hour, savoring it as though it were wine — the strengthening color, the stirred fragrance, the shining thought: With this day, I go forth into a new land. I am released from joyless years.

She passed the white, crumbled ashes of certain night fires, the shapes of men still asleep within their cloaks, the lance of Abram, symbol of his authority, thrust into the earth before his tent, gleaming in the light. Reaching the well, she paused for a moment to consider all that lay before her. It was her first morning with the encampment of Abram, her first moment to behold it fully, with clear and unhurried eyes. Darkness was already upon it when she and Sarai and the company from Egypt halted here the evening before, amid the noise and dust and confusion of arrival, to await the disposal of the vast caravan.

The night had been dark and moonless after the thinly gleaming crescent sank below the western rim of the world, and their last miles were followed in the light of torches. Many of the villages already slept. Dogs ran out, barking savagely, and watchmen came forth to peer from under sputtering flares at those who traveled by command of the pharaoh, and with his protection, to the grasslands of the border.

The company was large and the journey wearisome. Besides eunuchs, archers, runners, carriers, and emissaries, there were those sent as gifts to the son of Terah, menservants and maidservants in great numbers, shepherds and drovers and herdsmen with bunched and crowding animals. Thus, the villages entered upon the way were assailed by a sudden intrusion of bleating and bellowing, the snorting of camels, the shouting of men. Torches, flaring loosely in the night wind, brought into swift reality the walls of twisted streets, the doorposts of houses, the edges of leaves, the shapes of trunks and shrubs.

And when they had come to the encampment, one of the emissaries, a man of dignity and bearing, was received into the tent of Abram. Whereupon he read before the son of Terah a message from the hand of the king, unsparing in its tone of quiet reproach: "Why have you said, 'She is my sister,' seeing that I might have taken her to me? Now, therefore, behold thy wife. Take her and go thy way."

Yet Hagar's thoughts were not for the words and phrases of

emissaries, but for the maidservants and slave women. Since they had been given to her charge, she was concerned to see how they fared. There was one who had wept throughout the journey, fearing she would be eaten alive by these barbarians of the north. There were some made lame by walking, others who carried children in their arms or were heavy with babes unborn.

Then, out of the clamorous and stifling dust into the blown light of the torches there came a certain steward called Eliezer, who received the Egyptian girl and her women as though they were honored guests. Under his hand it was but a little time until all were disposed within the tents in quiet comfort, their lamenting stilled, their hunger appeased, their terror ended. In the same way the herds and flocks were dispersed to a darkened plain beyond the encampment, the new menservants given place among the old.

The Egyptians yet in the service of the king turned homeward without waiting for the dawn, and would consent to receive neither food nor drink. Archers, runners, carriers, they filled their mouths with water at the well, spat it forth upon the ground, and set out at a swift, untiring pace, disdaining the hospitality of foreigners.

Now is my sister returned to the arms of her lord, thought Hagar, and knew peace.

As she stood beneath the trees by the well, the leaves were pierced suddenly by shafts of golden light as slim and unbroken as arrows. And now a shadow fell across the ancient stones and, lifting her eyes, she perceived that a stranger had come forth from the tents to drink of the waters. It was a moment timeless and imperishable. To the dust of her grave she wore it like an amulet contrived against despair.

He wore a short tunic girded at the waist, and sandals fashioned of leather in the manner of northern craftsmen. His flesh, as warmly brown and firm as the flesh of a date, had a sheen of sunlight upon it. Behind him, the sharply green fronds of the palms moved slowly in the morning wind, light gleamed from the rich and tumbled blackness of his hair, and, beholding her, he greeted her with a smile both imperious and gentle.

" Peace be upon my lord . . ." she began, and knew an inexplicable flurry of heart, a sudden confusion of tongue, so that she forgot herself and spoke in the syllables of Egypt. Then, still in confusion, she amended the words, repeating them in the tongue of the north.

"How is it that the Egyptian girl speaks the language of my homeland?" he asked, with a measure of surprise. His voice, low and rich and gentle, flowed upon her like the touch of a warm and kindly hand.

"My nurse — she who was as a mother to me in the days of my childhood — was a slave woman of Kish," she stammered. And then, quietly, she added, "I am the handmaiden of Sarai, one of the gifts of parting sent by the pharaoh to the master of this tribe."

"May joy dwell beside you in the tents of Abram," he answered.

The heart of the girl was lifted up in gratitude. Were I a princess of the land, he could not speak to me with more of courtesy. Then, seeing that he would drink of the waters, she made haste to seize the jar, to fill it and hold it forth.

"May it please my lord," she said breathlessly, and was filled with a dizzying joy that she might serve him.

He took the jar, drank from it, and gave it back to her.

"The handmaiden of Sarai is gracious."

"I am called Hagar," she faltered and, with a surge of yearning, wished she might hear the name issue from his lips. But he said nothing further, save a courteous phrase of parting:

"The Lord lead you."

She stood in the ripening light and stared after him, the empty jar dangling from her hand. After a little time she was aware that she trembled, and of the uneven pounding of her heart. Upon the rising mist of the early day the image of the stranger drifted before her dazed eyes. A man above other men, she said to herself, even as the pharaoh. And there welled up within her a sudden blinding sense of discovery, a knowledge not to be denied: I would go forth with him even in death.

And a dream came upon her, as compelling as a mirage, and found utterance in breathless whispers on her lips:

"Day upon day I will serve him so that, in the end, perceiving the devotion of his handmaiden, he will desire me forever at his side. Then, may it please the gods, he will look with tenderness upon me, saying in his heart, ' This girl I will take as my wife.' "

Her thoughts were scattered by the coming of a shepherd to the well, his flocks crowding, pushing, behind him. He was old and bearded and unkempt, so that she drew back from him with fastidious distaste, aware of the stench upon him akin to the stench of his animals, of his broken and dirty teeth, his obscene leer before the diaphanous fabric of her tunic. Yet, driven by the necessity to know the truth, she lifted her head and besought him in courteous words.

" Peace, shepherd. There is a thing I would ask of you. Who is he who now walks in the direction of the tents? "

The filthy old man, shading his bleared eyes with a scaly hand, peered after her gesture and, perceiving the tall form of the stranger, moved his lips in a loose and knowing grin.

" You are not the first slave who entered this household asking the same question. Not the first, nor the second, nor the tenth, seeing that all look with pleasure upon him. Yea, he is comely to behold! Yet if you think he will follow you to the hills beyond the tents when the moon is high, then your head is full of sand . . ."

The face of the Egyptian girl paled.

" If the shepherd please," she faltered, " it is only that I would know his name."

The old man slapped his gaunt and hairy thigh in coarse amusement, sneering an answer through broken teeth.

" Know this also, daughter of idiots! He will not call you to his couch, nor any handmaiden, nor any woman, save one. For he is Abram, our master, husband of Sarai, and he will cleave unto her alone, even to the shame of his own name, and the name of his father's house! "

The pearly mist thickened, dissolved before her eyes. A vast emptiness, dark and stifling, came upon her. Then the silence was ravaged by a crashing sound and the howling laughter of the vicious old man:

" May the hand of Azubah smite you seven times seven! You have shattered her jar upon the stones."

# XIII

THE GOODS AND HOUSEHOLD OF ABRAM HAD INCREASED A HUNDRED-fold, yet the going up out of Egypt was no such matter of dread as the coming down. For now the desert had ceased to be a stranger in their eyes and, understanding the nature of its ruthlessness, they had girded themselves against it.

Grain in plenty was loaded upon the gift camels, likewise lashed fodder and bulging waterskins. Sheep and goats were led forth to be slaughtered upon the way. And, seeing that their poverty had been relieved by the generosity of the king, and that they had come to understand the way before them, those of the caravan were festive in spirit at the hour of departure.

During the moons the household had dwelt in the grasslands, the rains of early winter had fallen again upon the hills of Canaan. Wells were filled, stream beds flowed as rivers, and earth parched to the hardness of stone became as moss before the plow. Great numbers of the Canaanites turned back, rejoicing, to their homes, tilled their fields, retrieved their dwellings from the dust, dressed such vines and trees as were restored to them, went out to plant and sow. Yet the early rains had fallen but a little time before they ceased entirely. Thus, terror was again upon the land. For now the season of the latter rains was far advanced, and still no cloud had risen in the sky.

The caravan went up toward Bethel, a region of stony mountains with ribs naked to sun and wind and rain, like bleached bones protruding from shallow graves. Its lonely valleys were filled with huge boulders and shattered rocks — great stones, holy stones, left behind by giants whose hands had hurled them, in some primeval fury, upon this barren land. And there were yet other stones, standing tall and black against the cloudless sky, marking the worship places of the Canaanite priests, the abode of their gods of earth and growth and grain. Phallic and fertile were these stones, Elisheba said. One might touch them and be done forever with the barren womb. If by another feast of the new moon no heir of Eliezer was quickened within her body, she would steal forth on a night of the waxing crescent, when growth waxed also, and touch one of the stones, that she might take from it fertility and bear a child. And the heart of Sarai cried out to her, " Daughter of Canaan, take my hand and lead me before your gods, seeing that all others have been deaf to my pleading." Yet this was not to be, for, indeed, it would bring shame upon her husband and all his house.

" If the Lord has spoken no word before me," she said, " even after many moons, who can say that such a thing will ever come to pass? "

Whereupon Abram told her gently: " The Voice of holiness is denied to none. To Sarai also it will come."

But Sarai found no consolation in the words.

From Bethel the shape of famine came out again to meet them. The stream beds gleamed no longer with living water, but were drifted deep in sand. The tender grasses and flowering thorns of the early rains had long since crackled to dust beneath the sun. In the parched clods of the sown fields the plants withered even while they sent forth roots. Unripened fruit fell like stones from the stricken trees and vines. Many of the wells were again as empty as if they had never known rain, and wind like the blaze of a grass fire was borne upon them from the south. Once a jackal, made bold by hunger, came from the rocks and went before them, a creature gaunt and loathsome, smelling of mold, with small hating eyes, dirty yellow ears, and slavering jaws. Whereupon Urfa cried out that the omen was evil indeed, seeing that jackals were guides to the kingdom of the dead.

" The Lord lead us," answered Maacah, quietly. And thus it was known that she had taken unto herself the faith of Abram.

Indeed, it was as if the Lord walked before them, for the well near Bethel was more than half filled with water, and herbage from the early rains remained in the valleys thereabout. And thus the caravan halted.

This was a place as empty and silent as if forgotten by all save the Lord. Even those who stood guard at night were awed by the stillness, the high loneliness of the stars, the unyielding desolation of the hills, the black and unfathomed depths below. Yet in the light of day, it was like the high altar of some primitive ziggurat from which a man might gaze upon the far reaches of the earth. On one side lay the dry and empty sands they had left behind. On the other, and fading into distances beyond, were the purple Mountains-of-Those-Across. Below, in a broad valley, were the salt, unchanging waters of the Dead Sea, and five Canaanite settlements known as the Cities of the Plains.

Birah, a certain maidservant given to Sarai by the king of Egypt, had been born in Sodom, the largest of these cities, and many were the tales she told of their splendors. Indeed, the women of the tents were speechless with enchantment before all that she revealed concerning the valley below.

Behold, not even the land of Egypt knew such beauty and fertility! Trees without number spread their shade across the valley. The waters of the purple mountains streamed constantly upon it, so that the plains were well-watered even when rain had ceased to fall. Here grass grew as high as a man's shoulder, and there was no wind from the desert to scorch and wither the harvests, for certain hills rose up between. Indeed, there were meadows to sustain a thousand herds and flocks. There were fruits and flowers also, gardens the eyes of the stranger could not believe, and no ugliness in all the valley, save for certain slime pits. Yet even these were not to be disdained, for they were filled with pitch, certainly a substance valued in trade, and one to bring increase to any man.

Behold, this was no stricken wilderness of burning sun and waterless wells and death and hunger! It was a land of abundance and delight. Herein the lady Sarai, and all who served her, might dwell in a high house as magnificent as any of the northland.

And there rose up within Sarai a yearning that this might, indeed, come to pass. How gratefully, and with what rejoicing, I would dwell once again within shaded walls! And the same words were upon the tongues of many slave women. Maacah and Azubah had suffered much from the journeying up and down, likewise all others who had known life within the cities of the north. In truth, there was no woman among them who did not recall with nostalgia the coolness of the great rooms, the cheerful bustle of the vast kitchens, the pleasant order of the unforgotten days.

To dwell once again within walls, to gaze from a lattice window, to sleep on a carven bed, to walk in a flowering courtyard, and bathe on a roof top in the cooled dusk; to linger in the Common Room by the light of alabaster lamps, to hear the opening and closing of doors, the flurry of steps in a brick passage; to behold the light of braziers reddening the garden wall at eventide, hear the cries of fruit venders, the chattering of neighbors, the jangling bells of donkey caravans, the voices of home: such memories rose before her like the faces of beloved dead, so that Sarai could not close her eyes against them until half the night was spent.

With the first dawn she rose gently, girded herself, and stole forth in the mellowing light to gaze down upon this valley rich in all the heart of a woman might desire. And as she stood there, shivering before the ebbing chill of the night, yet looking with dread to the burning day, she recalled the words of Birah — that neither bitter cold nor fiery heat descended upon the city of Sodom, but only seasons fragrant with flowers and sweet with freshened winds.

Even in the first radiance of day dawn, there was no consolation to be taken from the barren hills rising and falling about her in patterns of unspeakable loneliness, scrubby plants white with dust, skies cleft by rocks. Yet when the latter rains had fallen, Elisheba said, these same wasted hills would spring to verdant fertility under the thin green grass and sudden flowers by which even the desert was clothed, in the watered seasons. The wells would be filled, the barren slopes would bloom as meadows. Flocks and herds, grazing there, would wax fat and strong in the care of shepherds and drovers, while the household of Abram dwelt in the valley below. May it please the gods, thought Sarai, in her heart.

And then, though she had heard no sound of footsteps upon the stony surface of the hill, she was aware that Abram had come forth from the tent and was at her side.

" How is it with my beloved? " he asked, in concern.

She turned to him slowly, speaking in a voice without life.

" Let my husband believe me, I suffer no illness, but a heaviness of the spirit."

" Wherefore? " he asked, gently.

She opened her heart to him utterly.

" In truth, I am disquieted by the manner of our life, which has become a weary thing in my eyes. Let my husband forgive me if my words are an offense before him. Surely it is known to me that Abram has a duty to the voice of his Lord and must cleave, therefore, to the land of Canaan. Yet is it forbidden that we dwell within the valley below? For I am weary unto death of tents, and yearn to know again the comfort of walls about me, as in our homeland."

And there was compassion for her in his face, for he perceived how their life must appear in a woman's eyes.

" If it is within the heart of my wife to dwell in a high house in a pleasant vale, why should this be denied? Seeing that, even so, we may graze our flocks upon these same hills, and go up to the altar where the Lord first spoke to me in the wasteland . . ."

Gladness flashed upon her, so that her face was glorified by a shimmering radiance, as in the days of her girlhood. And though she did not reach forth to him, lest she be seen by those of the tents, with the warmth of her glance and the grateful lifting of her eyes, she embraced him tenderly.

That night, she brought forth his words, as joyously as one would spread a feast, for those who lingered with her. For when the men sat beside the fires, after the going down of the sun, many of the women gathered within the tent of Sarai. Then Hagar brought the scrolled harp for playing and singing the songs of Egypt, half music, half laughter. Azubah and Maacah came also, and the gentle Elisheba. And there were certain maidservants who recounted stories of their homelands, others who delighted the company with riddles and mimicry. But the wife of Lot tarried with them not at all.

" We shall go down into the valley, Abram has said, to the city of Sodom, in the fertile plain. And we shall dwell again in a fair house, as in the days of Ur."

To the women of the tents, such words were as sweet as honey from a rock. Eyes dulled and faded were made bright, cheeks as pallid as the dust flushed with pleasure, excitement bubbled like wine in the lifted voices.

"To cook again on a brick stove," sighed Azubah, "and be done with crouching in the midst of smoke and flame . . ."

"Water in abundance," nodded Maacah, dreaming. "For the scrubbing of floors, the washing of linens, the dyeing of cloth . . ."

"To behold Eliezer as steward of a high house," whispered Elisheba shyly.

Then Urfa cried out in shrill and joyous tones, "Now surely our wanderings are ended and, having found favor with the Lord, we shall know only peace and abundance for the rest of our days."

# XIV

THE WELL OF THE ENCAMPMENT WAS A SACRED WELL, ELISHEBA said, which was never known to be emptied, even in the most merciless season of rainless days, for it was guarded by a powerful spirit. In truth, she never drew from its mouth that she did not pour out a libation upon the stones, an offering to the angel of the waters. And though the women filled their jars, and the men their goatskins, for drinking and the washing of linens, for the pious duty of bathing, for the going forth with the flocks, there remained an abundance. But after many days, when the herds returned at nightfall, the water was lowered. And there were those who, believing the spirit offended by the stench of the sheep, burned fragrant herbs and smoking incense to appease it.

Then, at the going down of a certain sun, strife burst out among those at the well. The sound of blows and curses brought men hastening from every margin of the encampment, Abram among them, Eliezer, and Lot. And the women came also. Within the space of a few angry blows, a multitude had run forth and were gathered to see two shepherds set upon each other with staves and curses and clamor.

" Are the flocks of Abram to empty the well while those of Lot, my master, perish for a single taste of water? "

" No man may behold my flock and say it has enough of food and drink! " cried the other. " Not even the wretch before me! "

" Son of a mangy camel! "

" By the life of my father! "

" May the jackals litter your grave! "

Like dogs of the wilderness, they seized upon one another, with curses spat between their teeth upon their panting breath, their arms locked in striving until the muscles stood forth in risen lumps, blood streaming from blows upon their faces and clotting in their mouths. Then Lot and Abram rushed forward and wrenched them apart, uttering words of fury.

" How is it that the herdsman of Abram has set upon the herdsman of Lot, seeing that we are one household? "

" Must we fear to turn our backs upon you lest you brawl in the manner of untaught children? "

The shepherd of Lot, young and hot-blooded and strong in loyalty to his flock, wiped his mouth with the tatters of his tunic and burst forth in words of defiance:

" No longer will I bear the greed and insolence of those who serve the flocks of Abram! They would have their sheep drain the well to its last drop, and leave not a spear of thorn for the animals of my lord! "

And the shepherd of Abram, flinging forth his hands in a gesture of entreaty, cried out against the words:

" For your sake alone, O master, did I strike this evil dog! No water would he yield to my sheep, nor any grass, that they might eat! "

" Misbegotten son of a liar! "

" By the very god! "

And they would have set upon one another as before, had not Abram and Lot halted their strife.

" Be done with shouting and cursing! " said Abram, curtly. " If there is a matter to be judged between you, then lay it before me in words of reason, and in the manner of men."

It was from the edge of tears that his own shepherd answered him.

"For days upon days the flocks of Abram have suffered both thirst and hunger while this . . . this servant of Lot hastened before them, leaving nothing behind, neither a drop of water nor a tuft of weed! "

"Say to me now," cried the other, " is the fault my own that within this well, and upon these slopes, there is neither food nor drink for the flocks of two masters? "

For the space of a moment there was no sound save the hoarse breathing of the shepherds, spent by their strife and by their fury. Beyond, crowding and pushing against each other in their seeking for water, the sheep of both flocks mingled at the well, lifting their voices piteously. Then, turning, Abram laid one hand upon the shoulder of Lot.

"Have our eyes grown blind, my nephew, that we did not perceive this thing? Indeed, there is truth in the mouths of both our servants."

"Even so," agreed Lot. He turned to gaze upon the dry and empty countryside. "These stony pastures, this half-filled well — truly, they bear neither food nor drink enough for our needs."

They stood in the silence of thought. Then Abram spoke in quiet tones measured by a sense of his duty to his brother, long within the dust, and to the son of his brother, and to the memory of Terah.

"Let there be no strife, I pray you, between you and me, and between my herdsmen and the herdsmen of Lot, for we are brethren. Is not the whole of Canaan before us? Separate from me, my nephew, and choose for your tents the portion most pleasing to your heart."

He lifted his arm that he might point out the land.

"Below, in the valley of the salt sea, lie plains well watered and fair to look upon, grazing lands, cities rich in comfort, even as Ur. Behind," and he turned his face toward the declining sun, "are the empty hills falling away to the south, the edge of the desert, grass scattered and sparse in the rainless seasons. Yet a man may find shade for his tents and substance for his flocks through all his days." He added: " Into the hands of my nephew

I deliver the choice. If you will take the left, then I will take the right. Or if you depart to the right, then I will take the left."

For a moment, Lot stood wordless. Then love for his uncle welled up within him like a spring of living water, so that his voice was clear and unsullied and without guile.

" Surely, seeing that my uncle is older and, by his kindness to me, has earned the better choice . . . Seeing that he would find fulfillment in the valley below . . ."

A sudden movement among the women halted the words and, casting a hurried glance upon his wife, he perceived outrage rising in her eyes, and remembered the nature of her vengeance. And so, as one stricken in the midst of an ignoble act, he fell to stammering.

". . . yet, if it matters not to the heart of my uncle, then I — I will choose the vale below, and dwell among the Cities of the Plains."

Then, silenced by his own shame, miserable in his own weakness, he stood without lifting his eyes, and it was as if he would cry out before them all: " Let my uncle forgive me, I am forever possessed by this woman! Therefore, rejoice that we go apart, one from the other, and do not meet again, for thus you shall suffer no more injustice at my hands."

Sarai's heart was as a stone in her bosom. Turning, saying no word, too cruelly stricken to care that those who watched might perceive her wretchedness, she went within her tent. And with her going, she heard the voice of Abram lifted in a tone of quiet, unshattered dignity:

" If this be the choice of my nephew, then let him depart with the blessing of Abram upon him."

Thus was peace restored to the encampment. The wife of Lot, and the servants of Lot, and all his house made ready to go forth into the valley with the rising of another sun. And all that the encampment possessed of goods and slaves and flocks was divided, in equal shares, between the two families. And Abram dealt gently with his nephew because of Lot's weakness and shame, and because they were parting, one from the other, for all that remained of their lives.

The small daughters of Lot, excited by the talk of their maidservants, ran to the tent to gather their treasures and to question, with shrill voices, that which lay before them. "Shall we dwell in a garden of flowers, as Birah has said? Shall we indeed wear golden dresses, and eat sweetmeats and honey cakes at every hour of the day? Then hasten, that we may journey into the valley without waiting . . ."

Yet thought of their departure brought no grief to Sarai's heart. The moment had come when she was pleased to see them go forth from her sight and from her longing. For out of the love she bore them, their nurse had taught them fear. "Lay no touch upon the wife of Abram, for she who cannot bring forth children is cursed, and may do you harm . . ." Thus the little girls stood before their tent and gazed at Sarai with round, fearful eyes. No longer did they run to embrace her, or to beseech her for stories, but huddled together in fright when she smiled upon them, or ran, shrieking, to the shelter of their slave woman's arms.

Yet when the first dawn had reddened the stony slopes, Sarai rose and went before the wife of Lot to speak, with pride and fitness, some word of farewell. And sorrow rose to her eyes as she looked upon the other woman, not for their parting, but for their joyless years.

"Who can say," she asked quietly, "whether we shall meet again?"

"Who would meet within this wretched waste?" Lot's wife answered. "Not even in my shroud of dust would I return to it!" She moved forward, that she might gaze below, her spirit already gone forth into the misted valley. "In the city of Sodom men live only for rejoicing. There shall I rediscover the days of my girlhood, knowing the sound of music and laughter through the night. Again will my anklets flash in the joy of dancing, my lips grow red with the sweetness of wine."

Sarai laid her fingers lightly, even tenderly, upon one of the smooth amber arms.

"Strive not after the past, which in the life of no man has ever come again."

For the space of a breath there was silence. Then Lot's wife smiled, malice glimmering in her dark, tilted eyes.

"It is only because of envy that you utter such words. For the lot of Sarai is dust and loneliness."

Thus the caravan of Lot set out, descending to the fabulous Cities of the Plains, with dust rising up like smoke behind it, to dim the widening bands of dawn, the flocks massed upon the hills, the sudden intrusion of broken rocks against the sky.

Then those who had stayed behind ceased to watch and returned, each to his own task, to the matters of his own life, as if the household of Lot journeyed, even now, in realms of the past. But Abram remained upon the hilltop, and Sarai likewise, standing a little way off, in the place from which the other women had departed.

In that moment her heart rose up against her husband, seeing that his generosity had deprived her, and all the household, of fulfillment. Yet, perceiving how his shoulders sagged, and the manner in which he stared after the departing caravan, silent and disheartened, she ceased to reproach him even in her thoughts, and would have gone to him with gentle words and hands. But even while she lifted the hem of her tunic, he turned and, looking neither at her nor at any other, went apart to the altar of the Lord.

And when she had gone in to the slave women, she saw that the measure of their disappointment was no less than her own. The face of Maacah was marked with wordless misery, the mouth of Azubah was hardened and stilled. And though Sarai did not lay her bitterness before her maidservants, both Hagar and Elisheba perceived how it was with her, and sought to comfort her with a score of trifling services in her name. Throughout the day there was neither talk nor laughter from the women, but only such words as they required in their tasks, and frequent, gulping sobs from the weeping Urfa.

Near the going down of the sun, when the shadows of the great rocks lay in purple masses upon the darkening sands, and a single star glittered in the distance above the Great Sea, then Abram sought his wife in the quiet dusk, that he might disclose what passed within his heart.

"This day," he told her, "out of the bitterness of my despair, I went up to the altar of the Lord, and he has made his will known to me."

He spoke simply, for, seeing that they had walked together for many days, he no longer trembled before the Lord, looking to him as to a stranger, but received him gladly and easily, as a beloved Friend.

And it was in this manner, he said, that the Lord led him:

"Lift up now thine eyes, and look from the place where thou art northward, and southward, and eastward, and westward: for all the land which thou seest, will I to thee give it and to thy seed for ever. And I will make thy seed as the dust of the earth: so that if a man can number the dust of the earth, then shall thy seed also be numbered. Arise, walk through the land in the length of it and in the breadth of it; for I will give it unto thee."

He fell silent, restored and at peace, but with Sarai it was otherwise.

Unto thy seed! she thought, with scorn. Already I approach the latter years of bearing, yet my prayers are unanswered. Is a man to raise sons from seed sown upon a barren wife?

Then Abram, stirring, took her hands within his own and spoke gravely.

"Let Sarai be comforted," he said. "Within this alien land our lot will be dust and famine and a great striving. Yet there is no fear upon me, for the Lord obliges no man to do more than he has given him the ability to perform."

She turned to him in sudden shame and tears.

"Let my husband forgive my weakness," she whispered, " and remember how it was that once, long ago, I said, ' Where the gods would lead you, there would I be also, for in the love of Abram I am blessed.' For these words I would say again, even as then."

"It is no weakness, but a womanly thing, to long for the comfort of a fair house," he answered gently. "And though the hope of dwelling in the valley is lost to us forever, still . . ." And he laid before her a consolation. " To the south lies a broad plain shaded by trees of God not planted by the hands of men. And a city called Hebron, in which we may barter. Here, even a man of herds and flocks may possess a ripened field, some boughs of fruit, a few vines heavy with grapes in the season of harvest. Thus shall we go forth, when the latter rains have returned — and surely this will be soon, since they are long delayed — to dwell in this place of peace. And there is a hill whereon I shall build an altar to Him who has made me the promise . . ."

She stirred, set upon my doubts not to be revealed: Can any man say the Lord looks with tenderness upon the House of Abram? If this be true, wherefore has he turned his face from us in the hour of our despair? How is it that he reaches forth his hand to Lot, and to the wife of Lot, who have sacrificed not so much as a dove before him? How is it that Abram, who has obeyed the voice of the Lord in all things, is forsaken, cast forth upon the wilderness? Wherefore has she, a woman without honor, been given that which my heart has yearned to possess, even a child? Is this the way of a just God? Such a thing cannot be! Either he is weak and unhearing, or our sorrows concern him not at all.

And she stared, in loneliness and bitterness, out upon the empty hills.

# XV

A SUNSET OF BARBARIC VIOLENCE FLAMED BRIEFLY IN THE DIRECTION of the Great Sea and went out from a sky as pale as ashes. Darkness came swiftly and, with it, the first stillness of night by which men are saddened, made aware of the loneliness of existence, and stirred by a longing for that which is forever ended. Thus, there were those of the household of Abram whose thoughts returned to the eventides of the north, to hymns chanted from a high altar by a temple priest at the going down of the sun.

Days without number divided them from the familiar gods of their homeland, and these were not to be remembered without a sense of irrevocable loss. Around the watch fires smoking in the purple darkness of the wilderness night, men lifted voices troubled and perplexed to speak of this thing.

And their words were cries of desolation. Woe, a man must have a god! How was a man to live out his life with none to hear his petitions, to lead him as a shepherd who goes before his flock? Woe, the gods of this land are alien to us, and we have forsaken our own. What is it that we may do? In the manner of troubled children they turned their faces to Abram and awaited his words.

" No man," he said to them, " is cast adrift upon the tides of existence without a God, for Such has created the earth and all who dwell thereon.

" Has anything under the sun been brought forth save by the hand of a creator? Nay, not in all the distance of time. Were a man asked, ' Whose hand fashioned the seal about your neck? the sickle with which you reap? the house in which you dwell? ' could he then answer: ' These things were fashioned by no one. They but exist. They were not created.' Such words would be scorned by the veriest fool!

" And with whatever he has created, the Lord will abide. Wherever you walk upon this earth, he walked before you. For the earth is the Lord's, and the fullness thereof, and his hand is reached forth to receive his creatures. If you turn to him, you will need none else. If you depart from him, where will you find a path? "

And while he spoke in this manner, there were many who came forth from the tents to hear his words, among them Urfa and Maacah, and others among the slave women. But Elisheba went apart and sat alone in the darkness, made suddenly sad and remote.

Yet it was not fear of discovery that drove her to loneliness and concealment, for who, emerging from her other life, would recognize her now? Elisheba, wife of the steward of Abram, was utterly unlike the starved and bloodstained girl who, out of her wretchedness, had cast herself upon the desert to die.

Her little child, plump and brown and merry of face, had long ago laid hold upon the heart of Eliezer. It was Eliezer who named him for a certain forefather of the House of Abram — Shem, a man mighty of heart and deed. For there was an ancient tradition, " The Lord shall dwell in the tents of Shem," and Eliezer desired that it should be so with the little lad.

For a time he and Elisheba had known joy in the child, and in one another. Yet now there was a burden upon her, so that she was often silent, even in the presence of her husband and her child. Indeed, Maacah feared the little Canaanite was suffering from some wasting illness. Her face was pale and shadowed, and she was often disquieted. Word of the famine seemed to bring a sickness upon her, causing her to shrink from talk of empty wells, scattered bones, and desolate fields where thin and ragged crows stared down from withered branches.

How was it that the latter rains had not fallen? No traveler came within the encampment who did not ask this question. What iniquity is among us? What transgression is abroad in the land?

And there came a certain trader, whose camels were seen against the sky at the going down of the sun, his slaves and camel boys following after. Whereupon Abram went forth to meet the wanderers, and bade them take rest and food within his tent.

The tent of Abram was divided into two rooms, for it was both rich and spacious, stretched upon sturdy poles. The larger portion, which served as a Common Room, was spread with deep-colored rugs from northern weavers, furnished with cushions, chests, mats, low tables, lamps, and a gleaming brazier. Beyond the heavy, patterned hanging which divided the tent was the workroom, where Sarai and her slave women made ready festive dishes for the guests of Abram. Here were skins of wine and milk and grain, water jars, stone mills for the grinding of flour, pots and ladles and lifting forks, trays and bowls and ewers, braziers and lamps, all things needed for the bringing forth of meals rich in hospitality and flavor.

And when food had been spread for the trader and his host, the women lingered, silent and unmoving, in their own places, that they might hear the words of his mouth. For such men were both bearers of news and tellers of tales.

Yet his talk was concerned only with the misery upon the land, now deprived of the latter rains which had blessed it for more years than any man could remember. To the Canaanites gazing upon their wretched fields, this disaster was beyond understanding, but to the prophets of Baal, it was otherwise.

Surely my brother has heard of this matter . . . And again

the story rose up, a shape of fear and guilt before the listeners: " Let my brother believe me, she refused obedience to her master, the father of her child, and fled with it and hid it in the wilderness, that it might not be made a sacrifice. Yet the iniquity lies not upon the child, since it could not lift its voice against the deed, but upon the mother only."

Not until the people brought her forth and offered her upon the altar of Baal would the gods cease to afflict the harvests, cease to stop the mouths of old and young with dust. Not until that day would Baal look with mercy upon the wretched land, though a thousand drums were beaten before him, a thousand petitions chanted.

The voice of Eliezer was lifted sharply, slashing across the silence of the tent.

" If there was indeed a slave girl who fled into the wilderness in moons past, has she not perished before this hour? "

" Not so." The trader shook his head slowly, sagely. " Had she died, the latter rains would have fallen in their accustomed season. It is because she lives that the hand of Baal is heavy upon us. Only when she lies still in death, and her blood is offered for our sin . . ."

Then Eliezer would have leaped to his feet and seized the stranger with violence and fury, had not Abram restrained him from this deed of disaster. But the man, concerned with nothing save his own words, had already begun the telling of a tale, the story of a well a day's journey to the south. Upon its dusty rim, he said, with hands stretched pitifully toward the hope of deliverance, lay three skeletons rendered clean and bare by vultures.

" A young Canaanite peasant and his wife, it was told, striving to return to the Mountains-of-Those-Across. For want of a cup of water they died, together with their babe, a crumpled heap of small and tender bones."

Whereupon Elisheba uttered a faint and smothered wail and, turning from the inner room, fled into the darkness beyond and remained there, weeping, until the women found her.

" Give no heed to the words of the stranger," urged Maacah, " seeing that they were spoken in ignorance and fear. For I swear by the setting stars — and surely this is a great oath — that the

144

rains are the Lord's, and no Baal of this land possesses the power either to withhold them or to make them fall."

But Elisheba, ashen and weeping, would not hear her.

And afterward, even when the trader and his men were three days beyond the encampment, the sorrow remained with her, so that she came forth from her tent not at all, but kept to its silence and darkness. Nor would she eat of the food prepared for her, with unaccustomed tenderness, over the cooking fires of Azubah.

" Let my wife believe me," said Eliezer, pleading. " She has no cause for fear."

Her small, groping hand went out to him and, almost without movement, her pale lips began to whisper:

"It is not in fear, but in grief, that I live out these days, seeing before me the young peasant and his wife who toiled and loved and hoped and dreamed, even as Eliezer and Elisheba. And now they lie dead, and their little one also, because . . . because . . ."

Her voice rose wildly, and she began to tremble and could not stop, and he seized her and shook her fiercely, as he had done to men stricken by panic and beyond reason.

" Because of what? " he demanded harshly.

The terror departed as suddenly as it had set upon her. She stood lifeless before him, her hands hanging limp and still at her sides. And her voice, when it came, was as dead and dry as the whisper of sand.

" Because of me."

He stared at her, rendered wordless by the dazed look upon her face. Then, possessed by sudden fury against the teachings of the ungodly, he cried out, " Is there a madness upon you, that you would speak such words? "

And now she was suddenly strengthened and given peace. She lifted eyes grown clear, held forth hands steadied and gentle.

" My lord and my husband, let us not strive against that which we are powerless to resist or deny. The priests of Baal have demanded my life, and not until they are appeased will rain return to these ruined fields and . . ."

" Be silent! " cried Eliezer, and his face was white with unavailing rage. " Did I not love you more than all of life, then truly I would strike the words from your mouth! You are my own, I possess you utterly! To me belong your body, your loyalty, and your obedience. Then how is it that you speak of obedience to a Canaanite priest instead?"

Her eyes, heavy with sorrow, gazed up at him.

" Indeed, it is well known to you, my husband, that I bear you such love and devotion as are given to few men upon this earth. Yet how am I to defy the gods, seeing that they have dominion over us all?"

His hands opened convulsively, closed again, and then, groping and unsteadied, fastened upon her small, bowed shoulders.

" By the life of my mother, I swear to you, Elisheba, the gods of Canaan have no portion in reality."

He saw that she winced, unbelieving and afraid, and in tones of unleashed desperation he cried out before her: " The gods of Canaan are false gods, conceived in fear and born in the ignorance of an unholy land! They cannot see what passes upon the earth, neither can they hear or act, for they live not at all! And if a god be false, then his priests are false, likewise, and the words of their mouths as worthless as dust before the wind."

" Say to me, then," she whispered, " how is it that no rain has fallen upon this piteous land?"

"It is not the first year such rains have been delayed in their falling. Even tomorrow, a cloud may arise . . ."

" And if this does not come to pass, then all who dwell within this stricken land will perish. And we alone shall be left alive and, seeing that the gods seek revenge against me, surely you and Shem will be slain before my eyes . . ."

A shriek of terror from beyond the tent shattered the words. Putting her from him, Eliezer rushed forth and she, hastening after him, saw him snatch up a stone and hurl it down, again and yet again. Urfa, white and ashen, had fled a little way off, leaving a load of brushwood fallen and scattered upon the sand. Yet it was not she who screamed, but Azubah, bearing the little Shem in her arms, clutching him until he too cried out.

And all who were within the tents rushed forth, to behold the evil, crawling thing upon the sand.

" See now, it is dead," began Maacah, striving to ease the terror of Azubah. " See now, it cannot harm the child, for Eliezer has slain it."

"It fell from the brushwood," whispered Urfa in awe. "From the brushwood, out of my arms . . ."

"Often these creatures are gathered up with thorns and brambles," said Hagar quietly. "In truth, it is a matter for caution, seeing that one who is bitten will not live to behold another dawn."

Urfa began to weep.

"I did not mean that it should touch the little one!"

"Nor did it," said Azubah, sharply, "for I caught him up in time to save him from its poison."

"A viper," said Eliezer and gazed, revolted, upon the dead shape, the white belly, swollen and repulsive, the ugly head, the horns.

Suddenly Elisheba spoke in the silence.

"It was no viper."

They turned to gaze at her, startled by the cold and flat words, the strangeness of her voice. Eliezer went to her and touched her gently.

"Beloved, it is indeed a viper. Do you not see it, there upon the sand?"

"It was no viper." Her lips, white and stiffened, were scarcely able to shape the sounds. "It was Baal."

And now terror fastened upon him, for her eyes were clouded and unseeing, her spirit elsewhere. He took one of her small, chill hands in his own and strove for words.

"Nay, Elisheba . . ."

She stared beyond him, and beyond those who stood near him, and her lifeless voice brought forth that which she had long concealed in the dark and fearsome regions of her thoughts.

"It was Baal, and he is not dead, for none may slay him. And though he has departed from the skin of the viper, he will come again. For the gods of Canaan come in many forms, to offer favors, to take revenge, and so it is with him. Because he was deprived of my blood, he seeks the life of my child."

And suddenly she cast herself upon Eliezer in desperate weeping.

"Shem will die, and my husband also, for who can escape him? Yet my blood could save you, my blood given in atonement for my deed . . ."

Then, slowly, she lifted her ashen face. Slowly, the torment departed from her eyes, and there was an edge of soft and gentle crooning to her voice.

". . . and rain will be again upon the land. Rain will fall, and the hills will be as pastures, sweet and green. And those dead of famine, because of me, will rise from the dust and live again, and drink of the rain, and lie dead for my sin no longer . . ."

Slowly they drew apart from her, chilled by horror, knowing it was not Elisheba who spoke, but some alien voice within her. A shuddered murmur rose among them. " A demon has seized our sister . . ."

" In the darkness of night," she whispered, " he has come to seek me. I have heard him dragging himself across the stones, and the sound of his voice, like sand before the wind . . ."

Beholding Eliezer's stricken face, Maacah came forward.

" Let her be led within your tent, and I will bring a broth of herbs to give her peace."

Lifting her as one would lift a child from a nightmare, he bore her to her bed mat. And for her sake the evening bread was eaten in silence, the voices and laughter hushed, and those who came and went spoke in tones filled with concern. But when Elisheba had drunk the broth of herbs and fallen into slumber, her breath came softly and evenly, and there was no uneasiness upon her.

The shepherds watered their flocks and led them forth into the hills. The women, weary from the disquieted day, went early to their rest, and Hagar bore the little Shem within her tent and comforted him.

It was a night of vast emptiness and silence, with the wails of jackals, faint and moaning, in the distance, and the deeper, lonely sound of lions far away. A wind stirred and sighed in the trees by the well — stirred and sighed, and was lost in silence. Then a muted, monotonous throbbing was borne across the hills, an intrusion of drums from some ancient shrine where the Canaanites besought their gods for rain. For now, by reason of their desperation, their evening sacrifice to Baal was prolonged into the deep night hours.

Suddenly there was a slight motion, a faint glimmer of white before the tent of Eliezer, and Elisheba stood there, her hair fallen in disorder about her dazed face. For a little time she listened to the sound of the drums, and her head was lifted as though her spirit cried out to them. Then, soundless and unseen, she went forth into the darkness, trailing her skirt upon the sand, that the path of her footsteps might be effaced entirely.


# XVI

To walk in the path of Lamech, the oldest shepherd, was of Jarah's own choosing for, in following after the browsing flocks, the lad had come upon his own destiny. Indeed, it was as if his forefathers had risen with their desert dust and summoned him forth from the tents to behold the beauty of the wilderness. Here he looked upon the mightiest works of the Lord, and his heart was lifted up in rapture before them — the unyielding mystery of the stars, the voices of silence which rose from the darkened valleys, the dreaming purple distances beyond.

With these things I would hold communion all the days of my life, he thought, even as Lamech . . . And he was unable to frame with words the tenderness that rose up within him at the sight of the weathered old man, leaning upon his oaken staff and gazing, with wise, inscrutable eyes, beyond the quiet sheep, into the declining colors of the day.

"Then shall my own flock be given to my keeping," he told Azubah, "knowing my voice, following after my call." And her thin, ugly hand went forth and rested like a blessing upon his shaggy head.

Since his illness on the burning road to Egypt, they had ceased to deny, even in jest, the strength of the affection between them. For there was a certain night when, at the extremity of his pain, he had opened his eyes and been comforted because she watched beside him. Out of the boldness brought upon him by fever, he had cried aloud, "Azubah is as my mother!" and had seen her eyes glisten with swiftly risen tears. After a little time, her voice, strangely thickened and faltering, had replied, "My son is my son." Thereafter it was a matter understood by all the household. Indeed, many had ceased to remember that Jarah was a desert orphan, adopted into her care, and not the true son of Azubah's flesh.

Of the three shepherds to follow Lamech, he was the youngest, since Henoch had dwelt for ten years in the tents of the men, and Irad for more than twenty. Yet both had been shepherds when less than half the age of Jarah, were the sons of shepherds, and the grandsons likewise.

For a little time after the tents were spread at Bethel, they went out from the encampment every morning and returned with the going down of the sun. But, as the splintered herbage grew yet more scant, they moved farther and farther into the hills. Going before the feeding flock, they had traveled many days, yet a runner could have covered the distance in the space of little more than an hour.

According to the ways of shepherding, the lad set out upon the paths of the wilderness bearing a staff in his hand, wearing a sling and a pouch at his girdle. And before another moon rested upon the hills, he knew how it was that a shepherd might come to look upon his sheep with a love greater than the love of his own life.

Touched by their helplessness, their meek and unquestioning trust, he reached forth to save them from peril, to lead and to comfort them as did Lamech, with both rod and staff. Through dark and rocky valleys sheltering the dens of serpents and the lairs of wild beasts, he walked before them that they might fear no evil. Laboring beside the other shepherds, he anointed with oil the sheep that had suffered wounds from stones or thorns or brambles. At folding time, he lent his strength to the building of an enclosure of rocks and watched, respecting and astonished, while the sheep entered in by the narrow gateway under the rod of Lamech, who, though unlearned, and unable to count their number, knew whether all were safely within, and none lost or fallen behind. Filled with the wonder of that hour, the lad inquired, "Are they to know safety in a fold without a door?" And Lamech, with the dignity of years, and the gentleness of the kindly toward the ignorance of the young, replied, "I am the door " — and laid himself down to sleep across the opening of the rocky shelter.

And now, for the first time in Jarah's life, the fixed and unchanging patterns of the stars were made known to him, pointed out by the gnarled finger of the old shepherd as he himself would one day bring them before the eyes of other lads. And afterward he had spoken of them to Azubah, his voice hushed before the awe of his discovery.

"There is a cluster of seven small goats which huddle together forever in the sky, likewise the face of an ox framed in stars, and a giant with a jeweled girdle. Indeed, my mother, these things are true! With my own eyes I have looked upon them! "

And, though she answered him in quiet words, she stared at him so strangely that he was both bewildered and disquieted.

Nights in the wilderness were spattered with stars, edged with a vast and brooding loneliness. Indeed, it was as if the four shepherds were the only men who dwelt upon the face of the earth. Against the chill of darkness and the boldness of prowling creatures, they kindled a brushwood fire, which burned with crackling and splintering sounds, loud in the silence. Beyond, in the hilly wastes, the cries of jackals and hyenas echoed from the rocks, though their number had dwindled with the famine.

Henoch was a teller of tales and, with the yellow flames wavering upon his face, making hollow his cheeks, emptying his eyes, he could bring forth high stories of courage and peril, legends of the sands, wisdom of the weather, the skies, the earth, the ways of wind and sun and growth.

"This very night," he stated, " the latter rains will begin their falling. For three days the clouds have been gathering beyond our sight."

And Jarah wondered how it was that the others gave heed to such words, for the night was bright with stars.

Irad, a singer of songs, possessed skill with the flute also, and made a flute for Jarah so that, in springtime, the lad might know the most delightful moment in a young shepherd's life, the pouring forth of sprightly notes to which the smallest goats would skip and dance.

The lad listened to their music and to their talk until his eyelids were heavy, his scrawny shoulders were shivering in the chill, and his unkempt head, as matted as the back of any ram, had fallen to his chest beneath the heavy hand of sleep.

"Go now, Jarah, and take your rest," said Henoch, kindly. "It is soon enough that you will be required to stand watch for the flocks of your master. And a shepherd's vigilance, once begun, ends only in the burial cave. Behold, both Irad and myself . . ."

Thus, drunken with sleep, his legs stiffened and awkward, he stumbled beyond the fire, rolled himself within a cloak, and fell into the deep, instant slumber of the young and untroubled.

At what dark and hovering hour was he awakened? By what strange and disquieting echoes from the wilderness beyond? He sat up, staring and confused, knowing that it was neither the sound of a voice nor the cry of a beast that had shattered his slumber, but a thing compelling and mysterious — the steady and unbroken rhythm of a drum.

Yet the sound was not new to him, nor to any of the household of Abram, since more than once it had been driven across the hills to them by the winds of night. And Eliezer had said, "Give no heed to the drums of the ungodly, for they are calling forth the sons of Baal."

"The drums of the ungodly"! The very phrase held syllables of fascination for the ears of the young and audacious. What were they like, the lad asked himself, taut with listening — these native drums consecrated to the worship of such gods as sometimes were serpents, such goddesses as suckled doves at their breasts, their myriad breasts, and stood, uncovered and shameless, before the world. To what strange and ancient rites were they offering this dark and moonless hour?

Assailed by the feverish rhythm, Jarah felt it taking possession of his flesh, quickening the movement of his heart, thudding in his blood stream. A strange excitement came upon him, and a sense of subjection, as though he were being drawn slowly, unresistingly, into the realms of Baal. Making no sound, he rose and moved backward until he had gained the shadow of a rock, away from the sheep huddled within the fold, away from the small and glimmering fire, from the solitary figure of Irad pondering upon what mystery none could say, as he stared into the coals with Henoch stretched, sleeping, upon the earth beside him. If Irad heard the drums, they roused within his simple soul neither wonder nor question, but were like the famine in his eyes, a bewildering portion of an alien land, which would never be understood.

" Now, surely," said the lad, " they lie beyond this very slope."

And, groping in the blackness, he clambered up the single rock until he had reached one higher, and thence up one and yet another until he had gained the very crest of the hill and could gaze out upon the reaches of the wilderness.

A tongue of light sprang suddenly from the hills on the left, and was gone. After a little time, it leaped forth again and then sank to a red, unwavering glow. The watch fire of a hermit, a holy man such as dwelt in certain caverns among the rocks, the stronghold of a robber band returned from a raid upon a plundered caravan — in truth, it was none of these, but a ritual blaze kindled by Canaanite worshipers before the shrine of some native god.

A breathless desire rose up within the lad as he stared into the throbbing distance, a consuming need to know how it was that the worshipers of this land called upon their gods in the darkest hours of the night. For afterward — then surely he would stand in his own place among the men of the tents. " Only Jarah has beheld the manner of their worship," these would say. He saw the face of Azubah lighted with pride in his valor. He saw a thousand shepherd fires glowing down the years, and heard his own voice lifted in the telling of the unforgotten tale: " It was such a night as this, with the moon not yet risen, and the stars grown faint, when I rose up and followed the sound of their drums."

The sudden, familiar assault of hunger intruded upon his dreaming and brought him back to the hilltop where he stood shivering in the cold, his stomach empty, his shoulders unclad. He felt in the pouch at his waist for such foods as shepherds carried, the cheese and olives, the dried figs and bread. Then, cramming portions into his mouth, he set off down the hillside toward the glimmering valley, across the sanded earth and dusty water courses.

Days earlier, he had woven a sling from tufts of wool plucked from bushes where the sheep had passed, that he might practice the casting of stones and thus become skilled. Lamech could strike a hair with a stone; Irad and Henoch could cast wherever they desired — to turn back a straying sheep, to kill a serpent, to halt a wild beast, even to slay it. Truly, a sling in the hand of a skilled shepherd was a weapon unfailing and deadly. But in the hand of Jarah it was little more than a jest, and he could not look to it to defend him upon a journey of peril. The dagger given him by Eliezer was a better choice, and he touched it with affection as he hastened across the wilderness, in the direction of the drums.

Once he stumbled in the darkness, twice he fell upon the stony earth, and once he cut his shoulder upon a certain sharp edge of rock, so that blood came forth. Yet he stanched the flow quickly and easily and went forward until at last, after the space of more than half an hour, he came upon the gently curved summit of a dust-laden hill where the yellow light of many fires flared suddenly before his face, and he looked down upon a valley aflame with torches.

Suddenly, he dropped and lay like a lizard in the dust and, like a lizard, crept forward upon his belly until he was concealed by some shattered rock, and his eyes peered from above it. It was the way of the natives, Elisheba had said, to build their worship places upon the heights, and now he saw that what had seemed a valley was, instead, a plateau reached by a tortuous path from below. The ascent was traced in torches borne in the hands of the ungodly.

The sound of drums was clamorous in his ears, yet muted by reason of being brought forth from the skins by the beat of bare hands. The drummers sat within the shadows, and he discerned them only when a flaring torch cast light upon them, bringing into sight the swift motion of brown hands, the edge of a drum, the gleam of a smooth, squatted thigh, the thinly traced contour of a face flung back in primitive ecstasy.

Yet there was only silence from the natives climbing the steep ascent, moving as though they walked in sleep, or were possessed by a consuming awe. And after a time the plateau was thronged to its very rim, with scarce the space of a hand between the torches, and the night seemed filled with strange, wild faces, dark and silent and waiting, with a look dazed and sensual in its unconcealed thirsting.

A fire had been kindled upon an altar stone and was burning with a rich and steady glow of coals, like a fire prepared for the sacrifice of a lamb. Behind the altar, higher than a man's head, black against the night, were pillars, phallic in shape, strange and ritualistic.

A hush fell suddenly upon the drums and then, slowly and with measured steps, a Canaanite priest moved out of the darkness and ascended the earthen steps to the altar stone. Almost at once lesser priests came forth, running, and cast themselves into a frenzy of religious ecstasy, gashing their flesh with knives, uttering howls not unlike those of wild beasts, leaping, rising, and falling. And there was one whose mouth spattered foam as he leaped, and another who fell into a seizure and was dragged from view.

Now the drums began again, their insistent rhythm quickening, strengthening, pounding, until Jarah reeled before it, and felt as if he were drunk with it, and wanted to rush forth and tear his garments from his spare brown body, and leap and shriek and dance for the unholy Baal in his nakedness.

But, abruptly, all sound ended. The priests stood motionless, the musicians were stilled, the worshipers waited, tense with some fearful knowledge. For a little space there was silence. Then the high priest turned from the altar stone and began a strange, mournful song, so despairing, so sorrowful, so filled with agony of spirit that even the shepherd lad knew it to be a death song, and cringed before it. And, as the last wailing note ebbed into the darkness, the sacrificial victim was led forth between two priests as powerful and sinewy as giants. A single gasp, a fragment of horror, was torn from the lad's lips as he beheld what had come to pass, seeing that the victim was no beast, nor yet an offering of the fields, but a young girl.

Save for a thin garment, she was unclothed, and the bronzed loveliness of her flesh was touched by a sheen of light cast forth from the torches. Her hair, long and dark, fell about her shoulders and down the length of her straight, small back to the slender shape of her waist. Her head was lifted proudly, and she moved forward with simple dignity, unflinching, unprotesting, to the wide top step where the high priest awaited her.

When she had reached him, and turned toward the multitude, the light shone fully upon her, and the heart of Jarah turned within his bosom, the blood of Jarah chilled within his veins. For a moment he was stunned beyond moving even his lips, as he stared, in wild disbelief, upon her face. And even as he stared, his heart as cold and shattered as the stones about him, the arm of the high priest was swept upward, the voice of the high priest cried out an alien phrase, and a lifted dagger flashed red in the torchlight. Then the dagger was plunged into the breast of the girl upon the altar stone, again and yet again, so that her flesh was rent, and her blood poured forth into the clay bowl prepared to receive it. And at that moment, the lad, driven by the horror that possessed him, leaped to his feet and shrieked out a single word of agony and despair:

" Elisheba! "

Yet there was none who heard, for his voice was lost in the voice of the multitude, the howls and shrieks and screams and wails, the slashing and leaping and bellowing of the frenzied priests, the wild beating of the drums, the moaning and screaming of the women.

Wildly, and without his own knowledge, Jarah turned from the rock and fled into the wilderness, away from the shape of horror behind him, from the leaping shadows of the ungodly, striving to outrun panic and terror and grief. His teeth had bitten through his lower lip and, within moments, his garments were made tatters by his heedless flight among the rocks, across the empty stream beds, through the choking dust of rainless days, running, sobbing, crying out in words meaningless, inarticulate. Sounds like the throaty cries of animals were torn from his chest as he sped. His jaws hung loose and uncontrolled, his body trembled until it seemed that the flesh shook upon his bones. A little way ahead, yellow eyes gleamed suddenly in the darkness, but he was beyond the fear of lions or evil spirits, or the creeping things of the night. And then, as he tripped upon the edge of a jutting stone and fell, he began to vomit convulsively, and after that lay still.

Slowly reason returned to him, reason and tears and sober grief. He climbed weakly to his feet and thought how a duty had been laid upon him, how he must bear to Eliezer the sorrow and the anguish, there being none other who could tell of this thing. Standing in the darkness, he groped about him, unable to sense the direction of either the sheepfold or the encampment. And then, recalling the teachings of Lamech, he turned his face upward, that he might behold the patterns of the stars. " The lion crouched upon the serpent of the north " — yes, truly, it was there, unsetting and imperishable, wrought in the brightness of stars by the merciful hand of the Lord. And if he kept it at his back, he coud not fail to come upon the tents of Abram. Yet, when he again looked northward, the shape was blotted from his sight, though, after a little time, it reappeared. Even the skies have given themselves to madness in this hour, he thought, shivering.

Surely now he had walked all night, and dawn should be glimmering upon his left hand, and a dawn wind rising from the silent hills, smelling of stone and dusty scrub. Yet the darkness was still heavy about him when, from afar, he beheld the watch fires of the encampment, and the shape of the goat's-hair tents against the sky. Calling briefly to a sentry, he stumbled on until he had reached the tent of Eliezer and uttered his name in a voice so hoarsened by anguish that he knew not whether it was his own.

" Let my uncle come forth and hear what I must say."

At once the tall figure of Eliezer was before him, the strong brown hands of Eliezer were upon his shoulders, steadying him against the faintness which had come upon him.

" What is it? Has harm befallen the men, the sheep? Speak quickly, my son — yet softly. For Elisheba is ill."

Jarah began to weep, his mouth wide open, tears — hot and blinding — coursing through the dust upon his face, his words brought forth in gulps of anguish.

" Elisheba is gone. She is not within . . ."

He was aware that a swift fear had come upon the face of

Eliezer, that he had turned quickly into the darkness of the tent where he and his wife had slept through the early hours of the night. And then he burst forth again, and had seized Jarah cruelly by his scrawny shoulders.

"Where is she? Speak, lest I tear the words from your throat!"

The lad moaned.

"How am I to answer the words of my uncle? How may I bring sorrow to him whom I love above all men . . ."

"*Where is she?*"

Jarah was spent and numb. His lips moved stiffly, his body grew limp, and his voice was dazed, the words dragging, one upon the other.

"She is dead. I saw her die — a sacrifice upon the altar of Baal. It was with a dagger that the high priest killed her, and when her blood ran forth, they drank of it, screaming . . ."

"*You lie!*"

The horror of the lad's words sent Eliezer reeling upon the edge of madness so that, wild and beyond reason, he struck out at him with strength and violence. And then he knew that Jarah was sprawled upon the sands, with blood upon his broken lips as he gasped: "May my uncle show me mercy! It was no easy thing I did — for his sake . . ."

Eliezer stood swaying upon his feet. His lashing hands had fallen to his sides and hung limp, without life. His eyes grew dull, his lips faltered with his own words.

"May Jarah forgive me. It was as if a demon rose within me . . ."

He fell to his knees and gathered the lad into his arms and, with a shaking hand, tried to smear the blood from the bruised, brown face.

"May Jarah forgive me," he muttered, in drunken accents. "It was the serpent — the ancient fear — "

And his throat gave forth deep and heart-shattering sobs.

"For the sake of her slumber, I did not awaken her to tell her what had come to pass. Yet when I lay down beside her, a little past nightfall, the storm clouds were gathering in the sky . . ."

Then, falling back upon his heels, he lifted his arms to the blotted heavens, and to the rising wind, and the sudden lightning, and cried out in a voice that was fearful to hear: "Now may the Most High God receive my words! By the love I bear my wife, I swear that all my days shall be spent against the ungodly, and against the abominations of their worship, *even to my last breath!*"

And it was as if the dark fabric of the clouds were rent by the jagged edges of his cry, for the skies were opened, and there came forth upon him the saving and torrential waters of the latter rains.

# XVII

AND THE NAME OF ABRAM, SON OF TERAH, BECAME A LEGEND ON the lips of those who dwelt within the land of Canaan, and those who dwelt beyond.

On a certain fair plain at the edge of the desert, it was told, there abides a man mighty of heart, strong in wisdom and in possessions. For a space of years he has dwelt among us, has received us into the shelter of his tents, has given us both meat and drink, bound up the wounds of the afflicted, lifted his hand for the sake of the oppressed. And not once, but many times, he has helped us to drive back into the sands the painted tribesmen who would have raided our homes, plundered our fields, dishonored our wives, and enslaved our children.

There are many among us who call him friend — Eshcol, Aner, and Mamre, landed men of Hebron, elders and captains, even kings of the east, and the king of Salem, which is of the north. And he is a friend of his God.

Yet he is still as a stranger among us, a man of the north abiding in the laws of his homeland and the ways beloved of his heart. The encampment of his household is no mean scattering of tribal shelters, but like unto a city, with tents as many as houses, and each man knowing his own.

Truly, the herds and flocks of Abram seem too vast to be counted, reaching far into the hills, requiring more than ten score of shepherds to go forth with them. The wealth of Abram is very great, the wisdom likewise, and there are many who come to sit with him in council.

To him belong certain tenting and grazing rights, and the rights of certain plowlands, acquired at the beginning of his sojourn from our brother Mamre. These were inscribed upon clay in the form of a solemn vow witnessed by the seals of Abram and of Mamre. And afterward an admonition was laid upon them: " May he die the death who breaks this bond."

Yet, in truth, the vow had been broken not at all, but fulfilled ten times over. And so powerful were the fighting men of Abram that his neighbors suffered no further fear for their flocks and fields and families. He had chosen and trained more than three hundred men, so that he possessed a small, swift host skilled in the use of the spear and the bow, taught to bear unrelieved hunger and fighting and riding and thirst.

Behold, there was a day but a little time past when, in the valley of the Dead Sea, four kings warred against five, and the king of Sodom went down in defeat. Then the victor, a certain Elamite king of the north, hastened homeward with many captives, among them Lot and the family of Lot.

And one who escaped came running to Abram, a speck growing larger and larger across the plain until it became a terrified man, who cast himself down and cried out the bitter tidings. And wrath rose within Abram's heart that the warriors of the north should have dared to dishonor a son of the House of Terah. Thus, calling together his fighting men, he rode forth, and Eliezer also, to pursue the enemy. And, riding without rest or pause, he followed them even to Dan, at the foot of the sacred mountain, and set upon them in battle, and recovered the captives and the plunder.

Thus did Abram return the goods and men of the king of Sodom and save from bondage the household of his nephew Lot. Nor would he receive any of the spoils for himself, but only for Mamre, Eshcol, and Aner, the three brothers who had ridden out with him.

And, as Abram and his men turned homeward, they came to the city of Salem, ruled by a holy man who was both priest and king, Melchizedek, priest of the Most High God. And, coming forth from his city, this holy man gave Abram bread and wine, and blessed him, and said, " Blessed be the most high God, which hath delivered thine enemies into thy hand." For it was known to him that Abram was chosen of the Lord.

And still does his tribe dwell upon the fair plain of Mamre, sheltered by mighty trees near the city of Hebron. And each day he ascends the hill of the Lord, for he is a man very holy of heart, and he has built there an altar and a shrine.

So said those who entered into the tents of Abram — the merchants, the peasants, lords of the land, couriers, elders, warriors. And it was no matter of surprise that all should wish to behold this man of the north, his tents, his goods, his servants. For of him were told tales of valor and wonder. Yet, even so, he had not escaped the searing touch of shame. For Sarai, his wife, was barren, and bore him neither daughters nor sons. And all sorrowed because of it.

For of Abram, son of Terah, men said, " He will be known and honored when kings and conquerors lie unremembered within the dust of their graves."

# XVIII

THOUGH IT WAS KNOWN TO ALL THE HOUSEHOLD THAT SARAI WAS ill, even Urfa could discern that it was an illness of the spirit and not of the flesh. Her days were spent in solitude and, of late, she had come forth from the gloom of her tent only after the setting of the sun. And none who beheld her could doubt that she suffered great heaviness of heart.

" Often it is thus with women who approach the end of bearing," said Maacah, quietly, but her face was filled with grieving that it should be so with the darling of her heart.

And the matter was murmured among the women of the tribe, over their weaving and mending and spinning, above the plucking of fowls, the rocking of butter churns, the tending of children.

"The end of bearing is upon her." And they sighed in compassion, and in understanding.

"With many women, there is sadness at such a time."

"And ill temper befitting the demons themselves! Behold my aunt, the eldest sister of my mother . . ."

"She who has passed the years of bearing has reached the desert of life."

"Is there then to be no heir to the House of Abram?"

"If the master would but take a secondary wife, a concubine young and plump, and as fertile as a ewe!"

Knowing what it was that enlivened their tongues, Sarai shrank from the necessity to go among them and turned, instead, to joyless hours of loneliness and silence. Not even the delicacies of Azubah would bring her forth.

"Nay, say I have no wish for food."

Often she lifted her voice and spoke sharply to the slave girl upon the threshold.

"Let no one enter, save only Hagar."

In the rich devotion of Hagar she was blessed, for apart from it how was she to have endured the fruitless years, the loneliness of this alien life in an alien land? They had never ceased, even briefly, to be other than maidservant and mistress, yet in their affection they were as sisters passing their days together.

According to the custom, Sarai set her hand to a thousand tasks, knowing pride in the doing, and Hagar with her. Together they shared the raising of a tent, the grinding for bread, the cooking of meats and pastes and cakes, the kindling of lamps and fires, the fashioning of garments, the searching out of honey and herbs and wild fruits and greens in the hills.

Thus the years had flown like chaff before the wind. And there came a certain morning when Sarai knew that youth had gone forth from her tent and would return to it no more.

On the evening before a man from a high house of Damascus had been given the hospitality of the tents. His caravan was vast, laden with precious goods, a multitude of animals and slaves. And in the dawn light, Sarai, awakened by the clamor of his departure, had risen and looked out upon the company, since it was large and rich and of splendor, and had heard his words of farewell.

" May you be requited, O host! "

" The Lord give you to arrive well."

" May the son of Terah live forever. May his sons be as many as the stars."

And, beholding her husband in a moment when he thought no gaze upon him, Sarai saw him wince before the words as from a wound, and knew that he bore within his heart a measure of shame and sorrow unrevealed to her.

For a time he stared after the departing caravan and she, from the shelter of the tent, stared upon his face and, at length, upon reality itself: *It is not I who will give him sons. The words of the prophecy were spoken, not of me, but of another.*

For her the years of youth had borne only despair, and even these had reached their latter days. Soon the manner of women would no longer come upon her. *I must lift my eyes to the face of truth and behold it without crying out against it. The sons of Abram are not to be the flesh of my flesh.*

Maacah spoke to her no more of bearing. Even Hagar, closer to her heart than any other save Abram, had ceased to comfort her with promises. The hour was past, the hope departed, the dream ended.

Once she had encountered, upon the face of the wilderness, a Canaanite woman who told her of a soothsayer dwelling in a cave in the rocks. This man, it was said, knew incantations that could bring fertility upon any woman within the space of a single moon. Thus Sarai and Hagar, together, sought his aid, crouched with him in the gloom of his abode, listened to the drooling words of his mouth.

The flames of the hermit's little fire shone forth from the depths of his eye sockets, so that his eyes became as coals, burning and malevolent. His frame was as gaunt and wasted as a skeleton stretched with parchment. The hair falling down about his face and shoulders was wild and white and ragged. A beard, thin and befouled, covered his hollow chest. Sarai could look upon the soles of his feet, as he sat cross-legged before her, and they were thick and dark and horny, like the feet of a great lizard. The stench of him was the stench of death and mold and filth, and she retched before it.

His hands, like crusted talons, dealt with a thorn branch, a

163

tuft of wool, a wilted leaf, a shred of stone, and his wavering voice chanted:

> " As the leaf is torn,
>> So shall the evil spell be.
> As the thorn is burned,
>> So shall the evil spell be.
> As the wool is scattered,
>> So shall the evil spell be.
> As the stone is broken,
>> So shall the evil spell be."

His rhythmic, monotonous voice was akin to a spell. Sarai could see him swaying to the words and felt that she was swaying also, unable to prevail against his magic. She and Hagar emerged from the cave dazed and sickened. And, like all the other seeds of desperation, this also had been without fruit.

And the sorrowing cry of many years rose again to her lips: " Oh, my husband, how is it that you should possess so unworthy a wife? "

Here upon the edge of the desert, Abram had become powerful beyond other men. For his sake many had departed from the gods of Canaan and worshiped before the Lord. But Sarai was not counted among them, and because of this her heart had never ceased to reproach her.

It was not that her faith remained with the carven gods of her childhood. Indeed, the years in Canaan had all but effaced them from her thoughts. Even in the watches of slumberless nights, when memories were strengthened by darkness and silence, it was difficult to conjure their images before her eyes. The moon also had ceased to afflict her with terror.

It may be, she reasoned, that Nannar possesses power only within the walls of his own temples, the gates of his own cities. Surely he was a lesser god, seeing that he had not prevailed against the faith of Abram.

The God of Abram was a great Lord, said those of the tents. To one and then another, his voice had come, so that now it was no small gathering which went up, morning and evening, to sacrifice before the altar consecrated to his name.

" Yet how may I ascend the hill of the Lord," Sarai asked,

aloud, " seeing that he has summoned me not at all? " And suddenly, the thought came upon her: It is because I am barren and unworthy that he has turned his face from me. And she hid her face within her hands, in guilt and shame.

Throughout the day, even to late afternoon, she remained within the cool dimness, the undisturbed silence, of her tent. Not since the early years in Haran had she known such bitterness of spirit. And now she recalled how she had passed the torment of those hours, fearing Abram would put her away and take a secondary wife in her stead. Perhaps he waits for me to make the choice of such a one, it occurred to her, according to the custom.

And her thoughts were turned to the laws of the north, which her husband had in no wise abandoned. Indeed, it was by these laws that he lived and led his people.

*"If a man's wife has borne him no children, and he takes to himself a secondary wife, that children may be borne unto him, the secondary wife shall not be made equal to the first wife . . .*

*"If, instead, the wife give a maid to her husband, that children may be borne unto him, the children of the maid shall be the legal children of the wife, and subject to her."*

The heat strengthened. It was a burdensome afternoon, plagued by flies, disquieted by the sound of grinding, the lowing of a bullock, a noisy quarrel which flared between two slaves and was stilled by a word from Eliezer. Sarai lay staring at the taut black ceiling and considered again the words of the law.

" If . . . the wife give a maid to her husband, that children may be borne unto him . . ."

After a time, the familiar tokens of evening intruded upon her, the light twittering of birds nesting in the olives and terebinths, the plaintive voice of the youngest camel, suddenly aware of hunger, the smoke of supper fires, the redness of sunset stealing between the edge of her tent and the sanded earth. And then, from a distance beyond, came the elation of the returning men, the laughter and calling out of the women who awaited them. The lad Shem cried out that he had shot an antelope by his own hand. Yet she neither went forth nor ceased to reflect upon the ancient law.

If the wife give a maid to her husband . . ."

The smell of the returned camels assailed her suddenly, and she turned her face from it, into the cushions. She heard, from beyond, the light tapping of camel canes upon soggy necks, the muted thud and heaving of breath as one of the great beasts dropped on his forelegs, the sandy shuffling of his body as his hind legs were folded, and as he lurched from side to side, settling into the cooler earth below the sun-heated stones, lifting his voice in loud complaint.

" If the wife give a maid to her husband . . ."

And she rose and stilled the protesting cries of her heart and spoke aloud, her voice harsh in the silence: " By what other means am I to be the mother of sons? " Slowly she went to stand in the tent door now edged with the first shadows of the declining day. Thus does time alter the shape of our desires, she thought, in bitterness. Once I would have closed my eyes in death sooner than to give him a concubine.

She gazed upon the dispersing men, their pleasure that Shem had taken game, Eliezer's pride in the lad's skill with a bow. Beyond the approaching figure of Abram, she beheld these two, side by side, absorbed in their talk and in their laughter, the arm of the man across the shoulders of his adopted son.

And Abram, halting beside her, said quietly, " In truth, Eliezer has found the means to fly from grief."

The heaviness of the day was in her voice.

" Eliezer," she said, slowly, " but not my husband."

He followed her within the tent.

" Seeing that I am blessed beyond other men . . .," he began.

But she was not to be comforted and cried aloud: " Do you believe that I, your wife of many years, cannot perceive what passes within your heart? Can you think it is unknown to me that, beyond all else upon this earth, you would ask a son? Nay, the yearning stands forth in your eyes, as sharp and searing as pain, each time you look upon the children of these tents! And if a man be denied the blessing nearest his heart, all others are as dust! " She added desolately, " Had a son been born of our flesh in the first years of our marriage, he would now be as tall as Abram himself . . ."

"I would not have Sarai mourn that for which there is no help," he began.

She moved from the touch of his hands and spoke sharply:

"How am I to be released from mourning, seeing that my guilt and shame are always before me? At the dawn of this very day, hearing the departure of the Damascene, the nature of his words: 'May the sons of Abram be as many as the stars —'"

"Such words are but a courtesy of the tongue."

"A courtesy that wishes for a host the best that may come to him," she answered miserably. And then, swiftly, she covered her face, and sobs came forth between her shaken fingers. "Oh, Abram, my husband, the same thought is in both our hearts, and the same sorrowful understanding! For the years of our youth have reached an end, the hope for a son of our flesh is finished!"

And when she had turned to him, he held her close within his arms, not as though he would console her, but as though he would not have her look upon his face.

"In truth, every man cherishes the hope of sons. But if such a thing is not to be . . ."

"To the lowliest herdsman sons are born!" she cried. "One after another, year upon year! But to Abram, whose name is honored throughout the land, neither sons nor daughters. Yet there is a thing to be done . . ."

She paused, feeling as she had felt in the cave of the hermit, sickened and shamed and terrified. But the decision was strong upon her, and not to be abandoned.

"In the first years of my barren hopes, I said in my heart, He will send me forth, and take another in my place . . ."

He spoke quickly, sharply, as if to halt the words upon her tongue:

"Nay! Not even for the sake of my father!"

"Yet if a slave of my tent bore you a child in my name, according to the laws of our homeland, which are sacred in our eyes . . ."

"Not even a slave wife!" he said, shortly, and then, wearied and troubled with the day, he cast aside his headcloth and flung himself down to rest against the heaped cushions.

She followed him, relentless and insistent.

" Wherefore does a slave exist save to fulfill the needs of the master, and of her who is his wife? A maid chosen by my own will would be no more than a shadow passing across our life together, and then gone — as a cloud is gone, or a moth against the moon — gone and unremembered in our hearts. Yet from her we would have taken a son."

She drew near to him and, falling down beside him, put her arms about him and gazed beseechingly into his face.

" And when she had borne, then a child would rest in my arms, a cradle would hang within these walls. And there would be feasting and rejoicing for the sake of our son, and he would grow sturdy and tall and would be a blessing, learning the wisdom of Abram, walking in the steps of the Lord."

For a moment it was as if the vision, rising before him, was not to be cast aside. Then, swiftly, he rose and spoke with such coldness as she had never received from his lips.

" Let Sarai say no more of this matter, for it is grievous in my eyes, and not to be heard."

And he strode forth into the early darkness and would have returned to the men assembling for the evening bread, but she hastened after him and caught the edge of his sleeve and cried out to him from the depths of her despair:

" Do not depart from me in my wretchedness! Neither say to me that we will live out the years that lie between us and the long silence without a son! Comfort me in my affliction, lift the burden of dishonor from me! For I can no longer come forth from the tent, with their eyes upon me, staring . . ."

He turned slowly, and a cold fear came upon him, for while he beheld her standing before the dark tent, in the light of the risen stars, it was as if he looked again upon Elisheba — the face made white by misery, the desperate eyes, the disordered hair. And he took a single step toward her and demanded hoarsely, " Wherefore do you speak of staring? "

She passed her hand across her forehead, at once confused and sorry.

" Let my husband forgive me," she whispered. " I had not thought to speak of this thing, for it possesses no reality, but often it is as though — as though all the world were witness to my shame. The slaves, the wayfarers, the natives of this land, even the vultures from above, the prowling creatures of the night — as though it were whispered by the spirits of the wilderness, the evil ones who rise with the wind and dance with the dust: 'Barren . . . barren . . . she who is wife to Abram is barren . . .'"

He seized her shoulders in his hands and cried out, "Enough!" and her lips fell silent, yet when she lifted her face before him, he was heart-stricken by the measure of her wretchedness.

"Barren . . .," she whispered. "If they came forth calling: 'Harlot! Harlot!' and struck me down with stones, it would be easier than to stand before their pity, their scornful smiles, the words I need not hear to understand."

He sought to comfort her with words murmured against her face.

"Let my darling forgive me that, not until this hour, did I perceive the fullness of her sorrow. Thus, for the sake of my love, I will not deny you this child . . ."

And she cried aloud with joy and wept against his breast, trembling and incoherent. And when she had drawn apart from him, and cleansed her face of tears and smiled again, her voice was filled with unconcealed eagerness.

"Before another sun has set I will choose a maid. A tent shall be set apart for her and, after the ancient custom, I will lead you to the threshold . . ."

But, moving abruptly, he put her aside, and his voice was cold with anger.

"I will not be led forth like a ram to a ewe!"

And he departed from her.

Yet she turned to the tent with undiminished joy, her thoughts full of dizzying dreams and vows.

"No common woman of the tents shall be the mother of our son," she said, half aloud, "but one of wisdom and gentleness, of family. Hagar only shall be the mother of this son, for a child born of the body of my sister shall be even more my own than the law has declared. In him shall we know the fulfillment of our sisterhood, the love and tenderness and kinship of years brought forth in the warm and lovely body of the little one."

And she hastened to summon Hagar, that she might tell her what had come to pass.

The lamps had been kindled and the tent was sweet with the

winds of evening, its purple shadows edged and softened by the yellow light of the flames. In the gathering eagerness of her desire, the words of Sarai fell like ripples upon water, and spread into silence grown wider, and yet wider, until it became a pool of stillness reaching beyond the tent, the hills, even beyond the night. Wordlessly, Hagar stared at her, her lips parted and unmoving, her eyes widened and dazed, like the eyes of one in a dream.

" I . . . to be the slave wife of Abram? " she stammered. " Slave wife and . . . the mother of his son? "

Made suddenly fearful by the uncertain tones of her voice, Sarai cried out, " Surely, knowing how it has been with me through these fruitless years, Hagar would not deny me the child! " She reached forth both her hands in undisguised pleading. " For the sake of my husband's honor, for the sisterhood between us, surely Hagar, whom I love . . ."

A cry, faint and tortured, sprang from the lips of the slave, and then, stricken by guilt, she fell to her knees at the feet of her mistress and bowed her head.

That night Sarai ceased to stir, tormented and restless, upon her bed mat, but lay quietly and at peace, her thoughts dwelling upon the child. And when at last Abram came to the tent, she would have spoken of it further, but he said, in a tone courteous and remote, " Let us say no more of this matter, for I am weary and would sleep."

It was always at a late hour that the men dispersed, each seeking his own tent. And when they had ceased to talk, one after the other, and had departed from the fires, then Sarai would rouse in the darkness to the sound of Abram entering — his step upon the threshold, the rustle of cloth as he cast his garments from him, the sudden warmth of his body as he lay down upon the bed mat — and the sense of his nearness was like the gates of day closing upon fulfillment.

Yet afterward there was a certain night when, stirring into wakefulness, being roused by that which she neither heard nor understood, she opened her eyes and found him seated at her side, gazing quietly upon her, saying no word. Warmed and made drowsy by slumber, she smiled up into his eyes and her face, cleansed of bitterness, was the face of his bride. And suddenly, he flung himself down to her, his head upon her bosom, in the manner of a child who would be comforted. His voice, low and shaken, cried out in a tone akin to anguish, " Sarai is my beloved wife." And she held him tenderly, knowing only that they were undivided and inseparable as never before this hour.

# XIX

IT HAD BEEN RAINING AND LIGHTNING STILL GLIMMERED, PALE AND fleeting, upon the darkly massed clouds receding into the morning sky. Behind them rumbled the awful voice of the Lord, which, only a little time before, had thundered above the roiled and foaming storm with a crashing vehemence that set the hills to trembling: " Behold thy God in all his might, and lift not thy strengthless hand against him . . ."

For many days the clouds had cast their consoling burden upon the earth, bringing into being the season of abundance, so that the silvery grass of spring had come forth in the sanded places, and the desert bloomed as a rose. Scarlet and blue and gold and pink, a thousand lilies of the field moved in the wind — along the weed-tufted sand, in the green thorn thickets, among the stones, in the patches of sunlight and moss beneath the tere-binths, the olives, the tamarisks, the figs. Into the sweet and sunlit air rose the smell of flowers and wood smoke and leafy dampness and blossoming vines.

In this season of fecundity, of mating and life and growth upon the earth, the animals brought forth young, and the fields brought forth barley, and the blown clouds brought forth the waters of deliverance. Rain pools lay in scooped sand and stone, and the blue of the sky was upon their waters. The wild bees were drunk with the sweetness of flowers and grass. Birds nested and mated and sang in the trees of God. The herds and flocks spread into the hills, and sought out the thick new grass from among the rocks, and with them went newborn lambs, damp of fleece, unsteady of legs, and little black goats skipping and playing like children in the sun.

Milk, new and foaming, was borne from the sheep, the goats, and camels. Shepherds and slaves drank of the clear, sweet water and filled the jars and waterskins from pools and springs and wells. The tribe of Abram rejoiced, and the women sang as they washed the garments and linens of the household, bathed their children in the abundant waters, and set about the mending and cleaning of the tents, the churning of butter, the drying of milk, the searching out of greens and wild fruits. The men dealt with the increase of herds and flocks, and some went forth to plow and sow. The hills were filled with gladness, and the desert sang with joy.

Then those who belonged to the land of Canaan sang and danced and sacrificed before their gods with unsparing merriment, and their joyous spirit flowed like a heady wine from the gates of Hebron, a little to the south of the tents of Abram. And when the moon had reached its fullness, at the time of the spring equinox, they kept the feast of Astarte, goddess of fertility, that abundance might remain with them.

Streamers, bright and festal, fluttered from the white roof tops of Hebron to mark the season of worship and rejoicing. Children clad only in flowers danced in the streets of the city, honoring Astarte, whose image was sacred in the eyes of the ungodly — a lewd unclad figure with suckling doves fastened upon her breasts, and the Baal of increase, in the form of a serpent, between her thighs. To Astarte, the earth mother, giver of fertility, many offerings were made, that fruitfulness might come upon the fields and vines and pastures, upon the cattle and ewes and wives.

Daughters of Canaan, clad in white and wearing chaplets of spring blossoms, danced before the shrine of the goddess, their songs shaped to the rhythm of their timbrels. Children brought bread and wine to be placed upon the altar. And when the high priest entered, with the soothsayer beside him, their voices were mingled in a chanted summons to the myriad gods to come forth and partake of the feast.

" Eat of the bread with me, drink of the wine. . . ."

And the merriment was suddenly stilled before the awe and

wonder of the worshipers, who felt that, in this sacred moment, the gods were before them.

Many of the tribe of Abram were stirred by the festivities of the Canaanites and turned their eyes from the lonely hills to gaze, with the quickened pulse and unfathomed yearnings of youth, toward the sound of dancing and singing and unrestrained revelry beneath the glorious moon. But Eliezer, passing among them, uttered an admonition now familiar to their ears: " Turn not into the paths of the ungodly but, instead, lift your hearts to the Lord for this season of blessing! Go forth to labor in the fields and pastures which he has given you, and rejoice in their abundance! "

In truth, a harvest of plenty lay before them, for the floods had been beneficent, the Lord had defended their crops from locust swarms, and so mindful were the watchers set to guard the fields that these had been plundered neither by thieves nor by the cattle of the wilderness. Already barley rippled like the waves of the Great Sea from whence came the pleasant winds of morning.

Certain of the Canaanites befriended by Abram had long since imparted to his tribe their wisdom in plowing and sowing and tending and reaping in this alien land. Among them was Aner, brother of Mamre, and one who had ridden out with Abram in the saving of Lot. And between Aner and Abram there was a kinship and a brotherhood, though Aner cleaved to the gods of Canaan and worshiped before Astarte, and gave one of her un- holy images into the hands of Zilah, his little daughter, that Zilah might be made desirable in the eyes of worthy men, and possess both beauty and fertility, even as the goddess. Because the child Zilah had no mother, she came often to the tents of Abram, joined other small girls in the playing of games, ate sweetmeats and honey cakes prepared for her by Sarai. And no longer was Sarai given sorrow by the sound of childish revelry, for in the pledge of Abram she was content.

Indeed, it was of the promised child that she had been dream- ing when she lifted her eyes from the mending of a torn head- cloth to find Hagar within the tent. At once she perceived some subtle change in the Egyptian slave, a strange and troubling shy- ness of manner, a singular hesitancy of speech. But when words at last found shape upon her lips, they were uttered in breathlessness and wonder:

" Now, let the heart of my sister rejoice! "

Sarai gazed at her, suddenly disquieted.

" Wherefore? "

" With the coming of another spring a child shall dwell in the tents of Abram, the child for whom you have uttered a thousand prayers."

Slowly, Sarai rose to her feet.

" How — how has this been made known to you? "

" The moon is long past its waxing, yet the manner of women has not come upon me. Thus, it is no longer to be doubted that a child of Abram is quickened within me."

Sarai stared at her, striving to conceal dismay. He has then begotten a child upon her — our child — and has said no word to me! Of this, I — the mother of the child — have known nothing!

The voice of Hagar was lifted in swift concern.

" Has my sister an illness? "

Sarai moved her head in dissent, too shaken to utter as much as a word. Thoughts dizzying and violent rose before her: Wherefore has he concealed this matter from me? Not, certainly, to spare me sorrow, seeing that it was of my own choosing? For what cause, then, did he go forth to her in secret? And a deep, wrenching suspicion stirred within her. God of gods, have my eyes been blinded? Silently, and to his own shame, he has yearned for her these many years . . .

Suddenly Hagar was as a stranger in her eyes. Not in all their time together had she perceived that the Egyptian slave might quicken desire in the heart of any man, even Abram. Only now did she behold the ripened beauty of Hagar's mouth, the slenderness of her thighs beneath the fabric of her skirt, the clean lines of her bosom, fair to behold. How had he possessed this graceful slave with the dark, compelling eyes, the shadowy hair massed softly upon honey-colored shoulders? Her beauty was slight, even when she came to me in the harem of the king, in the earliest days of her youth, yet now . . .

A sudden loveliness shone forth in Hagar's face and shimmered in her eyes. It was as if she had blossomed with the desert, a part of its strange and unforeseen enchantment. In truth, her delicate arms and slender throat were as tawny as the desert itself, as the sands of the desert, the polished stones. The radiance of the lamps was caught up by the necklace upon her bosom, by her bracelets, the jeweled rings in her ears. There lingered about her a fragrance cast forth by the yellow blossoms in her hair.

When had he gone to her? At what dark and hidden hour? Had they whispered together in the manner of conspirators, laughed together in the sweet-scented darkness because Sarai and all the household slept, and not even the guards were aware that the master of the tents had gone forth to take a secondary wife?

*Wife* — the thought was like a viper, its striking swift and relentless and deadly. And rage flared within her, denying the word: She is no wife to him, but a means of fulfillment only! It is I who am his wife — I, and none other! Yet now he is known to her even as to me — the warmth of his mouth, the tenderness of his hands, the nature of his desire . . .

Then Hagar, shrinking apart from her, cried out in a voice edged with panic, " How is it that my sister looks upon me as she looks? "

And the words of Sarai lashed out at her:

" Leave me! "

" May my mistress forgive my thoughtlessness," said Hagar in sudden shame. " Let her cease to remember that I came to her thus, desiring her to share the blessing of this day with me, when it is with Abram she would rejoice, instead."

Abram, thought Sarai. Behold how she utters his name — in syllables lingering and tender and familiar — as though she were the beloved of his heart, and I a wife cast forth from his bed, despised in their eyes . . .

And she cried out harshly, in a voice unknown to her, " Leave me! "

Bewildered beyond utterance, and at the edge of tears, Hagar stumbled from the tent. For a moment, Sarai stood unmoving and in silence. Her hands were chilled and sweating, her heart pounded with a violence that made her sickened and breathless. Beyond the tent the trunks of the olives and terebinths swam be-

fore her eyes, as though she beheld them through torrents of rain.
And now she recalled the night when she had wakened and
looked into the face of her husband, when he had flung himself
down to her as though he would be comforted, and had cried
out, "Sarai is my beloved wife."

It was from Hagar that he had come in that dark and moonless hour. And not in love did he turn to me, but in guilt . . .

Possessed by a blinding fury, she began to pace up and down
the length of the tent, unleashing in her thoughts words violent
and incoherent. He is mine, and he shall cleave to me utterly —
and to my body, and to my child — and never again go forth to
this Egyptian slave!

And suddenly the taste of hate was in her mouth, as sour and
bitter and nauseous as poison. And because she could not bear
its flavor, nor the sudden cruel wrenching of her heart from
Hagar, she flung herself upon the floor and wept, and cried words
of lonely anguish into the cushions beneath her face, and bit the
edges of her hands.

# XX

HAGAR CREPT AGAINST A SUN-WARMED ROCK AS TO A REFUGE, AND
stared desolately at the desert loneliness about her, the far untrodden sands, the scattered stones, the smoky shapes of thorn. In
this whispering realm of dry and drifted sand she lay silent and
without movement, striving to give no thought to the night. Yet
it was not unknown to her that, within the space of an hour,
darkness would be upon her.

And, despite the burning of the day, she shivered. Then a sick,
familiar weakness assailed her, her hands and brow grew chill
and damp with drops of gathered sweat. Suddenly she was cast
forth upon waves of nausea which seemed as endless as the waves
of sand.

"With one who bears a child, it is often so," she whispered,
striving to soften her own fears. "With one who bears a child,

Maacah has said . . ." Whereupon her lashes quivered upon rising tears, and her heart went out in bitter yearning for the comfort of the slave woman.

Yet, even though she had wished to turn again to the black tents of Abram, she was too wearied for the journey. Since the morning of this day she had wandered in the desert alone, driven forth by the lashing words of Sarai, too blinded by heartbreak to behold the full measure of her incautious deed.

For more than three moons she had known illness without ceasing. Often she was seized by such dizzying faintness that the world dissolved before her eyes, and she sank into pain and retching darkness. More than once both Azubah and Maacah had knelt at her side in pity for her wretchedness. Maacah laving her face and wrists with cooling water, Azubah loosening her garments, lifting the sandals from her feet, urging a cushion beneath her head.

And it was thus that they had been, in the early hours of that day.

"I would not trouble my sisters," said Hagar faintly, "but when the darkness comes upon me, I am helpless before it."

"With the rising of another moon . . . ," Azubah began, in consolation, and then stayed her words, for a shadow had fallen across the slight figure of the Egyptian slave, and Sarai stood gazing down upon them. At once both Azubah and Maacah were stilled, knowing her displeasure, fearing, for Hagar's sake, that which she would say. In the trees beyond the tent, some winged creature of the morning set up a shrill, persistent humming which seemed unbearable in their ears. Then the lifted voice of Sarai shattered the tense and guarded silence.

"Indeed," she said, and her words were cold with courtesy, "is it again that Hagar moans with pain?" The slave women neither spoke nor stirred. Then Sarai tilted her head, that she might look more fully upon Hagar's wan face, and added, with a faint and mocking smile, "Yet this is but the beginning — the very least you shall have to bear!"

Hagar spoke in bewilderment.

"Surely my mistress does not rejoice in my distress . . ."

Sarai made no answer, but turned upon the slave women.

177

"Go forth!" she said, shortly. And when the two had departed, she came again to Hagar, speaking with unconcealed scorn. "Like all others of these tents, I am wearied with your manner of ever suffering illness."

"In truth, I have suffered much," answered Hagar, quietly, "yet to me this is a small matter, and not to be mourned. A thousandfold would I suffer, until I died of it, for the life of my child."

"Your child?" cried Sarai. "By the law of our land, it is *my* child you bear, the son of my prayers, my dreams, my sacrifice, and of my love!"

Tears rose to Hagar's eyes, and her words trembled upon her lips.

"How is it that you have turned upon me with such hardness of heart, seeing it is for your sake I bear this child? By your bidding alone did I become slave wife to Abram . . ."

"*Wife!*" cried Sarai, and fury rose with her voice. "You are no wife, but a slave only — a slave to bear a child, as camels bear, or ewes!"

Strengthened by anger, Hagar lifted herself from the cushions and stared into the face of her mistress, and her own voice, when she spoke, was not without mockery:

"Even though I am a slave, to the dust of my grave will I remember that once I was young and fair — and wife to Abram!"

"Fair!" cried Sarai, driven to malice. "Surely some time has passed since Hagar beheld the sight of her own face! Let me then bring a mirror, that you may behold the sickly color of your skin, the sweating forehead, the bloated walk. Where now is the beauty by which Abram was beguiled into your tent?"

Stricken to the heart, Hagar broke into weeping and gasped, from her uncontrolled sobs, a piteous entreaty:

"Leave me!"

Sarai came forward, deliberately and with scorn.

"Does a slave give orders to her mistress? Or is it that, having been chosen to bring forth young, like a beast of the fields, you would hold yourself higher than the true wife?"

Hagar lifted her face, made wet and streaked by the bitterness of her tears, and cried out in undisguised grief: "My sister, my sister! How is it that this dread thing has come upon us? Behold, there is now, in all the earth, no path which we can walk together! Thus, let Sarai send me forth! Send me forth to my homeland, lest I die of my sorrow! For I must know peace, if I am to bring the child safely to birth . . ." Her voice became a wail of wretchedness: " Bid me dwell no longer within this tent of hate! "

Hope rose like a light in the eyes of Sarai, hovered there for the space of a moment, and departed.

" Should you return to Egypt, the child would be lost to us," she said, coldly. " Therefore, speak no more of the matter. You shall go forth from this household only when my son is delivered to my arms! "

But no sooner had she gone from the tent than Hagar rose and fled into the wilderness, passing beyond the well, the tents, the trees, the sown fields. And to a shepherd encountered at the edge of the desert, she said, " If any ask of me, say I have gone to gather mint," and hastened her steps.

For a time, her wandering had the unreality of a nightmare. Again, and yet again, the thought beat like a storm gust upon her: Surely it is not Sarai, my beloved sister, who has turned in hate and bitterness upon me, reproaching me for a child of her own bidding . . . Unable to believe that such disaster had come to pass, she was dazed and staring before it.

In truth, so bitter was the wrath of Sarai against her that it had spread like a plague throughout the encampment, burdening and disquieting all who dwelt therein. There were those who, having suffered the sorrows of the barren, knew how the taking of a secondary wife could shatter a woman's heart. There were others, concubines of many years, who turned as sisters to Hagar, and hardened their hearts against the name of Sarai. And the seeds of quarrels were sown, not only among the women, but between husbands and wives lying at night upon the same bed mat.

" And if it is within your mind to go in to another because the master has done so . . ."

" Who has said I desired another? Still your tongue, that I may sleep! "

Even the slaves quarreled over the matter. Indeed, the words between Urfa and Azubah could be heard as far as the vineyards. But Maacah was silent, seeing that her heart sorrowed for both Sarai and Hagar.

It was with dignity that Abram bore the disquiet upon the household. Not even for the sake of the beloved would he deal harshly with Hagar, and in the level glance of his eyes she read the full measure of his regard: In truth, it is known to us both that I have never looked upon you with love, yet you are my secondary wife, soon to bear my child. Thus let it be understood that you are honored in my heart for all the days of my life.

Even yet, he had not perceived what she felt for him. In all the years since her coming up from Egypt, she had avoided him, silently, faithfully, hastening from a tent when he entered, lifting her voice before him only in answer to his own words. And it was not unknown to her that, in his eyes, she was but a humble shadow of a fabulous land, departing with his coming, abiding with singular devotion beside his wife, turning away, for reasons unspoken, from the men who had sought her in marriage.

All that day she had wandered beneath the dizzying sun without thought of what might come before her. In her mind was some notion, clouded and obscure, that a caravan might come upon her and bear her to another encampment, a far city, even to Egypt.

In the first hours of her journey she had known neither fear nor loneliness. And indeed she was not alone, for small sand-colored lizards scuttled among the rocks, a frightened hare halted near a clump of thorn and stared at her with begging eyes, a dove called from some distant refuge in the hills.

Near noonday she came upon a rock pool holding sweet and untainted water from the clouds of another day. And here she paused to bathe her scorched face, her aching feet, her eyes burned by the glare of sun on sand.

Later in the afternoon a shadow upon the horizon caught her gaze, and she thought, Behold, it is a caravan, and hope rose within her. And she knew no fear, for the law of the desert dealt mercilessly with any who harmed a woman alone in the wilderness, and even the most depraved of men would shrink from such a deed.

Past midafternoon, when the sands were dragging at her feet and the sickness had begun to gnaw within her, a flock of small birds rose up a little distance ahead. Now surely they were taking water, she thought, and went to where she had beheld them, for thirst was again heavy upon her. And she came upon a small desert spring which rose from the midst of some wet and mossy rocks. Then, having drunk of the waters, she cast herself upon the sanded earth by a sheltering stone, and knew the full measure of her loneliness and weariness and danger.

After a little time the sun was gone from sight, and the purple darkness sifted down upon the wilderness, and the first stars came forth in the sky. Hunger smote her suddenly, and shivering cold. Dark stretches of cloud lay along the horizon, and she thought with terror of storm and lightning, of the chill lashing of wilderness rain.

Again the sickness rose within her, the retching, fainting terror. And then it was as if she were adrift upon some far and murmuring realm of darkness, as if a Voice, out of the echoes of all eternity, spoke within her ears:

" Hagar, whence comest thou, and whither wilt thou go? "

She stirred, her pale lips moving in a faltering answer scarcely to be heard. And the echoing Voice was strengthened in her ears.

" Return to thy mistress, and submit thyself under her hand. Children beyond number shall be descended from thee. And thou shalt bear a son, and thou shalt call his name Ishmael."

And the Voice faded farther, and yet farther, into the reaches of the wilderness, until it had departed from her.

Strength came upon her then, and warmth, and peace, and she opened her eyes and cried out in words that trembled with wonder:

" Lord, you have looked with mercy upon me! "

Slowly, humbly, she rose from the sands, fixed her way by the patterns of the risen stars, and turned again to the tents of Abram.

# XXI

IN THE WAY OF THE LAW, SARAI AND HAGAR, TOGETHER, WOULD bring forth the child. Thus, when the pangs had come upon her, Hagar would seat herself upon the knees of her mistress and Sarai, with her arms about the laboring slave, would strive with her against the agony, weep with her, cry out with her in pain.

Yet even this was denied her, for Hagar, strengthless and ill, gave birth to the little Ishmael suddenly, and very simply, at a silent midnight hour, before even Maacah could be summoned. And in the haste and clamor that came afterward, none thought to bear the tidings to Sarai. Thus she knew what had come to pass only when she heard the child's crying.

After a little time Maacah brought him, oiled and swathed, and laid him in the arms of Sarai, and drew the kindled lamp nearer. To Sarai, the moment was of such wonder that her heart trembled before it, and she was both dazed and blinded by her joy. And then, looking upon him, she saw the dream become dust before her eyes, for he was utterly the child of Hagar. Even Abram, hastening forth to behold his son, saw how it was with him — the honey-colored face, the dark tilted eyes, the curling black hair, the look of high but alien blood.

And it was as if a light went out before them.

"He is neither my child nor your own," said Sarai bleakly, nor did she strive to conceal the tears that rose to her eyes.

"A child has many faces," declared Maacah smoothly. "A new face for every season of his life, until his years of growing are at an end."

"Let us rejoice that this son has come to us," said Abram, with gentleness, "for he is both strong and beautiful, and already my heart finds pride in him." He added, absorbed in touching the child, " His name will be Ishmael, Hagar has said."

" Hagar has said," thought Sarai, and the words were as fierce spurts of anger within her. How is it that you have talked with Hagar of names, seeing that it is I who am the mother of this child? And she clutched the babe to her breast with such violence that he broke into desolate cries, and Maacah hastened to take him from her.

" He hungers, the little one," said the slave woman, with tenderness. " Let me bear him to Hagar, that he may be fed."

And thus it was that each time Sarai took him to herself he wailed aloud, and was borne away to Hagar to be comforted. And later, when his own mother's voice was known to him, he would have none other, but shrieked despairingly when he was taken from her. Yet to Abram he turned in utter delight, and the love between them was no ordinary thing.

In truth, there was no year in all his boyhood in which Ishmael was not loved and defended and counseled by all the household save Sarai.

When he grew frightened, at eventide, by the bellowing of the returning camels, it was Urfa who took him in her arms and taught him courage.

When he watched, entranced and envious, the women shaping the evening bread, it was Azubah who gave him small lumps of the new-mixed dough, that he might make small bread flaps of his own.

Later, he delighted in running forth to meet the shepherds at sunset, in watching while they lowered leathern buckets and chanted, in chorus, some song of the well. And when they had filled the trough for the striving flocks, they gave a portion of the water to Ishmael, that he might take pleasure in serving the little lambs.

Zilah, the Canaanite girl, brought him toy animals formed of clay — a lion, a camel, a gazelle. It was Irad who pointed out to him the hare on the face of the moon. When he fell ill from eating unripened berries on the hillside, Maacah healed him with a nauseous potion of buttermilk and garlic. And, seeing that he was indeed healed, Azubah fed him delectable pastes of honey and nuts.

After his fifth year the lad had morning lessons with Eliezer and his father. Thus he learned the counting of the days and moons and seasons, to weigh out money rings for bargaining, to write upon clay tablets, to read that which his teachers had given him. He practiced his lessons by writing in the sand, and sometimes chanted to himself, in the way of childhood, certain of the things he had learned.

"A full year must pass before the newborn camel leaves its mother's milk. Sorrel plucked and eaten will stay the thirst. There are seven planets which direct our lives. If a man have misfortune, let him change his name, then the spirits of evil cannot seek him out, and all will go well with him thereafter."

From Hagar, he heard the tales of Egypt, and those she had learned from the lips of her nurse, who came from Kish. Eliezer told him stories of the ancients, how a tower was raised up to heaven, and a flood came upon all the earth. But it was Abram who taught him the ways of holiness, and the manner in which God brought forth the earth:

"No reed had sprung up, no tree had been created, no city built, no throne established. The earth was not formed. All the lands were sea. The Great Lord brooded above the face of the waters, and formed mankind of dust. And he declared the names of the mighty rivers, and he brought forth marsh grass and reed, brushwood and land, the wild cow and calf, the garden and the forest, the ewe and the lamb."

Often the gentle Maacah, busy with some household talk, would turn to him, as to many before him, with some lesson to be taken from matters of the day.

"Only see, my child, how it is that the black goats are heedless and mettlesome and wild, even as black-hearted people. While the lambs, so meek and obedient and good, are dear to the heart of the Lord."

Even from the sharp tongue of Azubah such teachings were given to his care.

"How is it that I must bring wood for the fire?" he demanded. "There is nothing here to be cooked!"

"The ways of life are the ways of life," she retorted. "Make your fire ready, and the Lord will send you meat."

184

In the seasons of plowing and reaping Shem taught him the labors of field and vineyard. From the fighting men of his father he learned the use of a bow, the thrusting of a dagger, the hurling of a spear. Jarah showed him the kindling of a shepherd's fire, the playing of a flute, revealed to him how it was that by striking the surface of a rock one might bring forth water stored within.

With Jarah, Ishmael shared an unchanging love of the wilderness. After the seventh year of his life, he went forth into it alone, took from it flowers and fruits and herbs and greens, even game. And there was a day when he returned in pain, and near to tears, his face welted with bee stings. But Hagar, bathing his wounds gently, embraced him with a tenderness between laughter and weeping and said to him, "Even you must learn, my darling, that the Lord has made no river without a crocodile."

Between Hagar and Ishmael there was a love and understanding not to be told. And for the sake of this they dealt tenderly with one another, sharing all things. Yet Ishmael was such a lad as turned with gentleness to all the household, and to Sarai also. Often he brought fruits and flowers of the wilderness and laid them before her, saying, "It came to me that these might please my lady . . ."

And Sarai, receiving them with little grace, thought in bitterness, She has said to him that he must be kind to me because I am old and barren and accursed, and the wound upon her was too harsh to be eased by tears.

Because of Ishmael she suffered unceasing jealousy of Abram, knowing that he rejoiced with Hagar in their son, witnessing flashes of pride and mirth and tenderness between them because of the lad. She had looked upon their shared fear when he was ill with a fever, and once when they had believed him lost upon the wilderness. And she thought, in desolation: I, his wife, am an intruder upon the sacred ground of their parenthood.

"All things pass away," she said to Maacah, "and thus are gone from me the things for which I was beloved in his eyes, youth and a fair countenance and the promise of sons. He abides with me only because he remembers that I was once the wife of his heart and, being a godly man, he looks with pity upon my years and weakness." Nor would she be comforted by dissenting words.

Hagar came no more to the tent of Sarai and when, by some ill-favored chance, they met upon a path or beside the well, there was not so much as a glance between them. Yet, covertly, Sarai beheld the slave's unaltered grace, her dark and radiant witchery, and cried out within her own heart: Wherefore does she not grow wasted and stooped and ugly, that my burden may be easier to bear?

Then Abram, seeing how it was with her, said gently: " Let there be no more strife between us, my darling. It is not within our power to restore the past. Therefore . . ."

And it came to her that she had once counseled the wife of Lot in the same manner. " Strive not after the past, which in the life of no man has ever come again." And she knew with what glibness of tongue one may speak of a path never trodden.

Yet she did not reject the words of her husband, but turned to him with sudden, yielding tenderness, out of her loneliness, and out of her weariness with the long sorrow between them.

" Both life and death are dust," she said, slowly, " and there is only love. Thus, let us be happy together, and afflict one another no more."

And she clung to him and wept.

But the solace of this hour was no lasting thing, and when she heard the name of Ishmael lifted up before the tents, her wretchedness returned to her and would not be cast aside:

" Behold, a son with the wisdom of his father and the beauty of his mother — Ishmael, son of Abram, son of Terah! "

And Ishmael also went up to the hill of the Lord and worshiped as Abram, and said, in humility and meekness, " Teach me a prayer, my father, befitting the lips of a child."

Then Abram, with his arm about the lad's slight shoulders, taught him a prayer befitting all upon the earth:

" Lord, defend me from myself."

And there were many in the plains near the city of Hebron who walked in the way of Abram, and went up to the hill of the Lord.

Some were of the household and some were of the land. Among them were counted Maacah and Hagar and Eliezer; Shem, the son

186

of Eliezer; Jarah and the shepherds, Henoch and Irad; Urfa and Birah, the slave women; and Eschol and Mamre, Canaanites who had ridden forth with Abram, to the rescue of Lot. But their brother Aner, father of the girl Zilah, clung to the gods of Canaan.

And there was a day when Azubah heard the voice of holiness within her, and entering the tent of Abram, she stood before him, twisting together her ruined hands, and asked in a voice both humble and afraid, " Who may ascend the hill of the Lord? "

Then Abram rose and took her hands within his own, and said with tenderness, " Such as possess the heart of Azubah."

Thus she went up to the altar and worshiped there, and it was understood that she stood before the stone of sacrifice with her heart cleansed of bitterness at last.

" Even to this hour," said Maacah, " she prays for him who is unworthy to walk in her shadow. Say to me now, is it not well for her if Rahim lies dead? "

But Azubah believed that he lived and, believing, prayed unceasingly, " Lord, that he might turn to me again, even with the years upon me, the scars of sorrow and of toil . . ."

And there were others, even children, who went up to the altar stone, among the beautiful and tawny lad Ishmael, with his hand in the hand of Abram, hearing the ways of worship from Abram's lips.

" Let my son remember that he is a servant of the Lord, and no worthy servant stands before his master unwashed and ill-attired. Therefore, cleanliness is a duty before the Lord. A man must wash his body and gird himself in unsullied garments and cleanse his life of inglorious thoughts and deeds, before he approaches the altar of sacrifice. The sandals must be taken from his feet, that no stain be put upon sacred ground, and he must cover his head in the manner of humility.

" Do not go empty-handed before the Lord, but remember that a single word of prayer from a faithful heart is more pleasing in his eyes than a bullock offered by a man of sin."

The altar stood upon a trodden hill, a little distance from the encampment. About it was a low wall of stones shadowed by moss, strewn with blossoms in the season of spring. Above it were the strong and spread branches of an ancient terebinth.

The altar was of unhewn stone, with a smoke-stained slab of sacrifice where morning and evening ritual fires burned to reddened coals, and their smoke was lifted upward on the mist of dawn and on the wind of sunset.

From the hill of the Lord might be seen the whole of the plain, the trodden lanes, the scattered patches of light and shade from the figs and olives and oaks and tamarisks, the black tents of the great encampment. Beyond lay the slopes of the wilderness, the sown fields, the terraced vines. Farther to the south, at the edge of the desert waste, gleamed the flat white roof tops of the ancient city of Hebron.

Those of the faith of Abram went up to morning and evening sacrifices, but Sarai remained within her tent. Indeed, it was no matter of surprise to those of the household that the first and secondary wives had no wish to go forth together. Thus, they believed that she worshiped alone.

And it was told how, on a certain night of stars, the Lord made a covenant with Abram, son of Terah:

"Thou shalt be a father of many nations. Neither shall thy name any more be called Abram, but thy name shall be Abraham; for a father of many nations have I made thee. . . . This is my covenant, which ye shall keep . . . Every man child among you shall be circumcised. . . . And the uncircumcised man child . . . shall be cut off from his people. . . . As for Sarai thy wife, thou shalt not call her name Sarai, but Sarah shall her name be. And I will bless her, and give thee a son . . . of her."

Then Abram said, "O that Ishmael might live before thee!"

And the Lord said: "Sarah, thy wife, shall bear thee a son . . . and thou shalt call his name Isaac: and I will establish my covenant with him . . . and with his seed after him. And as for Ishmael, I . . . have blessed him, and will make him fruitful, and . . . will make him a great nation."

And, having spoken, the Lord departed from Abram, and left him alone with the silence of the night.

# XXII

AND NOW THE SEASON OF THE GRAPE HARVEST HAD RETURNED TO THE land, and the Canaanite people went forth, at the time of the full moon of the autumn equinox, to keep the Festival of the Vintage in the manner of their fathers and their forefathers.

Amid shouting and singing, they plucked the grapes and, in great stone vats, trod them beneath their unshod feet until garments and thighs were stained to purple redness. And the blessed blood of the vines ran forth from the vats and from the troughs into the jars and the wineskins.

To their gods, they offered the earliest and best of the ingathering, grain and oil and fruit and wine, and the firstlings of flocks and herds. Their great god, Adonai, was carried forth in processionals to the sound of ritual music, that he might bless the fields and make them fruitful. Their feasting continued seven days, with dancing and singing and unsparing merriment, and they cried to one another, "Be altogether joyful!" for this was the season when the year was reborn.

The vineyards of Abraham bore rich and heavy fruit. They were enclosed in a low stone wall, and hedge had been massed upon it, that the little jackals of the wilderness might not steal in and spoil the vines. Here Shem raised a jackal-scare, like a stone demon from the wilderness, and with him, laughing and enchanted, toiled Zilah, the dark-eyed daughter of the Canaanites.

At the season of harvest, women and children went forth with the men to cut the fruit from the vines and heap it into baskets. And a tenth of the vintage — indeed, a tenth of all the ingathering — was put aside for the aged, the helpless, the widow and her child. For, according to that which Abraham had taught them, they said, " He who gives to the poor lends to the Lord."

This day, with all others of the ingathering season, was warm and sweet and fair. Hagar, with some of the other women, had gone down to the vineyards, but Sarah and Azubah stayed behind and now, in the heat of the day, were spreading forth grapes to dry in the sun, dipping them first in oil and then in ashes, that they might be properly softened, yet at the same time made unsavory to insects.

As they sat together, it came to Sarah with sudden disquiet that there was some illness upon Azubah. The slave woman, she perceived, had grown yet more wasted and angular. Her hair was streaked with lengths of gray, her eyes were sunken within purple shadows and framed deeply in lines.

About her thin and unlovely neck, against the coarse folds of her tunic, she wore a bauble ludicrous and astonishing beyond measure, a beautiful jewel brought to her by Jarah. The year before, he had found it in the ruins of a plundered camel train at the edge of the desert.

" Being a thing of splendor and from a distant land, it is of no small worth," Abraham told him.

Jarah shrugged.

"What have I to do with riches? May it please the son of Terah, let it be given to Azubah, for the jewels of half the earth would not repay her kindliness to me."

And she had worn the bauble since that hour.

There was a sudden intrusion of voices upon the stillness of the moment, the creaking of cart wheels, the sound of a youth's laughter. Shem, the son of Elisheba, brought the last of the grapes and hastened with the unloading of them, it being in his mind to join the revelry in the streets of Hebron.

Grown to manhood, he was tall and lithe and brown, dark of head and light of heart. Though he was beloved of all the tribe of Abraham, and as dear as a son of his own flesh to Eliezer, none could deny that his spirit was wholly Canaanite. He desired neither the gentle, wandering life of the shepherd nor yet the fierce and rigorous life of the fighting man. Instead, he yearned for the tilling of the soil, thought better of the raising of a house than the raising of a tent, and took delight in the joyous Canaanite festivals.

The lad Ishmael had come with him from the vineyards and, together, they lifted the fruit from the cart.

"Behold," cried Azubah, starting forth to meet them, "you have spilled the last basket upon the ground! Must I suffer the carelessness of the young all the days of my life?"

Whereupon Ishmael cried out in mock dismay, "I would not have Azubah lift her voice to me in anger, for truly she is gentle and soft-spoken beyond all women."

Which caused Shem, even Azubah herself, to break into laughter.

How much he is like *her,* Sarah thought, turning from her task to gaze upon the dark and beautiful lad. The merriment in his eyes, the proud lift of his head, the witchery of his spirit, alien and strange. If he were the son of my flesh, I would know unending joy in him, but because he is of *her* flesh and Abraham's, I despise him utterly. And her heart smote her with the desolate knowledge.

Now, grudgingly, Azubah turned to Shem.

"Already it is noonday. If you would wash and gird yourself in time to behold the senseless revelry of the ungodly . . ."

"I also would look upon the senseless revelry of the ungodly!" declared Ishmael, suddenly. He besought the tall youth beside him. "Suffer me to go up with my cousin, even to Hebron, that I may look upon the games . . ."

But Abraham, coming forth, stayed the words upon the lad's lips.

"Let Shem make haste to dress the young calf I have taken from the herd," he called, "for strangers tarry with us."

And, hastening to the quiet shade where Sarah dealt with the grapes, he told her: "A moment past, as I rested before the door of the tent, I beheld three strangers walking across the plain and, in truth, the sun was merciless upon them. Thus, I went forth to meet them, that they might know themselves welcome, and, commanding a slave to bring water for their feet, I bade them pause and break bread with me. Even now they wait beneath the tree. Therefore, let Sarah take three measures of fine meal and knead it, and make cakes upon the hearth."

"As my husband has said," she answered readily, and summoned a maidservant to finish the dipping of the grapes.

Within the kitchen of Abraham's tent she took up a square of linen and wiped the oil from her fingers. Then, putting meal and flour and salt into a kneading bowl, she made a fine white dough and, when it was shaped into flat bread cakes, knelt by the heated stones at the door and baked the bread upon them.

Shem laid his hand upon the shoulder of Ishmael.

" If we hasten, little brother, we may yet look upon the wonders of Hebron. For, seeing that it is only noonday, and the dressing of a calf is a small task, quickly done . . ."

" And that a bed of hot coals is soon brought about," agreed the lad, with good nature. Thus he turned, with Azubah, to the renewing of the fire. Nor was there resentment in any of their hearts concerning these tasks, for hospitality to the stranger had been made sacred in their eyes.

Often, teaching his little son the ways of courtesy and goodness, Abraham had said: " Let Ishmael remember the words of my mouth:

" Even though it be a year of famine and, within your heart, you bewail the fate which brought a company of hungry men and animals upon you, go forth from your tent and welcome them with good grace. For surely the day will come when he who rides through dust and fast and weariness will be yourself, and these same strangers may come forth to you with bread.

" Ask no man whither he goes or why. If it is his desire to talk of these matters, let him speak, but ask him not at all. And when you sit within another's tent, say no word of food, but await it in silence, and profess astonishment when it is brought before you. For even though you have witnessed the slaughter of the calf and have smelled the sweet savor of its cooking, astonishment is the way of courtesy.

" Then turn back the sleeve of your right arm, even as your mother has taught you to do, and eat with the fingers of the right hand, but not before all dip into the feast together. And let no morsel pass your lips before you have prayed: ' In the name of the Lord, the merciful, the loving-kind.' "

When the calf had been cooked to tenderness and heaped upon a great tray, Azubah dressed it with melted butter and spread a wheaten paste around it, and Shem and Ishmael brought it before the men, with milk and the new bread.

Sarah sat alone in the inner room. There was little hunger upon her, but because it was the hour of the noonday bread, she ate a portion of fruit. Through the dividing wall of the tent came low, murmuring talk. The strangers spoke of the excellence of the food, the burning heat of the day, the gracious kindness they had received at the hand of Abraham, their host. Then, after a little silence given to eating and drinking, one of them lifted his voice in a question unseemly beyond belief:

" Where is Sarah, your wife? "

Her lips fell open in astonishment that a man should be questioned concerning the women of his household. Sudden quiet came upon the company. In the slow, controlled answer of her husband, she sensed the restraint of a courteous host before the incredible vulgarity of a stupid guest.

" Within the tent," he said coldly.

And the stranger declared, " Sarah your wife shall bear a son."

Behold, thought Sarah, in scornful understanding, it is one of the foaming prophets of the wilderness who sits at meat with my husband. For there were those in the land who wandered from village to village crying out things to come, who dwelt like beasts in the caves of the hills, afflicted themselves with gashes for their own transgressions, or bore the yokes of oxen upon their necks. A seer, indeed, she thought in bitter amusement, not even knowing that the manner of women has ceased to come upon me. And she laughed in scorn of his words.

But the stranger called: " Is anything too hard for the Lord? Wherefore did Sarah laugh? "

Startled, she stared at the dividing wall, a tremor of fear possessing her. How is it that this man knows that which his eyes have not beheld? And she was moved to deny her laughter, yet he would not have it so.

" Nay, but you did laugh," he declared. And he said again, " Sarah shall have a son."

Whereupon he rose up, and the others with him, and went forth into the heat of the day, upon the burning road to the vale. Abraham, in the manner of a courteous host, walked a little way beside them, and she stood, dazed and wordless, watching him depart. The voice of the stranger had not ceased to fill her ears. Was anything too hard for the Lord? Yet, a son of her own flesh and Abraham's — it was not to be believed. She began the tidying of the tent and sought to put aside the thinly rekindled hope. But it wavered and rose and was strengthened before her, despite the years heaped like ashes upon it.

Returning, Abraham came at once to the shaded coolness of the tent, where she dealt with certain unfinished tasks, and the wonder of the prophecy stood forth in his eyes. Yet there was a constraint upon them, so they could not bring themselves to mention what had passed, but were awkward and wordless before it. At last, out of the necessity to speak, she asked, " The strangers have departed? "

It was an ill-contrived question, seeing that the answer was known to them both, but he seized upon it quickly, and with gratitude.

" Toward Sodom," he told her, " and I also, a little distance, to bring them upon the way."

" A burdensome journey," she commented, " in the heat of this hour."

Again they were silent, and the shape of their unvoiced thoughts stood between them, bleak and lonely. Deliberately, she moved about the room, taking up a wineskin, replacing a cluster of dried herbs, dusting meal from the grain mill, scraping the bowl in which she mixed the bread. In truth, she said to herself, the thought of a child has been such a matter of bitterness between us that we fear to speak of it.

She was aware, suddenly, that he had turned to her with a gesture of tenderness.

" Sarah . . ."

She stood still and unyielding.

" What is it Abraham would say? "

" If it should be as the stranger declared, the blessing of a son . . ."

But she did not turn and her voice, when she answered, was flat and cold.

" Has not my lord already begotten a son for himself? "

Nay, she thought wearily, let me keep my tongue from malice, seeing that there is still love between us, and we have had so little of joy. And she lifted her eyes and made her voice more gentle.

"It is known to us both that I am past the time of bearing. Therefore, give no heed to the words of this man."

"Yet who can say that he was not a prophet of the Lord?"

"Prophet . . .," she repeated slowly. And there passed before her eyes, out of the undimmed chambers of her memory, a long and fantastic processional of diviners and sorcerers to whom she had turned in her unending search for the promise of a son. Like shadows they came forth, each bearing his own pattern of signs and omens: the rising of clouds, the drifting of smoke, the courses of the stars, the flowing of water, the waning of the moon. And she smiled a cold and mocking smile and asked, "What have I to do with prophets, seeing that nothing is certain save the burial cave?"

Then, because of the bitterness upon her, he said no further word of the child, but spoke only of the stranger.

"On the way we walked together, there was a matter he laid before me, saying how he had been sent to reckon the sins of Sodom. For unless ten men of virtue can be found within it, then Sodom will be destroyed utterly, and the other Cities of the Plains likewise."

Sarah shrugged.

"Was there ever a city of such evil that ten worthy men could not be found within its walls?"

"In Sodom and Gomorrah," he answered, quietly, "it is said that no man has escaped iniquity. Yet, if disaster comes upon them, may the Lord deal mercifully with Lot."

And there was compassion for him in her heart, for she knew how it was that the child Lot had walked by his side and held to his hand, even as Ishmael.

In the eyes of many, the Cities of the Plains were an abomination before the Lord. Sodom, Gomorrah, Admah, Zeboiim, Zoar — not one of them was undefiled, it was said, but the name of Sodom was infamous beyond all others. In truth, those of Sodom dwelt in such mires of corruption that shame itself seemed a virtue in their eyes. And Lot dwelt among them, and the wife of Lot.

How had the years dealt with the smooth amber body, the beautiful and mocking face, the dark and contriving heart? She recalled how it was that Lot's wife had stood on the hilltop at Bethel in the ripening dawn, the folds of her rich cloak blown about her by the wind of morning, how she had declared, with unconcealed malice, " The lot of Sarah is dust and loneliness."

And Sarah turned and stared out into the shimmering hills and said to herself, Yet perhaps even she has come to know that nothing fulfills the dreams of our youth, or the hopes of our hearts.

At the dawning of the next day Abraham, being concerned for his nephew Lot, rode forth to a certain place from which he might behold the cities of the valley. And the smoke of their destruction billowed up against the sky.

Afterward, it was told how the stars were shaken in the heavens, and the plain rose and fell as though it were tossed upon a mighty sea. The earth was rent and shattered, and the trees writhed in anguish, and there came forth thunder and fire and flame, and the cities were destroyed utterly.

Yet because of the honor of Abraham, the Lord spoke to Lot and bade him depart, with all his house, that they might be saved. But even in this moment of disaster, his faltering will was such that others had to lead him forth, and his wife and daughters also.

And the Lord said, " Look not behind thee, but hasten to the mountain, for the sake of thy life! "

And Lot and his daughters escaped and fled into the mountain, to dwell there, but the wife of Lot looked back, since all that was dear to her heart lay behind her.

The smoke and fire and ash fell down upon her, and upon the salt-strewn rim of the Dead Sea before her, and upon all the plain.

And when the rain of disaster had ceased, there was but a crusted shape of salt where she had stood . . . and the dust . . . and the loneliness . . .

# XXIII

Jarah had spent an entire day with the household and, having gathered food for another moon, was returning to the shepherd camp upon his own camel. Night upon night, he rode her about the wilderness pastures, for so vast had the herds and flocks of Abraham become that they were no longer to be brought through the perils of darkness by a few men on foot.

The camel of Jarah was a noble, swift-pacing animal, fair and proud, with a high head and great brown eyes beholding the world with dignity and disdain. That no evil might come upon her, he had given her a blue-beaded halter and hung strings of smaller blue beads about her neck. There was a crunching sound beneath her feet as she traveled, and a rhythmic swishing of sand which set up a melody in Jarah's head. And, presently, his voice took up one of the chants of desert riders, ringing forth in the silence, echoing from the hills.

With him he bore grain in plenty, cheese and olives and dates and figs, flat loaves of bread baked for him less than an hour before by Azubah. And there were other delicacies she had prepared — skins of butter, honey-and-seed cakes, fermented camel milk, to delight the hearts of Henoch and the rest. For they had been so long away from the tents that little more than a handful of grain remained to ease their hunger.

Bidding him farewell, Azubah had hung about his neck a snakestone formed of onyx, to defend him against the vipers of the wilderness. "Let my son go forth unharmed," said Azubah, and the words on her lips were an incantation to stay the forces of evil. Maacah had brought him salves for healing the wounds of men and animals alike. And Sarah had given him a skin of honey.

It was but a little past the hour of sunset and a new moon hung in the curling clouds of the west, a silver sickle swung at plumes of flame. Reddened light lay upon the sand, and upon the scattered trees and thornbushes, the clumps of weeds, the edges of the dim and dusty stream beds. Already the voice of an owl was calling from some lonely, hidden branch in the dark and brooding hills.

Jarah, grown to manhood, was tall and straight and comely. There was within him that which caused him to fling back his head in challenge at the thought of fear, to plunge forward without waiting into that which threatened or was unknown. And the dark and ruthless strength of the desert, borne in his veins, was beginning to make itself known in the proud lift of his young head, the lean lines of his strengthening stride.

Suddenly his joyous words faded and trailed like smoke upon the rising wind of evening, his eyes widened before the measure of his astonishment. For a little way before him, in the light of the setting sun, lay a still, white figure which, aware of his approach, stirred a little and was still again.

" The Lord lead me! " cried Jarah and then, halting the camel, he made her kneel and release him to the sands.

Swiftly, he knelt beside the stranger and lifted his head and beheld a man too weakened for speech, too afflicted with thirst to move his swollen tongue. With his last strength, the stranger clawed at Jarah's waterskin but, putting aside his hands, Jarah fed him water in single drops between his dried lips until he was able to take a mouthful at a time.

Meanwhile the moon brightened, turning the sands to pale loneliness, deepening the shadows, edging the hills and rocks and bushes with a thin, luminous blue. In its light, Jarah looked upon the burned and swollen face of a man handsome to behold even in his misery, but well advanced in the years of his maturity.

" How came my brother upon this wilderness alone? " he asked gently.

The man strove to give some answer, but his words, single, unrelated, incoherent, made mention only of robbers and a stolen camel. And, indeed, it was as if he had been despoiled of his last possessions, for he bore neither food nor drink, nor arms, and had been for more than two days without water.

"Let my brother be comforted," said Jarah then. "We are but a little way from the tents of Abraham, son of Terah, a refuge for all afflicted and shelterless . . ."

And so it was that in the second hour of darkness, Jarah rode again into the encampment, bearing the fallen stranger to the healing wisdom of Maacah.

The man was too weakened to move as they traveled, and lay inert against the hard, unyielding strength of the youth. The camel shuffled, loose-legged and even-paced, through stream beds, up drift sand tufted with scrub, plunging a little in the depths, climbing forth again.

The night was filled with darkness now, and with stars. Sounds from the encampment were borne out to them with the wind of dusk, the bleating of a sheep, the mourning of a flute, the voices of the household. Then the glow of supper fires rose before Jarah's eyes, and he smelled the rich savor of the evening bread.

"It is I, Jarah, returning with one who fell among thieves," he called. And the tidings spread as swiftly as a grass fire, murmured by all the encampment. "Jarah has returned. Behold, Jarah has brought a stranger from the wilderness, one fallen among thieves."

The man was lifted from the kneeling camel and borne within the tent of Abraham, yielding to utter weariness and the sudden peace of deliverance. It was but the space of a moment after they had placed him upon the spread cushions, among the hastily kindled lamps, before he had fallen into slumber. The wavering flames cast a sheen of light upon his dark, arresting face and Abraham, coming within the tent and beholding him, was halted as if by some lash of memory from other years. And, this being true, he turned sharply to Jarah.

"How was it that you came upon this man?"

"Behold, he lay upon the sands near to death from thirst and hunger."

"Wherefore?"

Jarah shrugged.

"How he came there is unknown to me, nor was he able to

tell of the matter, though he muttered of robbery and of thieves."

For a little time Abraham stood beside the stranger, wordless and unmoving, yet there was that in his face which filled Jarah with sudden disquiet and caused him to speak uneasily.

" Say to me now, is he known to my uncle? "

Abraham turned and said quietly, " Bring Maacah."

And when she had come within the door of the tent, he beckoned her near and said, in a voice low and not untroubled: " How am I to be certain? I was but a lad, and only a single time did I behold him. Yet . . ."

Slowly she went forth and gazed upon the man, and her breath was caught in her throat upon a fearful sound, and Jarah thought, with a swift sense of panic: Is it hate I behold in the face of Maacah? Such a thing is not possible.

" It is indeed he," she said harshly, " and no other." She bent nearer and looked more fully upon him. " Nor is he upon the rim of death," she added, bitterly, " but only spent from weariness and fear."

They stood in silence, saying no word, the lamps wavering about them, the shadows moving upon the black walls. From beyond a girl laughed suddenly, a light and joyous sound, and memory akin to misery stirred in Maacah's face.

" Let me not be called upon to summon her," she said then, and departed from them.

Abraham lifted his eyes to the silent and wondering Jarah.

" It is the husband of Azubah who lies before us."

With a cry, the youth sprang up, his face wrenched even as the face of Maacah.

" Nay," said Abraham, gently, " go forth and bring her here, seeing that she has long prayed for this hour."

Slowly, and with unconcealed reluctance, Jarah turned from the tent into the darkness. And when he came again, his arm about the stunned and wordless Azubah, he waited with Abraham upon the threshold, that she might enter alone.

Rahim had stirred and was awakening. He heard no sound of her coming and, for a little space, she stood in silence and gazed upon him unperceived. The soft yellow lamplight dealt kindly with him, so that he bore no look of years, and was not unlike the lad of her memory — the lean, hard strength, the dark and curling hair, the languorous grace.

When she had drawn nearer, she beheld the whitened patches in his hair like blown sand, thin and fine. There were certain shadowed lines across his brow, and others at the edge of his mouth. Yet he was unaltered by the years.

And now her heart was quickened and her breathing labored, before the measure of her suspense. How will he speak to me when he has looked upon my face? Ah, God of mercy, can it be that he will hold forth his arms, remembering? Her shaken lips moved to breathe the music of his name, " Rahim . . ."

Hearing the sound, he opened his eyes and beheld her shadow upon the wall. And, turning slowly across the cushions, he lifted his gaze to her face. For the space of a moment they looked at each other. Then he spoke in sharp and querulous tones:

" Go forth, old woman, and fetch me a skin of water, that I may drink . . ."

Her breath went out from her on a gasping sound like a faint, unbidden moan, and once again her lips sought to shape his name.

" *Rahim* . . ."

" Are you a lunatic, that you stand there shaking and gibbering? Go forth and fetch the water."

She turned and stumbled from him, her face as white as the sands, set in lines of anguish. And Jarah would have thrust her aside and slain him for her sake.

" Let me go forth into the tent and make an end of him! For, seeing that my mother has suffered a thousand deaths at his hand, surely it is not unreasonable that he should suffer one! "

" Nay." Abraham seized the lad by the arms.

" Only see the sorrow he has brought upon her! Is this not a thing to be avenged? "

" Even so," said Abraham, quietly, " it is not in the hand of Jarah to do the deed."

" Wherefore? "

" Leave the shafts of vengeance to the hand of fate, my son. For, as Jarah will come to know in the years of his wisdom, Fate is no mean archer."

And when Azubah came forth from the tent, the light of the fires shone upon her, and she was as a woman old in years and ill unto death. Her shoulders sagged beneath the weight of her misery and there was an unsteadiness upon her, so that Jarah reached out to her in fear.

"My mother," he burst out, in desolation.

She lifted her hand and laid it upon his own, and the touch was dry and cold and without life.

"It is to my shame," she said, dully, "that I have sought this hour. For who can bring back a star that has fallen, an arrow that has flown?"

# XXIV

Times without number, she had thought how it would come about. They would go up to the roof top of the House of Terah, she and Abram, at some midnight hour when the city of Ur slept in shadowed silence below.

In the radiant manner of girlhood, she had said to herself, "My saffron tunic with the embroidered girdle, and the little gold moons in my hair . . ."

They would sit upon the heaped cushions and gaze beyond the parapet, beholding the shape of the temple against the moonrise, the flaring torch of the watchman at the gate, hearing the distant and haunting sound of camel bells from some caravan on the plain to the south.

And, in the dreaming stillness, she would turn to her husband, put her hand within his own, and say that she was to bear a child.

Nay, it would be in the garden of the high house in Haran, in the last red glimmering of the sunset, when the crickets began their saddened chirping in the grasses and the moths came, mist-winged and beautiful, to seek the lamps, and the wind was rising in the silvery boughs of the olive tree.

The fair vale of Shechem, the hilltop of Bethel, the grasslands of Egypt, a tent beneath the oaks of Mamre . . . again and yet again, the dream had fallen into decay. Still there was a portion that renewed itself, unaltered by the years: a fair tunic, a gentle darkness, a phrase tender and womanly . . .

But on the morning when Sarah came forth from the tent of Maacah, knowing that a child was at last quickened within her, such thoughts departed from her utterly. Reaching forth to Abraham, she cast herself within his arms and wept, " Oh, my husband, let them not laugh because I bear you a child in my latter years! "

Even Maacah found it no easy thing to believe what had come to pass. And, indeed, it was a matter of astonishment before all the tents, yet they rejoiced, even as Abraham, that the Lord had looked upon them and blessed them with a child of the true wife at last.

And now there came to Sarah enchanted days of unutterable peace. The mornings were golden, the evenings dreaming, the hours sang about her. Even Urfa declared that the days of her youth had been restored, seeing the change that had come upon her. Not for years had Sarah given more than fleeting heed to her mirror. Now she turned to it as to an oracle, and her heart was lifted up before it. The flesh of her body was still firm in its look of youth, nor had it lost its warm brown sheen, its tender softness. Her dark and abundant hair bore only tinges of gray, and neither her hands nor her face were marked with years. And she whispered in joy and radiance, " Shall I be fair again, as well as young, in the eyes of my child? "

That year the barley harvest was very great, and the men and women of the tents labored in the fields from the first tremulous ripening of dawn to the falling of dusk. Ancient harvest songs rang forth into the air as the reapers swung their sickles upon the bearded grain. Near the hour of midmorning, they paused that they might refresh themselves with water cooled in a stone jug, and with sweet parched grain. And there were those who cast themselves down in the shade of the trees and took rest, for a little time, with their heads pillowed upon smooth, flat stones.

Afterward, the straw-bound sheaves were borne in carts to the threshing ground, a space of broad, sun-hardened earth where the slow and heavy-paced oxen trampled out the grain. And neither that which remained in the margins of the fields nor that which fell unheeded from the sheaves was gathered up, but left by command of Abraham for the poor of the land, and for those who sojourned within it.

From a leaf-covered shelter, Shem and Ishmael watched through the night, that no thieves might plunder the threshed grain. And in the morning the reapers came forth again, bearing the wooden forks of winnowing. When, with these forks, they had cast the threshed grain upon the wind which came from the sea, then dust and sand and chaff were carried from it, and it could be gathered by the women, sifted and cleansed of stones, and stored against the season of famine.

The summer was burning and windless, and there were grass fires in the dried herbage of the wilderness, so that vipers and scorpions were driven forth, and certain of the wild beasts also, and the smell of smoke lingered, haunting and sweet, above the hills.

With the harvesting of the wheat came the strengthening of the sun, and rainless days of burning, unclouded skies. It was a year of uncommon abundance. Fruitfulness blessed the fields of Abraham, his vines and gardens, his flocks and herds, even Sarah, his wife.

And there were those of the household who murmured among themselves, " Behold, if a man suffers misfortune, he has only to change his name . . ."

At the end of the harvest season, Shem took to wife Zilah, the Canaanite girl with the laughing black eyes, the tossed black hair, and the little gold ring in her nose.

It was not a marriage to the liking of Eliezer, though he had known that it would come. Yet he did not withhold his blessing, seeing that Shem stood before him even as he himself had stood before Abraham on the morning, now trodden dim by the years, when he had asked for the Canaanite Elisheba.

And it was in the words of Abraham that he spoke before his foster son:

" Thus shall it be, though it is no happy thing in my eyes, and not according to my heart. Because of the love I bear him, I am distressed for my brother, for I would not see him turn to the paths of the ungodly. Yet, also because of this love, let it be as he asks."

And he counseled Shem, "Lead your wife before the Lord, and your children also, and shun the ways of those who worship before sheaves and serpents, the fowls of the air, and the swimming creatures of the sea."

Shem answered slowly:

"Let my father forgive me if I say amiss, yet — seeing that the hand of the Lord has touched all things, trees and stars and clouds, the stones of the earth and all else upon it — surely he has been reverently worshiped through his creations, even by those who know not how to call his name."

At the end of the summer, after the season of harvest, a little time before the beginning of the winter rains, the little Isaac was born.

He was a child beautiful and perfect and, beholding him, Sarah saw the dream lifted up from the dust and restored to her, for his face was the face of Abraham, and of their fathers, and of their people.

And when he had been tenderly cleansed and his body swathed in soft, washed linen, then he was carried across the tent in the arms of the joyous Maacah, and given to Sarah.

She lay upon the cushions, her dark hair spread forth against them, her eyes bright with gathering tears. When she had lifted herself from the bed mat, she held forth her arms and cried out in a voice shattered by sobs, "Give me my child!"

And, holding him to her breast, she rocked backward and forward, remembering the anguish of the years, and cried out again and yet again, "He is my son — *mine whom none can ever take away!*"

And Abraham came within the tent and fell upon his knees beside her, and together they wept with joy in the child in whose seed all men of the earth would be blessed.

Then those of the tents rejoiced with feasting and merriment, and cried out, "Behold the son of the true wife, even Isaac, born of Sarah!"

And Ishmael looked upon the child and adored him utterly.

Day upon day he stole in that he might behold him. " Only see, my lady, his eyes are as bright as rock pools! " . . . " Only see, my lady, the sunniness of his smile! " And later he came bearing wonders to lay before the babe. " Behold, little brother, this tiny new lamb."

Sarah turned swiftly, her heart both chilled and frightened by the words. *Little brother* . . . And she cried out in panic: " Nay, then, I will not have it so! There is no justice in it! This alien lad, this wild and strange intruder from a foreign land, this slave child in whom I have no portion of flesh and who is as the sting of a scorpion upon my days — he shall not be heir to the House of Abraham with my son Isaac! "

And from that day forward the thought was like a violence upon her. Yet to Abraham she said no word of it, but pondered upon it in secret, thinking to devise some means of bringing about her will.

And the child Isaac was blessed of the Lord and strengthened and beloved. And his father declared that, on the day of his weaning, the House of Abraham would rejoice in such a feast as none could remember.

# XXV

It was known to all the tents that Azubah was dying. for the space of a moon she had not risen from her bed mat, and, though she breathed, the hand of death had led her spirit forth, so that she lay silent and unmoving, lifting neither her eyes nor her voice.

With both morning and evening, those who went up to the hill of the Lord offered a sacrifice for the slave woman, and uttered such prayers as rose within their hearts. And there were some, still in the years of early youth, who wept: " Lord, save her from death. Deliver her from this terror." But those who walked in the quiet radiance of age spoke otherwise: " Lord, take our sister unto your peace, for she is very weary."

And there was a certain morning when Maacah, kneeling beside the wasted figure, said farewell to her in wordless, wrenching pain, and sent Shem forth into the hills to bring Jarah, that the young shepherd might once more behold his mother's face.

Even Zilah, the merry Canaanite wife of Shem, wept for the slave woman and, according to the faith of her fathers, made a vow to her Friendly Spirit for Azubah's sake. "Bring healing upon her, holy one, and I will cast my gold earrings into the waters where you abide."

And of all who came and went, with slow and silent tears, to the tent of Azubah, only Rahim kept apart. Though he had suffered a fever after he was brought to the tents, and though she had tended him with unceasing devotion throughout all the days and nights of his illness, he did not so much as inquire how she fared. Instead, he spent the length of the afternoon in wheedling and charming certain maidservants. Above the labored breathing of Azubah, their voices rose in laughter and in dalliance.

"Has Rahim no harem that weeps for him?"

"My harem is vast and filled with beauty and you, my gazelle, shall be its queen."

Whereupon Maacah went forth and spoke curtly to the slave girls, scattering them to their tasks. And she turned to Hagar and spoke with bitterness, saying, "In the dust of her grave, she will remember him no more . . . and for this, let us give praise to God."

And Hagar, going slowly within the tent, said in her heart: Thus shall it be with me . . . in the dust of my grave.

For the space of two hours she knelt beside Azubah, moving a fan of palm backward and forward above her sweating face to dispel the heaviness about her, bathing her wrists and forehead to bring coolness upon her.

"Even as she did for me in the days of my bearing," she said, and tears stood in her eyes.

And presently Ishmael came, bearing honey he had discovered in the rocks and, in the way of a child, was saddened because Azubah could not partake of his earnest gift.

Only later, when the others had departed and Sarah entered and spoke her name, did the slave woman open her eyes.

" How is it with my sister? " Sarah caressed the thin, grayed hair and strove against tears.

Azubah answered dully, " The spear of time has wounded me until I die."

And Sarah thought, with silent misery, So shall it be with me.

Darkness had fallen and a night mist was rising when Shem and Jarah rode in from the hills. And Jarah went into the tent of Azubah and came forth shattered with weeping.

" Do the thing in haste," he said to the son of Eliezer, and strode to a certain heavy blackness beneath some terebinths. And presently Shem came to him there, and Rahim also, though reluctantly and with little grace.

" What have I to do with Jarah? " he asked, insolently.

Whereupon Jarah lashed out at him with unrestrained fury.

"What have you to do with any creature above a viper — you who were cast out by your own tribe for violating a girl alone in the wilderness? Nay, do not seek to deny it! At a certain well, the story was told, and the name of Rahim spoken! "

The mouth of Rahim moved loosely:

" She was not unwilling, the girl in the hills."

" Filthy dog of the wilderness, she slew herself for shame! " Jarah struck him with such violence that he fell to the sands with a smear of blood across his mouth. Then, seizing him by the throat, Jarah hauled him to his knees.

" My brother is beyond reason! " gasped Shem, striving to loosen the shepherd's fingers. " Jarah, hear me — for if you slay him, how is she to die in peace? "

The face of Jarah cleared, the madness departed from his eyes.

" Even so," he said, dully, and dropped the gasping man to the earth.

" My . . . my brother wrongs me! " wailed Rahim, beginning to shake. " Let my dear brother have mercy. Let him hear the words of my mouth."

But the fury of Jarah sprang at him, the hand of Jarah kept him upon his knees.

" May your bowels wither, may the hyenas gnaw your bones — whining, lying, contemptible son of a misbegotten she-dog! Azubah the slave woman is dying in her tent, and there is a thing I would have you do, and if it is not done as I have said, then, by the fire that burns, I will slit your throat and cast your entrails unto the jackals!"

"Whatever is the wish of my brother I will perform," declared the man, quickly. "Only say what it is I am to do."

"You will go forth to the tent of Azubah and kneel by her side and repeat the words of my mouth, beginning: *In the days of my youth there was one known as Lia . . .*"

"In the days of my youth, there was one known as Lia," he echoed, and they saw that the name stirred no memory within him. He added in a whisper of terror, "What Jarah will have me say I will say, indeed!"

"You shall say it or die the death!" answered Jarah. And when they had done with him, had seen him cleanse his face at the well and smooth his disordered garments, they sent him forth into the tent of Azubah, where lamps had been kindled in the darkness, and awaited him beyond.

And his voice was made both gentle and earnest as he knelt beside her, for he knew not whether he was beyond their hearing.

"The . . . the pain of Azubah is as my own," he stammered out.

Whereupon her eyes opened, and she gazed at him as if from a dream.

"There is a thing I would say to Azubah," he went on, and wiped a sudden sweat from his brow.

"Let Rahim speak," she whispered, gently.

"In the days of my youth, there was one known as Lia," he said, and paused, again to deal with the sweat of fear upon him.

The memory of an old anguish flickered in the face of the dying woman, so that for a moment it was yet more wrenched and bleak.

"Lia . . .," she whispered.

"A girl of beauty," he said, lamely. Then, with her dark, believing eyes upon him, he recovered, even in this moment, some of the facile, lying charm that had belonged to his youth. "A girl of beauty," he said, speaking more easily, "and of grace and laughter and many delights. For a time she was dear to me, seeing

209

that I looked upon her as the love of my life . . ."

"And she was . . . otherwise?" faltered Azubah.

Rahim stared down at her. How was he to say, even in his disdain for truth, the words that Jarah had bidden him utter? The gaunt and shapeless figure beneath the coverlet, the veined and coarsened hands, the thinned and graying hair, the face pinched by the fingers of death, breath heavy with the smell of it — all these were abhorrent in his eyes. He bit his lip in unavailing disgust and then leaned closer, determined to have the sorry business ended quickly.

"Even so," he said. Then, loudly and hastily, he added, "There has been but one love in the life of Rahim — Azubah, his faithful handmaiden, who pitied him in his affliction, and gave him back his life."

A gasp came from the dying woman, and her eyes blazed with a wild, unutterable joy.

"Rahim . . .," she breathed and, as she moved, the coverlet fell away from her and he beheld, upon her wasted throat, the necklace Jarah had given her. It is no mean bauble, he thought, looking upon it with a merchant's swift, appraising eye. Indeed, in Egypt, it would bring a man the food and drink and shelter of a worthy inn, garments fit to wear before kings, the flesh of a dancing girl young and wanton.

"Lord, receive the gratitude of thy servant."

He beheld the movement of her thin blue lips and thought, How may I contrive to take it from her?

"Azubah, my beloved," he said, glibly, then, and slipped his arm about her, so that her head rested against his chest. Her worn fingers clutched at the fabric of his tunic and then, like a child worn from sobbing, she closed her eyes and was still.

He felt the breath pass from her body on a light shudder, yet held her in silence for a little time, wanting to be certain she would not rise with an outcry when she felt the knife against her throat.

"Now, by the name of my mother, I shall live again."

His eyes glowed as he cut the necklace free and turned swiftly, silently, to the back of the tent. Those who waited in the darkness would continue to be silent, thinking Azubah had taken a long time in dying, forbearing to lift their voices in either wails or laments until he had come forth to say that all was ended.

He slipped from the tent and made his way in soundless haste toward the western slope, where some camels were pastured in the care of a very old man and a very young and stupid lad. It was the dark of the moon, and a wind was blowing from the sea, damp and cold. Through the shadows he followed the smell of the camels, the bleat of one of the foals stirring against its mother, their long sighs. And then, as he crept closer, he beheld the circle of motionless, kneeling shapes, some lying with necks stretched forth upon the sand, some chewing their cuds in solemn content.

And suddenly his teeth gleamed in a smile.

" There are two matters in which I possess great skill," he said to himself, " the seduction of a maiden and the stealing of a camel."

And he went forward, into the dark.

There was none to look upon him but the vultures and now, in the breathless heat of the late afternoon, they had grown bold, sweeping so close that he could hear the flapping of their great black wings, could smell the stench of death upon them, behold their merciless yellow beaks, the savage brightness of their eyes. And, clawing at the endless and unrelenting drifts, Rahim pulled himself yet nearer the wreckage strewn before him. He had ridden forth in too many raiding parties not to know that here lay what remained of a plundered caravan, that the shape thrust from a certain patch of drift sand was the edge of a waterskin.

The thought of a waterskin only a little beyond his torn finger tips smote him with an eagerness that weakened and sickened him. Yet it was necessary that he move slowly, very slowly and with great caution, if he was to reach it before the weakness of sweat and thirst and hunger caused him to lose consciousness, and rendered him up to the vultures.

But even as he dragged his seared and wretched body nearer the bones of fallen men, the broken and plundered chests, the strewn remnants of death and destruction, he spent a portion of his ebbing strength to touch his throat with seeking hands, to know that he still possessed a certain jeweled necklace.

He had counted three days since the storm. He had fled from the tents of Abraham south to the desert and, since its face was as the face of a mother in his eyes, there was no fear upon him. A single skin of water, a bit of bread, a cluster of dates from the Hebron market — a man bound for Egypt would need no more, for the camel was swift of pace, untiring, easily ridden, and he knew the ways of eluding pursuit.

The next day was very hot, with the strange and dry heaviness of air that presaged a more than ordinary storm. Thunder rolled and echoed along the rim of the desert, above the slopes and among the rocks. The wind burned the waste like a wilderness fire, and the heat of the sand rose up and scorched his face. Later in the afternoon, great brown clouds came upon the sky. Suddenly, the lines of the hills were softened and dimmed, the world was filled with an evil yellow glow. Then, with a blast of flaming, screaming wind, the storm was upon him, pillars of sand rolling like demon spirits before it, leaping and dancing and whirling with the gale.

Rahim's camel was blown round like a desert *Lil* and he himself torn from it and cast upon the sand before the wind. He kept his face and eyes covered, but his body was assailed by blasts of stinging sand and lashed with pebbles. Thorn bushes were wrenched from the earth and hurled before the storm gust, likewise great tufts of grass, and a tamarisk tree he had passed but a little time before.

And then, swiftly and suddenly, the storm departed and there was only silence. Rahim struggled forth and sought to rid himself of the burden of sand. His garments were heavy with it, his eyes, his nose, even his mouth were afflicted with it. In sudden terror, he clutched his throat, but the jewel was unharmed.

And now he saw that the shape of the world was altered. The hills had been torn from their accustomed places and lifted elsewhere. Trees and shrubs had vanished, and his tracks likewise. The camel was not to be seen.

Three mornings had dawned, and with each he had struggled farther into the sands, having neither water nor bread, nor any food save a few dates in his girdle. And then, beyond a certain slope, he came upon this scene of raid and plunder.

His skin burned with torment, his throat was raw and sore and swollen, his eyes inflamed, crusted with sand, and his tongue so enlarged as to fill his mouth. And yet, the waterskin lay before him, the jewel was saved, and he was not to perish.

Thus he smiled, dragging himself a little nearer, and a certain triumph came upon his lean brown face. Through the turbulent years of his life there had been many who sought his death, yet he had escaped them all, had lived to turn back and regard them with laughter, like some evil spirit against whom even the gods are powerless to contend.

Earlier, terror had wavered before his eyes like the shape of a cobra. Now it had departed from him, and he could bare his teeth in a triumphant grin before the thought of it. No, his life would not be required of him, but instead, would be preserved, that he might know the joys that can come to a man who possesses a jewel.

Thus he crawled forward and, with his last remaining strength, dragged the waterskin from the weight of the drifted sands. And when he opened it that which had been concealed within it came forth before his eyes.

And he saw it had been filled, not with water, but with jewels.

# XXVI

THE YEAR FULFILLED ITSELF AND A FEAST WAS PREPARED FOR THE tents of Abraham, the feast of the weaning of the child Isaac.

All morning the fragrance of glowing wood had filled the air, and thin blue smoke crawled into the sky above the cooking fires. Countless bread cakes were baked and heaped, one upon the other, to be eaten with the gustful flesh turning brown upon the spits — small, succulent game birds, tender wild antelope and deer, sheep and calf and lamb and kid seasoned with herbs and savory spices. There were relishes fresh from the gathering, olives and nuts, sweetmeats and honey cakes, fruits worthy of a temple offering, figs and pomegranates, dates, berries, melons, grapes.

And the best of the wine flowed into the bowls.

Never had Sarah gone forth from her tent with greater lightness of heart. Her face was radiant with the wonder of this hour, and she had made herself festive before it. Her hair had been washed and scented with fragrant herbs of the wilderness, so that its darkness gleamed in the sunlight. She had garbed herself in a rich blue tunic and a blue girdle traced with gold embroidery. Gold earrings and necklaces adorned her tawny skin, gold bracelets met with light and tinkling voices upon her arms.

Indeed, it was a day to be remembered, thronged with all the household and many of the land, joyous with singing and dancing and music and merriment. And when the feast was ready, Abraham stood before the vast gathering and called out the words of his joyful summons.

" Come forth and share a father's pride in his son! "

And all was stilled, as the gathering drew near and waited to behold the ceremony, the feeding of the first mouthful to the honored child.

The little Isaac, as festive as any of the guests, was borne forward in the arms of Sarah.

" Nay," she whispered fondly, as he yawned, " do not close your eyes in sleep, my darling. It is for you this hour has been prepared. No longer are you a babe, but a boy-child who feasts beside us."

And as Abraham lifted the child from her arms, their eyes met and their hearts were joined in the pride of the moment. Behold, my beloved, how we are blessed of the Lord!

Suddenly there was a stirring among those who stood near, and Sarah heard one man murmur to another, " Make way for the firstborn son." Lifting her eyes, she beheld Ishmael edging toward the front of the gathering, that he might look upon what would come to pass. The firstborn son! She shrank from the words and would not hear them, yet resentment against them was quickened within her. Not even upon this day of rejoicing am I to know peace. But the thought trailed, incompleted, from her mind, for now Abraham had taken a morsel of bread in his hands and was saying the prayer before food:

" In the name of the Lord, the merciful, the loving-kind."

Whereupon he placed the morsel between the lips of the little

Isaac, but the child, disturbed by its alien taste, quickly spat it forth upon his chin. And Ishmael cried out, with a boy's sudden delight, " Only see, my father, it is with the grace of a camel that he eats! "

The gathering burst into unrestrained laughter, and the little one was frightened by the sound, so that he began to wail aloud. Sarah seized him from the arms of his father and sought to comfort him against her breast. The trembling of his small body and the damp warmth of his tears upon her shoulder roused her to unsparing anger. Behold the manner in which the misbegotten child of Hagar has shamed my son! My son, for whom this feast was made, has become the object of their mirth! It was an insult not to be borne. Thus she cried out to Ishmael before them all, " How is it that you have mocked the heir of Abraham before his father's people? "

In silence the lad stared up at her, the brightness fading from his face. But Abraham, laying a hand upon his shoulder, answered in tones of quiet dignity, " Do not turn in anger against a child who has spoken only in jest."

The words smote her with such hurt and shame that she could have wept aloud. Not to the true son did he turn, nor yet to the mother of the true son. Nay, it was the child of Hagar he hastened to defend, the true wife he reproached before the face of all the company. And, roused to defiance, she cried, " It was not in jest that Ishmael spoke . . . but in jealousy."

There was a little stir among the guests, murmurings of astonishment, whispered words, and then an avid, waiting silence. Suddenly Hagar, pale and cold, came forward and put her arm about the shoulders of the lad.

" Come now, Ishmael," she said, gently. " Let us go forth to the tent, lest the heart of Sarah be moved to greater injustice against you."

And together they moved away, the throng parting, awed and silent, to make way for their passing. Yet when they had gone, those of the company ceased to have concern for them, and were both lively and at ease, filling the air with quickened chatter, with the sound of laughter, turning heartily to the feasting, relishing the food.

Sarah stood wordless, unmoving. Nay, she thought grimly, she shall not depart and leave me standing before the gathering as though all were ended. If there is an end to be put to this matter, then it is I who shall bring it about, and not a slave of my tents. Thus, giving the little one to the arms of Maacah, she turned to a certain path in the shade of the ancient trees.

Her steps were swift and hard upon the trodden earth and wrath rose like a flame within her, possessing her utterly. Her ears were closed to the merriment behind her, her eyes beheld no portion of the languorous day, the patches of sunlight which lay among the deep-massed shadows of the terebinths, the boughs moving in freshened wind, but were fixed upon the tent set aside for Hagar and the son of Abraham.

Not until this hour had she gazed within it. In truth, it was a simple shelter, yet Hagar had adorned it after the fashion of Egypt, with like color and charm, so that it appeared both rich and spacious in Sarah's eyes. Behold, she cried, made aghast by the sight, he has given her a dwelling fairer than my own! And the flame of her wrath leaped like a demon within her before this new offense. Violently, and with neither word nor ceremony, she entered the tent, passing from the brightness of the sun into the cool, dimmed shelter of walls beautified by delicate hangings, a gentle gloom made sweet with sprays of freshly plucked mints and flowering herbs.

Years before this day, she and Hagar had parted in bitterness, and now it was in bitterness that they met again, Sarah halting upon the threshold, Hagar turning from the lad. For the space of a moment they stood in utter silence, neither lowering her eyes before the other. Then Sarah moved forward, her voice cold and proud.

" If it lies within the mind of my slave that by bearing her son from the feast she may save him from punishment, she is indeed mistaken. Ishmael shall not laugh in scorn of my child and flee to safety behind the skirts of his mother! "

" May it please my lady," the lad began earnestly, " I did not flee . . ."

Hagar spoke quietly.

" Go forth from the tent, my son."

He burst out: " It was not in my heart to mock the baby, seeing that he is dear to me. It was only that, being of such smallness, he is amusing in my eyes. In truth, my mother . . ."

She said coldly, "How is it that I am your mother, yet you do not obey me?"

Shamed, he answered bleakly, "I obey," and went slowly, sorrowfully, from the room. When he had passed beyond the hearing of her words, Hagar turned proudly to Sarah.

"Now let the insults of Sarah fall upon me as they will, for the years have weathered my heart against them. But upon my son, seeing that he is innocent of wrong, they shall not fall."

"Do you seek to tell your mistress whereof she should speak?" demanded Sarah.

Hagar smiled slowly, her eyes chilled and hard.

"The wife of Abraham brings no fear upon me, nor shame, nor anything further, save contempt. For her greed and jealousy and railing are such as would appear more seemly in the harlot at the gate . . ."

With a cry Sarah struck her across the face. For the space of a moment, they stared at each other, made wordless by fright, and the mark of Sarah's hand, narrow and sharp and ugly, welled slowly upon Hagar's delicate cheek. God of gods, thought Sarah, in despair, I have done the deed of a kitchen slut! I have brought dishonor upon my own name. Yet before she could lift her voice in the words of misery that rose to her lips, Abraham came swiftly within the tent. Unconcealed anger gleamed in his eyes and blazed forth in his voice.

"What has come upon you," he cried out before her, "that you have turned this day of rejoicing into a day of strife?"

She stared at him haughtily, her smile proud and bitter. Indeed, I need none to tell me how it was that Ishmael, the talebearer, fled to his father with word of quarreling between his mother and the mistress of the tents. And now he, my husband, coming upon us, turns not against *her,* the slave with whom he begot this alien child, but upon me, his true wife! Before her face he berates me. Before her ears he casts words of reproach upon me. And though she appears meek and sad of countenance, in her heart she rejoices at my shame.

And she cried out in white and shaken fury: "Never shall

217

strife depart from these tents while both Sarah and Hagar dwell within them! There is much that I have endured, but there shall be no more. I shall suffer her no longer, not even for another day!"

"Sarah knows not the words of her own mouth," answered Abraham shortly, and he reached forth his hand as if to still the torrent of her wrath, but she would not have it so.

"Now let it be known," she cried, "before all who dwell within this household and upon this land that I, Sarah, and no other, am mistress of the tents of Abraham! And because of this the life of the slave woman is within my hand, and I may deal with her according to my will!"

And, having spoken thus, she declared in accents stony and unyielding, "So shall it be that, with the rising of tomorrow's sun, both Hagar and her child shall be cast forth forever from these tents!"

A sound, faint and stricken, came from the lips of Hagar.

"Cast . . . forth?" she whispered, unbelieving.

"Cast forth!" Abraham flung the words from his lips with a gesture of utter contempt. "Where is it that Sarah would have her go?"

"Let her return to Egypt from whence she came!"

Abraham stared at her.

"This is a poor jest," he said coldly, and looked with concern to Hagar, for despite the heat of the day, the slave woman was shivering wretchedly, gazing upon them as if from some far and reeling distance.

"May it please my lord," she stammered painfully, "send us forth as she desires. By what other means may Ishmael be spared lasting sorrow? Let Shem bear us to Egypt . . ."

"Neither Shem nor any other," declared Sarah, with a merciless smile. "For it is my will that you go forth on foot, bearing food and water and nothing more!"

Abraham turned upon her.

"What demon of malice has risen within you?" he cried, and his voice was shaken with the measure of his wrath. "How may a woman and child go forth alone to Egypt, seeing that they must cross the wilderness of desolation which lies between?"

She stared at him insolently.

"Is it for the sake of Hagar that you voice such anxiety concerning this matter? Is there, then, love for her within your heart, secretly and in hiding, sending you forth to her tent in the darkened hours of the night?" Even while she uttered the words, she knew that they held no portion of truth. Yet the thought became real in her eyes, so that she beheld Hagar awaiting him in the scented darkness of this fair tent, beheld them embracing while they laughed together because she knew not what passed between them. And an agony of spirit possessed her before she was recalled to the moment by her husband's bitter voice.

"The jealousy of Sarah has never ceased to accuse me, yet it was by her will alone, and by her pleas, that Hagar became slave wife to me, on a certain night many years gone."

"And, being slave wife, she is not equal to her mistress," she answered, in triumph. "Thus it lies with me whether she will be cast out, and the manner of her going also, for this is the law."

He stared at her as though she had become a stranger in his eyes.

"Indeed," he said slowly, "since this is the law, and you know none higher, how shall I forbid you to invoke it, even in its injustice? For your maid is in your own hand, and I may not lift my voice concerning the manner in which you deal with her."

Whereupon he would have turned away, but Hagar cast herself before him and spoke desperately.

"May it please my lord, if indeed we are to depart, let it be said to Ishmael only that we visit Egypt. For truly his heart would break within his breast were it known to him that he must turn his face from his father for all the days of his life!"

At her words, the shape of reality rose up before his eyes, ruthless, terrifying. And, beholding it, he rushed forth from the tent, hoarsely calling the name of the lad.

"*Ishmael . . .*"

It was the voice of anguish and of loss — such a cry as one might hear before a burial cave.

# XXVII

ONE BY ONE THEY HAD TURNED FROM HER AS IF FROM A DEMON. When she went forth to the well, the women of the tents were there before her, gathered in small taut groups, speaking in muted tones, with hushed murmurings and sudden sobs, as though they stood before the dead. At her coming, they took up their pitchers and jars and went their way with neither insolence nor malice, but as if they beheld her not at all.

Such silence and emptiness lay upon the encampment as had not been since Azubah's death. Jarah was out in the hills with with the shepherds and the flocks; Shem and Zilah had gone to dwell in Hebron; even Abraham had journeyed forth, and Eliezer with him.

"The shepherds have been away for three moons," Abraham had said quietly, "and it is well to see how they fare. Surely by this time, they require both food and garments."

His tone was courteous, but Sarah perceived that his spirit had departed from her. A sense of panic smote her.

"A journey of more than a day?" she asked, tremulously.

"Even so," he answered.

And he would have departed from the tent with no word further, but she ran to him and clutched the sleeve of his tunic, and stayed his going.

"When is it that you will return?"

He looked at her strangely.

"All things are with the Lord," he said, and put her from him and went forth with no touch of farewell. She stood desolate, gazing from the doorway while the men rode out, Abraham and Eliezer before them, moving so swiftly that their cloaks were lifted and billowed by the wind.

Throughout the day no woman of the tents came to speak with her, nor could she gather the will to summon even a slave girl, knowing herself accused in the eyes of all. But a little past the hour of noonday bread, Maacah entered, bearing in her hand a toy bright with Canaanitish color. It was a small clay camel, a gift from Zilah to the son of Hagar in years past, and long beloved of his heart.

" It has come to me," she began, her eyes strangely bright, " that this toy might be pleasing to Isaac, seeing that Ishmael is past the need of it. Indeed," she added, " is past the need of all that is found within this world . . ."

Sarah spoke in the sharp and uneasy voice of one clutched by fright.

" Wherefore? "

" The way of the desert is known to you," answered the slave woman evenly. " And, seeing that four suns have risen since their going forth, who can doubt that they now lie dead before the vultures? "

Terror rose in Sarah's throat and was cast from her lips on a sudden wail.

" Go forth! Go forth and leave me in peace! "

But Maacah stood unmoving.

" Say to me now," she asked, thoughtfully, " what is the will of my lady concerning the garments left behind by Hagar? Seeing that she requires them no longer . . ."

Sarah turned upon her.

" Cast them into the fire! " she cried out, with violence. " Let them be burned to ashes! I want nothing before me to call her to my memory! Cast away all she left behind! "

Suddenly Maacah smiled, and Sarah perceived, in terror, that the face of the slave woman was grim and mocking, the face of a stranger.

" Can my mistress believe that the years with Hagar are to be cast away in the flames of a brushwood fire, or in its smoke? Nay, for there was love between you, and her face is forever woven upon the fabric of your days. In all the watches of the night you shall remember her, the radiance of her smile, the gentleness of her hands, the sound of her voice in its singing and its laughter — yea, and in its grief! From this day forward there will be within you a darkness not to be lifted, an emptiness not to be filled. This also Hagar left behind and neither your hands, nor any others, may destroy it."

Sarah rose, her face white with unrestrained fury.

"How have you dared," she cried, "even in the years of your age, to speak with insolence before your mistress?" Yet at once she was sorry, and sought to amend that which she had done. "Nay, turn to me, Maacah, turn to me in my misery! You, who are as my mother, do not forsake your wretched child!" And she covered her face with her hands and wept, but there was no answering tenderness in the face of the slave woman.

"In truth, a devil and an angel walk beside every one of us," said Maacah quietly, and she departed from the tent.

Sarah cast herself down beside the little lad and, gathering him into her arms, buried her face in the warmth and sweetness of his body and wept, "Oh, my child, let me hold you and be comforted for all else have forsaken me."

And the thought smote her: How is it with Hagar this day? In what distant loneliness does she clasp her son to her bosom and cry out with the very words of my mouth?

Then she put the thought from her and rose to her feet, saying aloud: "Nay, I will not condemn my own deed! There could be no peace upon these tents while we dwelt together within them. That which I did required no small portion of courage. When a thing must be done, there is no help for it, and now that it is done, it is ended, indeed, and I will not have it following like a hyena at my heels! Nor will I be despised in their glances because of it."

And she went to the well at eventide in a manner proud and deliberate. But there was none to behold it, for none stayed to look upon her coming, nor lifted a voice to her either in greeting or in disdain. It was as though she had died and now wandered, disconsolate, amid the unperceiving flesh.

At the going down of the sun she filled the tent with lamplight and lingered over the tending of the child, as if to stay the coming of night. Yet even when the hour had grown late, and the silence of slumber had fallen upon the tents, she was disquieted and without peace. For a time she stood in the doorway and gazed beyond. In the light of the moon, thin clouds, driven by wind from the sea, were streaming above the hills like the tattered veils of a beggar woman. The tents were crouching shadows, black and still. Near the margins of the watch fires, the soundless shapes of the guards moved up and down.

" If Abraham would but return," she said, uneasily. Then, putting aside her troubled thoughts, she strove to comfort herself with reason. " There is no cause for unrest. It is only because I have not broken bread this day that I tremble and long to cry out."

She turned hurriedly into the tent, bringing forth a crumbled loaf, some dates and curds. But the torment seized upon her again, an unyielding and mocking demon out of the night. Has Hagar taken food this day? Or is it that she hungers? And what of Ishmael, the gentle one, the little lad?

Suddenly there rose from the hills the long and desolate cry of a jackal. In truth, it was not unfamiliar, but this night she heard it as it would sound in the ears of a woman alone upon the wilderness, with none to save her from the night. Shuddering, she put the bread aside, quenched the flame of the lamp, and crept close to the comfort of the sleeping child.

That night the rains of winter began with a cold and lashing storm, a torrent of wind which swept vast sheets of water in from the sea. Awakened by the little Isaac, who wept in fright before the crashing thunder, Sarah beheld terrible lightning, flooded hills, and rushing stream beds. Even when she had lulled the child to sleep and the storm had departed, swept toward the east, rain did not cease to fall. She rose, shivering, kindled a brazier against the chill, and brought another coverlet from the chest. The flames of the new fire wrought glimmering shadows upon the ceiling. For a time she lay staring up at them, breathing the familiar scent of wood smoke and dampened wool, hearing the lonely sound of wind in the wooden rings of the roof.

A little past midnight the rain ceased, and the moon shone forth again. Suddenly, she sat up, taut and listening, for there had come to her ears the sound of the camels. The men were returning — indeed, were at the margin of the encampment, calling to the guards. And presently she beheld them, drenched and hurried, passing the tent door. The camels were wet with rain and their hair had curled in the dampness, so that they appeared strangely tawdry and unfamiliar.

Then Abraham was upon the threshold, a dark and sudden shape against the receding clouds. She longed to cry out to him, but instead, fearful of what words might pass between them, hastened to lie down again upon the cushions, to close her eyes as though she slept. He entered silently, going to the warm redness of the brazier, and she heard the sound of his garments, flat and cold, as he removed them. At least, she thought in forlorn comfort, I shall cease to suffer fear, knowing he sleeps beside me. But when he had been for a time in the warmth of the bed mat, she knew sleep would not come to him, that he would lie awake, gazing into the night, even as she.

Behold what has come to pass, she thought bleakly. Even while we lie together upon the same bed mat, in the bonds of years, of marriage, of parenthood, we are divided utterly.

Yet she perceived that this homecoming could have been none other than a joyless thing in his eyes, the silent and unwelcoming encampment, the barren earth whereon the tent of Hagar had stood, the empty path down which Ishmael had run a thousand times to his embrace. And suddenly she beheld some measure of the sorrow she had brought to him. The shape of it rose and accused her with her guilt. She had cast blame upon him for a child born of her own pleading, turned in bitterness against him because he loved the son of his own flesh. And now I have divided them, one from the other, and shattered the heart within his bosom.

Even then she sought to console herself with unvoiced words:

"It was according to the law that I dealt with her. Thus who can say I dealt harshly, or lifted against her a hand without mercy? The way of the law is the means of justice. And being the law of our fathers, it is sacred in our eyes. Therefore . . ."

But other words strove with the first:

" Shall Ishmael then depart from the heart of his father? Nay, such a thing is not to be! Though my own son should die with the dawn of another day, I would love and remember him to the dust of my grave. And if there came one who seized him, and cast him upon the wilderness, and I knew not whether he lived or lay dead, whether he suffered thirst or fear, or called my name . . ."

And, rising to her lips, the torment within her burst upon the night with a sobbing cry. The sound brought Abraham to her, and she wept against him in unconcealed anguish, pouring forth the dark stream of her shame and guilt.

" Let my husband believe me, a madness was upon me, a madness of jealousy, and of hate! Now, only now, do I recall how vast and savage the wilderness, how small and timid the feet of Hagar! If it were I, cast forth from all that had sheltered me . . ."

Thus she wept until her body was shaken as by a fever, her tears coming forth upon gasps and tortured sobs, wrenched from within her by a violence unyielding and terrible.

" Is it that I have destroyed them both? Yet even now, this very night, if the men went forth into the wilderness . . . Bid them take torches, my husband, and go forth calling! "

He lifted her and sought to cleanse the tears from her face, to still her streaming, heart-stricken words.

" Let Sarah hear me. If indeed they live, it is because they have found shelter with other wanderers, and are beyond the dangers of the wilderness. Yet whatever has befallen them, it is no matter to be mended by tears."

His voice thickened with bitterness, and silence came upon them, dark and chilling. Putting her from him, he rose and went apart and stood beside the brazier, staring into its depths with unseeing eyes.

" Let my husband forgive me," she whispered at last. " Let my husband forgive me, and send me forth from his tent."

He made no answer, but bowed his head and, in the diminishing light of the coals, she perceived that he wept. Whereupon she crept near to him and touched his hand, in the manner of a frightened child.

" Abraham," she whispered, " say to me now, and conceal no portion of the truth from my ears, is it believed in your heart that they live? "

There was a length of silence. At last, in a voice made hoarse by the strength of his grief, he answered: " Even so. For I have asked the Lord to go before them and lead them beyond peril. Yet though they live, what is that to me, since I shall never behold my child again? " He lifted his face, wet with the coursing of tears. " In truth, the love I bear our son is a great love, yet Ishmael is as dear to my heart. I would have wished that when at last I am gathered to my fathers, both Ishmael and Isaac might stand before my burial cave! "

She had no words with which to answer him, and so crouched against the cushions in silence and wretchedness. Beyond the tent the moon went out in darkness and the wind came forth again from the empty hills.

After a time she stirred and said, faltering: " Certain words which Hagar spoke to me on a day long past are not to be denied: ' Behold there is now, in all the earth, no path which we can walk together.' Yet if Ishmael lives, then surely he shall come again within the tents of his father. And may I lose all I love, now or evermore, if I look with anything save gentleness upon him! "

But no sooner had the vow fallen from her lips when the chill of an ancient terror was upon her.

" Yet it may be," she whispered, trembling, " that because of his wrath against me, the Lord will cause them to perish."

" Nay," Abraham answered her in tones of quiet rebuke. " The Lord deals not in iniquity, but in righteousness. The good that comes to men is from the Lord; the evil, from themselves."

Whereupon he turned to her and spoke as gently as he would have spoken before his sons:

" Behold, there is a moment in the life of every man when he hears the voice of holiness which summons him to the altar of God. There are those who hear it in the days of their childhood, and those who hear it only at the door to their house of dust. Who can say at what hour it may come to you? Some turn from it unheeding, and some turn from it denying, but it comes to all. Out of the silences of the night, at the crests of gladness, from the depths of sorrow, within the halls of sultans, upon the streets of beggars, since God walks in all places, among all conditions of men. For Sarah also such a moment has been set aside. Sleep now, my darling, and take your rest."

Wearied beyond answering, she lay down. The rain had begun again, drumming on the roof, splashing upon the stones, driving into the sand. The rains of winter are cold rains, lashing the wilderness without mercy. Remembering this, she winced before it, and murmured against tears, "That they may be delivered, that they may know peace."

And it came to her suddenly that never before had there risen from her lips a petition utterly apart from her own striving.

# XXVIII

SHE WATCHED THE STARS GO DOWN AND BEHELD THE FIRST GLIMMER of dawn along the edge of the sky. And she said, again and yet again, in a voice dulled and without life: "It is not I, Hagar, wandering in the sands, unsheltered, unwanted, unsought by the tents of Abraham. Nay, have no fear of this thing, for it possesses no reality. It is but an evil dream from which I shall presently awaken."

Whereupon Ishmael stirred in his sleep, and it came to her that she had spoken aloud. She passed her hand across her forehead and thought, in confusion, Indeed, I am very weary, if I know not the sound of my own voice.

She had rested but little, being both troubled in heart and fearful of the night. Until Ishmael fell asleep, they had lain side by side upon the folds of their cloaks, and gazed at the numberless falling stars. When these had ceased to delight the lad, and when he had wearied of pointing out the glorious patterns of the constellations, he had fallen silent and thoughtful. And after a time he said in a voice of unconcealed longing, "How is it with my father, I wonder?"

Anguish rose within, and she cried out wordlessly before her son: Do not shatter my heart with the mention of his name! Yet her voice, when she lifted it, was steadied and gentle.

"In truth, he sleeps, for the hour is late."

The boy lay quietly, staring at the sky.

"It is certain in my mind that he longs for me, even as I long for him. Never before this night have we been apart." He roused suddenly, and looked into her face. "Let us tarry but a little time in Egypt, seeing that my father and I would not be divided."

It was as if her heart broke within her at the words, but she said only, "Sleep, my son, for the journey before us is long and wearying."

He sighed, "It is within my heart now to wish we had set forth on one of the camels."

Later, when he had fallen asleep, she rose and went apart from his side, and from his hearing, and wept bitterly with inconsolable grief.

It had been three days since the morning when she and Ishmael came forth from their tent in the pale green light of dawn. The hills were white beneath the fading moon, the Star of the Fallen Angel burned with unutterable radiance in the morning sky. Beside the gleaming stones of the well, Abraham awaited them with food and water for their departure. His face was pale and set in lines of stilled despair, as though he went forth to the burying of his own dead. Yet he sought to speak easily, even lightly, before them.

"Nay, the wilderness is not to be crossed without food and water."

Thus he gave a bag of loaves and dates into the keeping of Ishmael, and fastened a waterskin upon the shoulder of Hagar.

"Should the heat of the day become heavy upon you, go forth in the light of the moon. And let Hagar have no fear, for surely there will come a caravan bound for Egypt, a kindly band of wanderers."

"As Abraham has said," she answered, numbly. Her head swam in pain, her eyes were dazed, and she stared, unbelieving, upon the moment. Nay, it possesses no reality. Such a thing is not to be.

Gently, he laid his hand upon her shoulder.

"Do not forsake the Lord, Hagar, but remember him in all your prayers, and in your teaching of our son. Let Ishmael walk in the paths of the Lord all the days of his life, and his sons likewise." And he added, in pity for her loneliness, "Forgive me, little sister, that I have brought you so much of sorrow."

She whispered blindly, her eyes gleaming with unshed tears, "I shall remember you at every sunset."

Then Abraham knelt and gathered his son to his breast, and

they clung together with all the tenderness of the love between them.

" If my father will watch upon my white lamb until I have returned," began the lad, anxiously.

" Even so," answered Abraham. And she saw how it was that, over Ishmael's shoulder, he strove with his own grief, his own tears, the anguish of his own heart. Then he blessed his son in words more heart-shattering than a farewell uttered before a burial cave: " The hand of the Lord lead you, and the spirit of the Lord go with you, and the love of the Lord be upon you, even as my own."

Thus Hagar and Ishmael turned from the tents, weeping as they went. And now, like a burning red coal from the heart of a brazier the sun rose into the sky. There was terror in the thought of the day, for the valley to which they had come was of utter desolation, without so much as the shadow of a rock to shield them from the burning heat. Their waterskin was all but emptied; only a few dates remained of the food; and they had come upon neither wells nor any wanderers.

Now Ishmael awakened and, rising, gazed about him with sleep-filled eyes. After a time he said in wonder, " Behold, my mother, there is no sound in all the world save the sound of my voice! "

And, indeed, the sanded valley, empty of life, was as silent as death.

She said hurriedly, " Let us go forth, my son, that we may seek a well."

And thus they set out across the drifted plains and slopes, and Ishmael ate the last of the dates and, together, they drank of the water, and when they had finished, no more than a sip remained.

The sun became merciless upon them and yet there was no means by which they could escape its burning, binding torment. After a time they came upon some tufts of dried and broken weeds, some scattered thorn. And, across the wilderness of glaring sand before them, they glimpsed a small, low tree.

" Where there are trees, there is often a spring," said Hagar, but Ishmael made no answer and, when she had turned swiftly to look upon him, she saw that he was deadly pale and trembling upon his feet.

And she cried out in fear, " Is there an illness upon you, my son? "

" Nay," his voice was thick, blurred. His eyes were empty, as though blinded by the harsh brightness of the day.

She put her arm about his shoulders, that he might walk more easily, and knew him to be aflame with fever. After a moment, he said pitifully, " If I had but a mouthful of water . . ."

Whereupon she gave him the waterskin, and he drained it of the brackish portion left within it. Her own lips were cracked and parched and her mouth as dry as the sand itself, so that she spoke slowly, thickly, and with pain.

The world swam in waves of heat, shimmering, gleaming, shining. There was no sound save the slow striving of their feet against the sand. After a time, it came to her that Ishmael was very ill. The fever upon him had strengthened, his eyes were glazed and unseeing, and he fumbled for the waterskin, forgetting its emptiness.

" Nay," she said, gently.

He stared at her blindly.

" If my mother would give me a single drop of water, a single drop to ease my thirst . . ."

She answered him weeping, though no tears came forth from her burning eyes.

" Behold the little tree, my son. Let us go forth to the little tree, for it will spread its shade upon you — and perhaps a spring rises beside it."

He stared at her, whispering: " I would lie upon the sands. Here, I would lie down and let the rain fall upon me."

She cried out, " No rain, my son, will fall upon us here! " And, with her arm about him, she fell to pleading, " But a single step, my son, a single step! "

" Nay, nay," he muttered, and sank at her feet, upon the sand.

In fear and anguish she began to cry out and, seizing him, lifted him in her arms and dragged him to the shadow of the tree. And there was such a stillness upon him that she feared for him even more, and put her hand upon his chest, and felt the thin, uneven flutter of his heart.

" Oh, God," she cried out, " let me not see the death of this child! "

And she stumbled to her feet and went forth, in the hope that, near the tree, she might perceive some small trickle of water rising among the stones. And suddenly she was wandering in the wilderness of the past, as though in a valley alive with the echoes and drifting with images called forth from the realms of her memory.

" I am Hagar, your servant . . ." and the alabaster lamps of the Egyptian palace rose before her eyes.

" Who is he who now walks in the direction of the tents? " The lean brown figure against the sharp green of palms lifted by the wind of morning.

" Why does my mistress look upon me as she looks? " And the face of Sarah came before her, white with unavailing fury.

" The Lord lead you . . ." the gentle voice of Abraham, bidding her farewell.

Suddenly terror came upon her, blind and unreasoning, so that she fled wildly into the sands of the valley, her voice crying out against its own echoes again and yet again, " Lord, who shall have mercy upon us if you do not? "

And then there rose up before her a flock of small birds, such as were often seen in the green pastures of the desert. She halted, astonished and confused, while they whirred across her face and were lost in the far, burning reaches of the sky. As though from a vast and echoing distance, the thought came upon her: Wherefore do such birds descend upon the wilderness, save for water?

Desperately she turned about, and strove toward the place where she had beheld them, stumbling, falling, crawling to her feet, stumbling forth again, through the endless drift sand, through the terrifying silence, the searing, swimming, liquid light. And suddenly she came upon a spring, rising from the sand and rocks, edged in thin green.

# XXIX

THE NIGHT WAS TENDER, SWEET, TREMULOUS, FOR SPRING HAD RE-
turned to the land, the rain had blessed it, and the wind of the
Lord was in the trees. Across the open hills, in the light of the
risen moon, there drifted the scent of spices and wood smoke and
blossoming vines.

With the going down of the sun, a caravan had come from the
strengthening dusk, seeking the shelter of the tents. It was a
large caravan of many slaves, many laden camels, and Abraham
hastened forth to meet it with undisguised pleasure, since Asshur, its leader, was known to him.

In the weary-hearted manner with which she had come to do
all things, Sarah summoned certain youths and slave women of
the household. Supper fires, newly kindled, burned with festive
crackling and splintering sounds. From the kitchen of the great
tent came the muted stir and whisper of women, the light patter
of their hands as they shaped the bread. In but a little time the
flesh of a calf, succulent and savory, was gathered upon a massive
tray, and slaves bore it forth, with melted butter and wheaten
paste.

Now the feast, spread both swiftly and abundantly, was at an
end. The slave women had returned to their tents, the children
had fallen into slumber. And because the child Isaac was restless
with the discomfort of a new tooth, Maacah had borne him to
her own bed mat, that he might not be disquieted by the voices of
his father's guests.

Within the spacious Common Room of the tent, lamps had
been kindled in festive numbers, and cast a soft yellow radiance
upon the dark faces of the men, their gleaming eyes, the sudden
flashing of their teeth in some word of scorn or laughter. To-

gether, they lingered about the vast plundered tray, leaning easily against camel saddles heaped with the comfort of cushions or rugs. The right hand of each hung downward, heavy with congealing butter, awaiting the slave who passed from one to the other with water for the cleansing of their fingers.

And now their eyes were lifted with eagerness to Asshur, for none was a more gifted teller of tales. Indeed, Asshur moved through each day like some gleaner of the fields, gathering wonders to be bound with the magic of his voice, and spread forth in some season of famine beside a lonely watch fire. Yet even Asshur could not lift from Sarah the unabating misery upon her. She lingered alone in the inner room, and his words came to her through the dividing wall, but she let them fall, unheeded, into echoes and silence.

She had become, Urfa said, like some spirit of the dust who walked among the living but dwelt with them no more. And slowly those of the household, perceiving the measure of her grief and despair, turned to her in pity, and sought to bring her consolation. Yet she said only: " What is this to me, seeing that Hagar is dead, and Ishmael also? Ishmael, who was a child of light . . ."

Five moons had passed since their going forth. The breathing silences of the desert had received them utterly, and who was to say that they had not perished?

And now, as she sat within the quiet room, with the flame of a single lamp guttering upon the last of the oil, she knew no pleasure in the words from Asshur's lips. Yet, after a time, being roused by a certain awed and compelling note in his voice, she lifted her head. In her thoughts she could behold him as readily as though he sat before her eyes — his dark and comely face lighted by the wonder of his tale, his dark and graceful hands moving with the telling, the crimson and blue and saffron of his garments resplendent against the shadowed wall.

" Of all that has befallen me in the days of my life, this was of the greatest strangeness. To the dust of my grave I shall remember it! The men were taking rest, and had fallen into slumber, and — by the life of my mother! — there was no sound, not even the clong of a camel bell, the scuttle of a lizard, the calling of a dove. Yet a voice was lifted within my ear: 'Go forth to the tree of God beyond the rocks.' And this I did, even though it was no slight distance, for I was sore afraid! And behold, I came upon a woman and a lad beside a spring in the sands, alone and weeping."

Murmurs of wonder rose from the men, and above them the voice of Abraham, suddenly urgent, "Wherefore?" Hearing, she knew how it was that he had leaned forward, his hands closed and tense, striving to conceal the measure of his torment, the pounding of his heart, the quickening of his breath.

"Bound for Egypt, they were — a tale to hear!" declared Asshur. "A woman known as Hagar, cast forth from the tents of her lord for a cause she did not reveal to me. Nor would she speak his name. Yet it is not to be doubted that he had taken another in her place. Thus I knew not what I should do concerning this sorrowing wanderer and her son."

He sighed and paused. Sarah, driven to her feet by his words, clenched the fingers of her hands lest she should tear aside the dividing drapery and cry out, "Speak quickly, lest I die!" Then she heard the voice of Abraham, taut, courteous, controlled.

"Let my brother make haste with the telling, seeing that this is no ordinary tale."

Asshur sat yet higher upon the cushions, knowing delight in the pleasure of his host.

"May it please my brother, with the evening of the same day, we halted at a certain well, and there chanced upon a tribe from the sands of the south, a sheik mighty of name, with uncounted slaves and herds and wives; one of justice and mercy, even as Abraham. Thus he received the woman and child to his protection, that they might dwell within his tents, in the land of Paran."

Blinded by the strength of her sudden tears, Sarah stumbled forth from the tent, and the joy that rose within her was like a mighty hymn of thanksgiving swept upward, and yet upward, on unending waves and billows of light, even beyond the stars.

For a little time she stood unmoving, dazed by the wonder of this hour. The moon shone high above the hills; the shadows had deepened. Near the well crickets lifted their dark and lonely cadence against the night.

Around the glimmering ashes of their supper fires the slaves of Asshur were spread upon the earth, motionless and shapeless, asleep within their cloaks. His camels lay like huge round stones in the darkness, stirring the silence with the gentle crunching of their cuds, with their long, soft sighs.

Sarah gazed upon them with a strengthening sense of awe. By the hand of the Lord had the caravan of Asshur been brought forth out of the dusk; by the voice of the Lord was he bidden to speak of the slave and her child. In truth it was as Abraham had declared: " The good that comes to men is from the Lord; the evil, from themselves."

And there rose before her, as pale and dissolving as mist, the faces of many who had tasted the waters of misery: Lot, and the wife of Lot; Elisheba; Eliezer; Hagar; Azubah and Rahim; even Sarah herself; Abraham also. And in truth their sorrow had come to them, not from the Lord, but from the striving of one against another.

She held forth her hands in the still blue light, and knew that they were cleansed of her deed, that hatred dwelt no longer within her, nor bitterness for what had come to pass. And suddenly, she said, in the hushed and whispered voice of wonder, " I have ascended the hill of the Lord."

And she perceived that it was not by the trodden path that one went up to the altar stone — by the sacrifice upon the coals, or the tithe of duty borne to the gate, or yet by words brought forth upon the lips — but by the yielding of the heart to the ways of holiness.

And there came forth, out of the dimmed recesses of the past, the memory of the night in Haran when Abraham had gazed beyond the blurred white silence of the sleeping city, and declared: " So have men prayed to idols, but their seeking is of another God — a God higher than clay — whose hands have made both the heaven and the earth . . ."

To him also had come the voice of holiness. Was it out of the passage of the wind, the whisper of the sand, the murmur of the waters in the deep and ancient river? No man knew.

" Who can say at what hour it may come to you? " he had asked. And, even as he spoke, it had echoed, in the falling of the rain, the anguish of her own burdened heart.

She lifted her eyes and beheld the moon, white and gibbous, beyond the mighty boughs, and a sense of strangeness stirred within her at the thought that once she had worshiped, not before the Lord, but only before his creations. She perceived the black tents against the pale risen clouds, the tamarisks shimmering in the radiance of the night, the silences of the desert beyond, and the land also became her own.

And, out of the wonder of the moment, she whispered:

"Lord, forgive me that my words are unworthy of your glory, but you are still a stranger unto me, and I know not the ways of prayer.

"But hear me, Lord, and do not depart from me as I have departed from you.

"For I have reached forth my hand to other gods, I have turned from your name, and from your voice, unheeding. You have seen my dishonor and my shame.

"Yet if you will walk before me, I will keep your way; if you will be my strength, I will keep your word.

"For I would go up to the altar of God and there abide forever."

The wind moved in the ancient boughs and was stilled. Veils of silence rose about her, one upon the other, dark and tranquil, closing out all else. It was as if she stood within a temple of eternal refuge, an unseen radiance of imperishable light. *This, then, is the Presence and the glory.* . . . And her heart knew peace.

"Have mercy upon me," she whispered, "and upon all women. For there is none among us who has not the soul of Sarah."